Surreal South '13

SURREAL SOUTH '13

edited by
Josh Woods

with Associate Editors
Alexander Lumans
Clint Stevens

Press 53
Winston-Salem

Press 53, LLC
PO Box 30314
Winston-Salem, NC 27130

First Edition

Cover design by Kevin Morgan Watson

Cover art, "The Key," Copyright © 2013 by Terri Yeske,
used by permission of the artist.

Printed on acid-free paper
ISBN 978-1-935708-96-4

For Laura Benedict and Pinckney Benedict,
founding editors of Surreal South

Contents

Acknowledgments

"An Ugly Monkey" first appeared in *Chiron Review*, Winter 2001

"Introduction to the Unofficial Reports" first appeared in *Fiction International*, November 2011, Issue #44

"Jackson" first appeared in *RFD Magazine*, Summer 1991, Issue #66

"Out from Under" first appeared in Roanoake Review, Volume 38

"Scavengers" first appeared in *Indiana Review* 34.2, Winter 2012

"Something Rich and Strange" first appeared in *Nothing Gold Can Stay: Stories*, Ecco, 2013

"The Bad That Can Happen the Day Jesus Rose from the Dead" first appeared in *The Word Made Flesh*, firthFORTH Books, 2012

"The Fox King" first appeared in *The Fairy Tale Review*, Issue 8, 2012

Introduction

Human sacrifice, dogs and cats living together, mass hysteria!
—Peter Venkman, PhD.

The dead will rise; witches will dance; swords will lunge; beasts will roam; gods will snicker; space and time will slip; slumbering horrors will shudder awake; innumerable eyes will watch your every move. Welcome to *Surreal South '13,* the fourth volume in the anthology series featuring stories embedded in the surreal and seen through the perspective of the American South, fiction that lives on the fringe.

As the editor of this volume, I was immensely fortunate to inherit the *Surreal South* series from its brilliant and bizarre progenitors, Pinckney and Laura Benedict. They started these anthologies six years ago against the grain with a goal that, now, most of us (writers, editors, and readers alike) celebrate and strive to find: a bridge across the gap between work that is perceived as "literary" and work that is perceived as "genre." They succeeded three times over in '07, '09, and '11, and I was terrified at the task of stepping in to succeed a fourth time, terrified, that is, until I saw this book of freakishly amazing stories come together. Then I was terrified for all the right reasons. I realized that good, surreal stories don't need me to keep them alive; they've been out there slithering and thriving, especially in American fiction, for decades and decades. I merely had to let the weird do the work.

Well, the weird did the work along with two mostly human beings: 1. Alex Lumans, who I'm pretty sure is either a reincarnated velociraptor or a taxidermy-golem, and 2. Clint Stevens, who for all intents and purposes was the Agent Fox Mulder of this book, and who might in fact be Mulder by way of some string-theory slipstream phenomenon—I'll have to look into that. These two men are the Associate Editors of the book, and without them, this volume would not exist.

And as is my style in introductions to anthologies, I wish to summon the spirit of the tour guide and leave you with a couple of quick concepts that I hope you'll find useful as you tear through these pages.

First, as I understand it, great bizarre and horrific stories have always and will always tend to use three archetypes as anchors: the dead, the beast, and the labyrinth. The dead will return to our world (as ghosts, undead in the flesh, etc.), beasts will intrude (as monsters, unnatural mixings in the animal kingdom, etc.), and we will discover that our world is not as straightforward as we had thought, that we are trapped in a maze we can't fathom, a winding madness, enveloped by immense and inhuman powers (sentient castles, conspiracies, cyclical curses, etc.). Dr. Venkman intuited as much when he warned (in the epigraph above) of death, of beasts, of insanity all around us. Beware as you read.

Second, bizarre and horrific stories succeed when they glimpse something just past the limits of our minds, a peek under the veil, even though, if both writer and reader are honest, they acknowledge that they can't know what it is they have seen. All they can know is that they are shaken by the thought of it, less certain of what they thought they knew, a little more afraid even of the little things. Take care, dear reader, and remember, when you see Gozer standing before you, glimpse at what's behind her.

And with that, in the spirit of Virgil, I shall simply say, Let us begin our descent.

Josh Woods
Breese, Illinois
October 2013

SURREAL SOUTH '13

Katherine Lien Chariott

Introduction to the Unofficial Reports[1]

There was *something* in that apartment that crossed from Georgia, 2015, into Poland, 1940—this is proven in the unofficial reports about the Savannah case, but official reports don't admit its existence and never will. So rather than begin with that *something* (wormhole? portal? bridge?), with questions about that *something's* nature and potential uses for travel across time and space, or details about its known dangers (how it managed to transform an ordinary American bathroom into a concentration camp, and an ordinary American girl into a European Jew, marked for death), as logic dictates, official reports invariably start at the moment the Savannah girl encountered the police. Such reports tell us that, when officers first spotted her on that summer sidewalk, half-naked and shivering, despite the brutal, humid Georgia heat, they thought she was a lost little girl, eight or nine at the most. Of course, when they got closer, her shorn head and skeletal face, her skeleton's body, gave her away, even before she told them the truth: that she was sixteen years old and starving, and just minutes away from her own home. According to the first officer to question her, the girl "looked like a victim of a Nazi concentration camp"; she looked "just like a Holocaust survivor, like she just got out of Auschwitz."

But you're already familiar with this version of the girl's rescue,

---

[1] An introduction to these unofficial reports—famous, or infamous, already— might seem superfluous. But the actual contents of the reports, and the risks and rewards of reading them, are understood by so few, that I ask you to bear with me for these few pages before making the decision that faces every person who opens a book.—C. L. Hou, Editor

and even with the particular words I have chosen to tell this part
of her official story. They've been repeated on your television and
in your newspaper, on your Internet and your radio, and not just
by the police and the media, but also by doctors and nurses, social
workers and lawyers, and government officials. In fact, the same
few pieces of information, told in the same language, and using
the same imagery, can be found in *all* official reports about the
Savannah case, resulting in a narrative whose uniformity is both
suspicious and disconcerting. Authors of the unofficial reports,
including my own organization,[2] have pointed out this unsettling
consensus from the beginning, but no official report has
acknowledged it, let alone questioned it. Nor do official reports
ask an even more important question: why the girl was imprisoned
and starved. Instead, they give a mere timeline of the case, relying
on chronology to imply causation; a timeline that reaches only so
far back as the moment the crime (they claim) began.[3]

   To quote one official report, which is, in a sense, to quote all
official reports, "the girl was eleven when she was locked in a
bathroom of her family's downtown Savannah apartment. She was
held there for five years." As we all know, on the other side of that
locked door were the ones the police arrested for the crime, the
girl's parents. The Savannah girl's mother and father: their faces
smile out at us from every official report about the case. It's always
the same snapshot, the one of them leaning against their old Buick
sedan in the middle of a motel parking lot in Florida; a picture

---

[2] CFUR. Surely, you've heard of us. We've been attacked in every possible forum from
    every possible angle, accused of being conspiracy theorists and kooks; opportun-
    ists willing to exploit even the Holocaust for our own obscure purposes. I have
    been attacked, in particular, as a madman and a fool and a liar, one who willfully
    refuses to see that time moves in only one direction, and that place is bound by
    specific coordinates that must never change; one who, worse yet, would dare to
    deny the singularity of an evil which is defined for so many by its uniqueness,
    thereby reducing its significance and increasing its danger at the same time.

[3] But, of course, that's all the official reports *can* do. To do otherwise would be to
    admit that we've entered a new age, one where past, present, and future, where
    here, there, and everywhere, where history and the news and our own diaries can
    and will collapse into one, whether we want them to or not, again and again,
    and, oh God, again.

that (as official reports unfailingly remind us) was taken during one of the many family vacations they enjoyed while their daughter was locked away in her cell. Surely, you're sick of that snapshot by now; surely, it makes you want to turn away. But you need to look at that photograph again. This time, ignore the foreground—those happy, healthy pink faces; those tee-shirts, a his and hers set with Mickey and Minnie Mouse beaming out at you, stretched over those round, self-satisfied chests and bellies; the battered blue of that car those two rest against so comfortably—and focus on the background. There is something there that shouldn't be: a ghost image of the kind we find in twice-developed film, blurry and incomplete but still there, and still clearly a girl, whose shaved head and sunken features give her identity away. She stands at the very edge of that parking lot, just a few yards from the entrance to that motel—where, you will argue, she could not possibly be,[4] but where she most certainly was, and where she most certainly remains—staring out at us with black eyes that challenge us to read countless secret meanings. Can you read her eyes with me? Or do you look at that snapshot, even now, and, even now, only see what the official reports tell you is there: those fat guilty adults, the same two who are now locked away in cells of their own?

Probably, those parents are all you are willing and able see.[5] Let's concentrate on them together. Memorize their images: the blue of those eyes that refuse to give a clue about the blackness of their souls; the soft pink-red of their mouths, which, you hate to admit it, seem kind, rather than otherwise; their awful resemblance to your neighbors and, maybe, yourself. Now let's take that hated pair back in time to their old lives, the ones described in your newspapers and on your TVs, and so the only ones you can believe in. It is the day before their daughter's escape, and those parents are at home in their apartment, in that white

[4] I will not now attempt to explain the Savannah girl's presence in this photograph, which was so famously taken during the time of her imprisonment—that is the business of the reports that follow.

[5] I know, too well, the limits of common understanding and vision, having come up against them countless times myself before I found CFUR, to pretend that they do not exist, or even to blame those who are trapped by such comforting boundaries.

building you have seen on the news, gracious, though slightly run-down. They are in the living room of their gracious, run-down apartment, watching a movie and eating peanuts outside a door locked against a girl so thin that her bones have started to wear away. Of course, we want to see that girl, but official reports won't let us do this—*they* reduce her, and her years of captivity, to a few meager sentences that refuse to tell us anything meaningful. The only way to get to her, and to get to that time, is by abandoning the safety of government-approved words and ideas, and following the unofficial reports, a dangerous thing to do, for so many reasons.

If you are willing to brave that danger, you will find yourself stepping, as she did, through that *something* and onto another land and into another millennia. There, you will learn that the room, known in official reports simply and ridiculously as the bathroom, is more accurately named the death room, and that this death room is amazingly, unbelievably, but truly, located within a concentration camp, one which is not merely *similar* to Auschwitz, but which *is* the very same Auschwitz that you had supposed (and who could blame you) to be on another continent, and firmly anchored in another time. Come with me into that awful place now, just for one minute. There is the girl, right in front of you. She sits on a hard tile floor, wearing only an old cotton tank top and worn cotton underpants, with only the thinnest layer of muscle and skin to protect her protruding bones. The other prisoners are conspicuously missing from her cell; the girl is alone, perhaps part of some bizarre experiment (she is covered with scars so strange they cannot reasonably be explained in any other way) whose results we'll never learn, because there's no one to collect them, no Nazis scrupulously writing things down. She leans forward to rub her frozen hands over her frozen feet, then falls back flat on the floor and lets the cold rush through her joints, hollowing them out. Now all that moves is her mouth. Her lips spell out words in slow motion with the seriousness of a prayer or a curse. But when we lean closer to hear them, we find that the girl is naming food, a list that includes that of her people, and that of her captors, too: apples and honey and collard greens, piled high on one plate; smoked salmon and pierogies and red velvet cake, eaten in alternating bites; shrimp gumbo and matzo ball soup, served up in the same bowl, and topped off with sweet potato fries; ham hocks and beans with gefilte fish mixed in. She names all of that food, and more, and all of it in the startling combinations of the starving.

When the list is complete, the girl crawls to the door and looks through the keyhole. What she sees—that man and that woman, that living room in America, in 2015—makes her tremble. Of course, she would give anything to go there, to join them, but she is trapped on the other side of that *something* (that wormhole, that portal, that ungodly bridge). She must stay where she is, but we can leave her behind. Let's go back to the official reports about the Savannah case. Stand with me in the hallway, just off that living room, invisible, where we can watch those parents, where we can forget, if we try hard enough, what is happening to that girl, just out of our reach, and just out of our sight. Now, we will see something that surely made her weep. There is a knock at the door and the mother rises from the couch to welcome a couple to her home. The husband is carrying a six-pack, the wife holds out a pecan pie, both destined for a folding table set up in the corner. Soon, that table is covered with Cokes and casseroles, with home-baked cookies and fried chicken and beer, and that living room is bustling with friends and neighbors, guests at a party who will later report that, even on this final day of her captivity, no one suspected the existence of the Savannah girl in the very next room. Amazing. More amazing is this: the door opens again and two boys walk through it. They go straight to their bedrooms, but, five minutes later, they are back in the living room, eating barbecue from Styrofoam plates.

These two children hold the key to so much that needs to be known about the Savannah case, but official reports barely mention them, and so they have remained mere outlines, up until this moment. Here they are revealed as thirteen- and fifteen-year-old boys, with light hair and light eyes, both of them sturdy and strong, just like countless other boys in this country, except that they share a terrible secret. Even now, you can see the weight of that secret in the stoop of their shoulders; in the slow steps forward that one of them (the younger boy) takes as we watch. He stops, at last, in the middle of the room. That plate of barbecue, tangy and delicious and almost untouched, is still in his hand. He stands where he is for a full minute, looking at that bathroom door with a blank expression on his face, with absolutely expressionless eyes, before turning to rejoin his brother against the wall, where they two keep their unbroken secret with an unbroken silence that lasts through the rest of the party.

The importance of that dual silence—ignored or glossed over, of course, by official reports—is impossible to overstate.[6] However, perhaps even more important than what those brothers didn't say in public before the Savannah girl escaped, is what they did say in private afterwards. For those words, we must, once again, turn to the unofficial reports. There, you will find the police interviews of the two brothers: a half dozen closed-door sessions that the State (of course) has not, and will not, make public. In the first of these

---

[6] Think about it: it was not just on this one occasion that those two were silent. Those boys left their home, day after day, to go out into the world, and they never said a word about what was going on in that apartment. They never once, singly or together, wrote a disturbing story for English class, one that might have drawn the suspicion of a teacher. They never once, singly or at the same time though in different rooms, burst into tears in the middle of a math lesson, as they copied down numbers and symbols, made poignant to them, if to no one else, because they were as incomprehensible as their own lives. Neither one of them, not once, told a friend or a neighbor or a policeman anything. This silence, surely inhuman, is impossible to account for if we believe the official reports about the Savannah case. If, in fact, what happened in that apartment was nothing more than an extraordinary case of ordinary abuse, then those boys (the girl's brothers) must have spoken out. However difficult, surely, they could have said, "My parents have gone crazy and locked up my sister in the bathroom." Or, at the very least, they might have whispered, "There is something terribly wrong at home." No, the only reasonable explanation for such silence is that what happened to their family was outside the realm of the known, a crisis unlike any that had ever befallen anyone in their acquaintance; in short, an unspeakable event, such as the one described in the unofficial reports. For, how could anyone expect a boy or even a man to say, "Listen to me. I have something to tell you. We have an Auschwitz in our apartment, and a girl locked away in there to die." Even a child would know the impossibility of speaking those words.

interviews, the officers asked why the family had imprisoned their only daughter. The older boy's answer was recorded in its sad brief entirety. "Look," he said. "There was a concentration camp in that bathroom, so *someone* had to be locked inside, and it sure wasn't gonna be me." But, in another room, the younger brother told a different story. That the girl, his sister, suddenly became someone else—a stranger whose dark hair and eyes were as foreign as the language that came out of her mouth—and then everything else happened as a result of this metamorphosis. According to this second son, it was the mother who first saw and heard the change, a discovery that sent her on a rampage through that apartment, one that left mirrors cracked and furniture broken, that left the girl running for cover, and then the girl cowering in a corner, and then, finally, the girl locked inside the bathroom, crying so loudly that she drowned out, even, the weeping and wailing of the rest of her family.[7]

If we believe the story told by these boys, then we must also believe the greater story told by this book about our own lives. But there are many who will insist on doubting this testimony: because it was given by children, or because it can only be found in unofficial reports, because it contradicts the words of the State, or because it contradicts so much of what we think we know (and what we want

---

[7] That son insisted that he was not sure how the girl ended up in the bathroom; the entire family insists that they do not know how this happened. However, a passage, written out, in a surprisingly beautiful hand, on scrap of paper found in one of the kitchen cabinets, seems to answer that question for us. It reads in part:

….the mother, looking at the girl she had always believed to be her daughter, saw at last who that girl really was, and, when she saw this, she began searching the apartment for what had to be there, if only she could find it. She was frantic in her motions, tapping against walls, tapping the floor, looking for a hollowness that might suggest secret passages, even lifting the carpet to uncover trap doors so subtle they did not make a sound, removing the grates from air conditioner vents which might open onto a tiny stairway that led to an attic in Holland, or a stop on some underground railroad to freedom. Silent and frantic, she searched for these things, which she was sure must exist, if her child was a Jew, transported to Georgia and the present from Poland and the past. But what she found, in the end, was that *something*, and that tiny piece of Auschwitz on the other side of it. And, as soon as that was found, into the camp the girl went, shoved in by her own mother's shaking hands….

to believe) about the world we live in. There are many who will
demand further proof, and proof that comes from outside of these
unofficial reports. To those, I can only offer this: the proof that can
be found within the official reports, themselves. Read those reports
again, but this time you must read them as carefully and as critically
as you read the words in front of you now. If you do this, you will
find that, not only are the official reports about the Savannah case
all suspiciously one and the same, but that they also bear striking
similarities to the *unofficial* reports. You will notice, for example,
how "the Holocaust" keeps popping out of every official mouth;
how "Nazis" are ever-present, as well, and on the tip of every official
tongue; how there is no escape from the words "concentration camp"
and "Auschwitz" (the very same camp CFUR has *proven* the girl was
held in, surely more than mere coincidence) in every single official
account. In fact, if you read carefully enough, you will find that,
more than similar, the two narratives are nearly the same.[8] Or perhaps
it is more accurate to say that they are two parts of one whole,
which can only be fully understood when they are read together.

Perhaps, as some in CFUR argue, there are those who meant for
us to read the two together, all along. It may even be the case that
the police officer who gave us our first information about the case
purposely wove in clues that would allow us to discover the truth
about the Savannah girl, even as he told the first official version of
her story to the world. Or perhaps it is as others argue and he gave
his lies a skeleton of truth only to more completely confuse us.[9]

---

[8] This claim may seem unfounded to you, at first. However, if we refuse to be
fooled by literary devices, by those too-common tricks of language, and, instead, read and understand all statements in the official reports as the literal
truth, then we can see that the difference between these and the unofficial reports lies almost exclusively in the amount of information presented, not in the
kind or content of that information.

[9] Both theories are equally plausible. By choosing, as he did, to tell that skeleton truth
about the case, cloaked only by the most clichéd of similes, the officer might have
been inviting us to understand that the things he was comparing were, in fact,
identical, not merely similar, and thereby giving us the power to arrive at the full story
from the partial one, if we so chose. However, by hiding it out in the open, where,
he might have assumed, no one would look for it, the officer might also have been
trying to conceal the truth about what happened to the Savannah girl all the better.

Whichever is the case, one thing is clear: that officer could not directly tell the public what he surely knew. The reasons for this are obvious: fear of punishment by the State for saying what he must not; fear of ridicule by so-called decent citizens who would refuse to believe him; fear of the panic and chaos that would ensue if he were, in fact, believed, and everyone in this country and then others searched their apartments and their hearts for secret portals leading to miniature concentration camps; fear of the consequences if even one fellow citizen found another such *something* and went through it, bent on erasing the wrongs of the past, and journeying as far back, perhaps, as the beginning of our species as we know it, when the very first one of us committed his first inhuman act (some long-forgotten brutality which may well have been his first act as a man), or, perhaps, really, just bent on inflicting new brutalities, in another time, another place; fear, finally, of the end of history itself, and so the end of any hope of escaping it.

That fear is legitimate. I felt it myself, when I first learned of that *something*. I feel it to this day, and more strongly each day, because of the path that I chose to follow, and that I continue to travel. You should feel that fear, too, and understand, before you read any further, before it's too late, that there is only one way to truly escape it. Close this book now. Close off all that you might learn if you turned the page: those terrible truths that might force you to change your mind, your heart, and your life. Give up on that *something*, and go back to the past, while it still exists for you. Go back to where you are safe, to the point when this story was one that a person could bear. Return to the scene of the crime, before anyone even knew of the crime's existence. Stand on the street, just outside that apartment building, under those Cypress trees, dripping with Spanish moss, and look up. Through the window, you can just barely see them. There is a family in that living room: a mother and father and their two strapping sons, all of them happy and smiling and full. If you turn the page, if you read even one word of what follows, you will, like me, never be able to see them that way again.

Shivering

Brandon needs a bag so he drives out to Snug Harbor, to a single-wide trailer there with no front door, a black trash bag hanging loosely in the frame. He walks inside and there's this brand new stereo and this brunette named Kimmy holding a naked toddler in her arms, and Kimmy has enormous tits full of milk. She's wearing a tank-top and men's boxer shorts. Brandon stares at her.

The husband and father and holder of bags, Jake is his name, whips his head around in the living room to Metallica's "Trapped Under Ice." His blond hair is long and liquid how it moves, waving, pulsing, spreading out and again and again, he chugs away at an air guitar, his wrinkled can of Old Milwaukee.

Once the song ends Jake turns a knob on the tuner, and the two of them, Jake and Brandon, they sit on the couch together. They don't immediately get to business. Jake starts going on about this new power he has, this God given ability that came on him while he was pissing outside three nights before. Brandon asks him to explain, even though he's mostly watching Kimmy walk around the room and the kitchen nearby, staring at her tits, and thinking how this girl could do better. She could have it all with a face like that, and a pair like that. She could have the big city neon and high heel shoes, the Jacuzzi tub, anything at all. But instead here she is, right here in a trailer with no door out in Snug-fucking-Harbor. With this fucking guy.

Jake says that one night he had looked up to an almost full moon and sighed on account of all the piss coming out—it was a long and good beer-piss, he made clear—and there came this sudden chill on him. Not an outside wind kind of chill, either. He called it a shivering, said it took hold of him like one hell of a shivering, and it lasted long after he was done with his piss. Jake had stood there with his dick in his hand just trembling, unable to stop, incapable of calling out to anyone. He says inside of him then must have been the ghost-hand of God, charging him up, bringing him to full ecclesiastical power. Brandon laughs a little bit at that. Then he apologizes, says go on.

So Jake takes him by the arm and walks him back outside, the black trash bag crackling behind them. They step onto the front lawn, and Jake leads Brandon over to a wide tree stump. He tells Brandon to watch, to just get a load of this, and he holds his hand out. A ribbon of flame then twists from Jake's palm to ignite the stump.

And Brandon hops backward. He licks his lips, looking from Jake to that stump on fire then back to Jake. This is impossible. How high he must be right now, except he's not, not yet, dear Lord. Brandon shields his face from the sudden heat. Flames tongue up toward the sky, wood starts to snap and pop, and there's a real fire now, that stump is fully on fire.

Brandon looks to Jake, asks what the hell he just did, and Jake says he only thought of what he wanted and there it was. Like, he said in his mind, let there be fire on that stump, and it was so.

"You can do that?" Brandon asks.

"Where you think I got that stereo?" Jake tosses his head back, flips the hair from his face. "I drove up to Wal-Mart, and I thought to myself, I thought let that well-dressed fellow there be generous. Let him offer up a thing with surround-sound speakers and a docking station, I thought. A sub-woofer, disc changer, turntable, everything, the silver one there, best one in the damn place. Let that fellow be kind unto me, and it was so."

Brandon shakes his head, tries to make sense of all this. He wonders why God or whatever in the sky would choose a man such as Jake for a shivering, and not himself. Why not someone from somewhere like New York or California, Washington, D.C., some big shot with a necktie and sunglasses?

Brandon frowns. "You just got a stereo? That's all you got?"

"So far," Jake says. "I got plans though. I got some good ideas."

"Like what?"

"Well, like I'm gonna get some lotto tickets, and win them all. Then I'm gonna reunite Pantera, bring Dimebag back to life and everything. Get them to play out here, in the yard. And I'm gonna make it so cops can't even see me anymore. Like I will be invisible, but just to these goddamn cops. Can you imagine?"

Brandon says that all sounds good, but maybe he ought to get a front door for the trailer too, and Jake says, "Shit, yeah, goddamn, let there be door." And it is so.

Kimmy opens the new door—brilliant white and freshly painted, just how a door from nowhere ought to look—and she peers out at them. The naked child is still in her arms. "Come get this boy," she says to Jake. "I'm gonna take a shower."

Jake and Brandon both move back inside.

Jake sits on the couch, Brandon does too, and they watch as the little boy waddles into a corner by the kitchen and begins to urinate. He has one hand on his hip. Jake laughs, says his son is a wild ass animal, and Brandon says nothing to that, suddenly noticing the stink of the place.

"Let that piss be now clean," Jake says. The puddle the boy made recedes, disappears, leaves nothing but unstained carpet. "I love it."

Jake ought to use his power for a house, Brandon thinks, or a mansion even, a jet plane and pilot to fly him and Kimmy and their boy clean off. Leave Snug Harbor and these Carolinas far behind them. But he doesn't suggest anything, he has his reasons.

They finally get to business.

"How much you want?" Jake asks.

"An ounce?"

"Sounds like a question."

"Well, I was just figuring. Since you can do anything now."

Jake shakes his head. "That ain't right, now is it? Me chosen by God, you looking for handouts."

"Sorry."

"That ain't how this works."

"Okay. Quarter then."

"Have some goddamn class."

Jake pulls an old metal lunchbox from under the couch and opens it, removes a cellophane roll of weed. Brandon hands him sixty dollars, which Jake places inside the lunchbox before reclosing it. They both relax on the couch, smoke a little, and maybe due to Jake's power it's the best kind of high Brandon has ever had. Inside of the air high, ultraviolet high. And they don't really speak anymore, they just sit there, feeling things.

After a while Jake is asleep. So is his little boy, small and fetal on the floor. Brandon gets up, walks back to the bathroom where the shower still runs. He knocks lightly. "Come in," he can hear Kimmy say.

Brandon steps inside and there she is, distorted behind a transparent shower curtain. Her skin is brown and yellow in the shitty light, and those tits stand out like globes from her chest. Excellent and profound globes, he thinks, they are perfect.

"What the hell?" Kimmy says.

"You said come in."

She makes no move to cover herself. "I thought you were Jake, dumbass."

"Pretend that I am."

"Why would I want to do that?"

"Look at this place, and look at you. Don't make sense."

"And I suppose you think that you and I do?"

"Well. I mean, why Jake?"

She tilts her head, grins. "His hair."

Brandon inhales deeply. "I can take you away," he says. "I been saving up, for a while, I can take you to the city. Any city you want, anywhere. I can work at a restaurant someplace or a bar. We can wear nice clothes and take cabs, limos."

"And my boy?"

Brandon frowns, thinking. "He can come too, if you want."

Kimmy smiles then turns back toward the stream of water. "You suppose I'm better than this, and I agree. I agree that I am better." She sends her hand slowly down her neck and chest to her belly, lower, closes her eyes. "I am better than this trailer," she says, "and that man with his gorgeous golden hair, and you. The smell of this harbor and the ground and trees, the weight of this atmosphere."

She raises her arms back up toward the ceiling, and tits are all that Brandon can see right now, glorious, pregnant tits.

"Better than this whole planet of men planning to save women, slapping shoulders, spending money and rutting and drinking and dying from prostate cancer and heart disease, liver failure. I am beyond your low biology. I always have been."

Kimmy seems to glow in that shower as she throws the curtain open, slick and with steam coming off her like smoke from the stump-fire outside. "A man may feel he is magic," she says. "He may feel a shiver and believe it is God that is the cause of his magic, but it is only his proximity to me. That man may have his every desire until the end, but he will end. I will go on long after he is bacteria, after he is broken down to planetary nutrients, as you, too, must ultimately be. And you think you can save me."

Kimmy presses her naked body against Brandon, wetting his clothes. He looks down at her, unsure if this is real or his high gone far ahead of him.

"You are very close to me now," she says, "for this short while. What do you desire?"

And he is at once full of need and too much truth, a wish to know more. He wants to see the scaffolding of time and the universe, schematics of these things, to know how energy came to be. He wants to know of himself before birth and after death, of souls and nightmares and dinosaurs, he wants to know who Kimmy is. If there are more like her. But he can only stare at her magnificent nudity, so she pulls away from him, grabs a towel from the rack on the wall. He sees sadness in her face, and figures he must be a disappointment to her. Not that she would have expected more. Sex is all Brandon wants, sex forever, hot swampy sex that bleeds and bawls in the night with this cosmic creature he has come upon. And Kimmy knows this. She is familiar with animals, knows much of their stupidity. But still, she grieves. Perhaps for that naked boy in the living room, pissing on the floor, babbling and mewling the way all men do. Now sleeping. Unable to be anything more.

A Test of Faith

Charles and Maggie lived deep in the hills of Kentucky. They had an old tractor and an orange ATV and a cellar stocked with smoked meats and canned vegetables, so they rarely worried about the distance to town—a gas pump, a country kitchen, and a church.

The snows, though, could be a cause for worry. The county-run plow wouldn't risk the four-mile dirt and gravel drive ascending from their cabin to the mountain pass, which took another twelve miles to meander into town. Charles rigged a corrugated metal roofing panel to the front of the tractor and strapped chains on its tires, and that rudimentary plow served well when God was kind for the winter. But, though the people of the hollers were kind to God, in prayer and services, He didn't often return that kindness in the cold months, when ice draped the trees and snow piled thick in the valleys.

As Maggie's pregnancy became apparent, the December sky roiled and heaved into slivers of steel, and winter's first blanket settled itself early. Maggie washed pots with a rag by the kitchen window and, with a small, calm smile, watched the menace building outside. She trusted her body as she trusted God. She felt wonderful, beautiful, and since spring, when Maggie's church friends first learned she and Charles were trying for a baby, they had passed along vitamins and onesies and bottles, nursing pads and rattles, a crib and a Johnny Jump Up, a portable food masher and little jars, booties and bibs and books. Their home was ready, and Maggie was ready, but Charles desperately wanted her to see the town doctor before the weather got any worse. He wanted the reassurance of facts, of medicine, but he only had the timeline for comfort—three months along in December meant a June birth, most likely, meant most any potential crises would fall outside winter's grasp.

The clouds murmured, dusted themselves, and by the second week of December began to salt the earth in earnest. At first, Charles spun out his makeshift snow plow once a day, then twice a day. He'd chopped wood all through September and October, stacking logs high in the den, piling them on the porch, along the outer walls, in pyramids between the shed and the cabin.

There was nothing Charles could do when the snow won, as it did for at least a short while every winter. Later, normally. January or February. The third week of December unfolded, and he awoke one morning to a bright white square where the sky and spruce trees typically showed through the window. He squeezed Maggie's arm.

Peeking over the down comforter, she said, "Mercy." The light was strange and muffled, as if the house were sunk in cotton batting.

"I don't imagine the tractor's gonna do a lick of good against that," Charles said. He pulled Maggie close, relishing her heat, the soft curve of her belly.

"How much of that was just the wind, do you think?"

"A fair portion, I'm sure." Charles looked at the window, like an oversized note card—so white! "But a draft that high, just on this one side, well…that still has to be a few feet all around, I imagine."

"My. Guess this means Christmas alone?"

"Just the two of us," Charles agreed. "Three of us, that is."

"Mmm…good."

Any thoughts of productivity laid to rest, the couple slept three more hours, happy to be warm, abandoned on their quiet homestead.

Charles heated handfuls of rags to press along the front door's edges, jimmied and plied the door until it finally pulled open—to reveal another wall of whiteness.

"Mags. Come look at this."

She padded around the corner in her slippers and thick bathrobe, her long black hair in tangles and knots. "Well I'll be. How deep? Is it just another draft pushed up?"

Charles grabbed the broom by the fireplace and, holding the bristled end, drove the handle into the wall of snow. They peeked down the narrow tunnel: no sky, sun, or trees. Charles tried driving the handle up high, at an angle: no light came down.

"We're buried. I don't believe it, but we're buried."

"But the chimney…?"

Charles nodded, "It'd be bad if the fire wasn't going all night. I mean, I have to think the snow couldn't go *that* high…but I don't know what to think, I just know it's good we had it going, 'cause even if the whole cabin's under, the heat kept that passage open. We'd be dead of carbon monoxide by now if it hadn't."

"That's very comforting, dear. Do you want potatoes?" Maggie asked.

They ate potatoes by lamplight, then read by the fire, taking turns feeding logs to its crackling orange tongues. They passed their sleepy days that way, aware of time only in that it had to be passing, and the grandfather clock clicked away the hours and nights in place of the sun.

Charles was checking the smoked ham hock in its pot on the fire, ladling the meat's juices over the potatoes to tenderize them, to make something like a holiday meal. It was Christmas Eve.

He heard a whimper behind him, and the sound mounted to a scream of instant, furious pain—"Charles!" At Maggie's scream he dropped the ladle and sprinted into the bedroom. "Mags— Maggie! Oh, God. Oh God, it's gonna be okay, Mags, hold on."

Blood soaked through her nightgown and stained the sheet beneath her thighs, an inky maroon puddle in the oil lamp's glow. Maggie's eyes were wet, the nightgown clung to her skin and she clutched at the blankets with bloody fingers.

"Charles, I'm sorry, I'm sorry help me I'm sorry, what's happening—"

He grasped Maggie's shoulders and pressed her forehead to his lips, kissed her cheeks, guided her hair behind her ears, off her shoulders, off her face. "It's okay. I'm here, Mags, we're fine. I'll be right back, okay, I'll be right back, we're fine."

Charles tore through the cabin. He pulled the ham hock off the fire and grabbed a large pot from the kitchen. He opened the front door and piled snow into the pot with his bare hands and shoved it directly into the fire to let the snow melt, then boil, and he grabbed a lantern and held it to the bathroom medicine cabinet, pushing bottles aside with shaky fingers, his mind stumbling to keep up with its instincts and reason. Maggie was in pain. Aspirin. Aspirin thins blood, she's bleeding, she'll bleed out—bleed out? Jesus, bleed out. No aspirin. A muscle relaxant. Wasn't a miscarriage something to do with contractions, with muscles—miscarriage. Miscarriage. Charles dug his shaky thumb into the cap of the muscle relaxants, fighting the childproof top. The pills scattered across the sink. He picked up one. Two. To the kitchen, poured a cup of water from the pitcher they'd been keeping on the counter, back to Maggie.

She looked sallow and desperate and primal in the unstable light. Charles put one hand behind her neck, craning her head up, and eased the two pills into her mouth, grabbed the cup and held it to her mouth to drink. The water dribbled between Maggie's lips and down her chin. She sobbed.

"It hurts. Charles I'm scared it hurts, it hurts, it hurts—"

Dizziness threatened his knees and heart. Charles told her to keep pressure on the wound, knowing that made no sense but having no idea what else to say, and ran to grab dishtowels from the kitchen and drop them into the water simmering in the hearth. The cloth squares bubbled and undulated in the pot like sacs of fish eggs ready to pop. Maggie moaned in the bedroom. Charles looked over at the pot on the floor with the ham hock and potatoes. A thin layer of fat was congealing on the broth's surface. He leapt up and squirted dish soap onto his hands in the kitchen, scrubbed it into his calluses and picked at the permanent oily stains about his short nails, plunged his hands into the water pitcher and shook them furiously until they rinsed as clean as they could be. He pinched the dishtowels from the boiling water and barely registered the pain.

Time slowed for a moment, looking down at his beautiful wife, his wife, lost and suffering in a fortress of snow. It slowed for a moment. Sanitized rags were for childbirth, weren't they. They weren't for child deaths. Charles had no idea what to do: surely and calmly, he realized that, surely and calmly for no particular reason. He peeled Maggie's nightgown away from her thighs. He pulled down her panties. He'd first done that ten years before. They were wet then, too; she was nineteen, had waited nineteen years for him, and she was beyond ready. He'd waited twenty for her, and when he first saw it—saw *her*, glistening, pink—it nearly sent him over the edge before they could consummate the marriage.

Now, there was nothing of that pinkness; all the colors ran red and black. Since it was the only coaching Charles could remember, he commanded, "Push." And Maggie did, and it was messy. Charles pressed the moist, boiled dishtowels against her inner thighs, around that opening from which this hell was springing.

"Push." What in God's name was he saying?

"Push." Push what, blood until she dies?

"Push." And Maggie was screaming again.

"Push." And Maggie was quiet.

Charles said, "Push," and there was something in his hands that wasn't blood.

She pushed one final time, without his guidance.

Charles looked at what lay partially cradled in his hands. The dizziness was back. Maggie was out: eyes shut, inert. That was best. He looked down again, and what he saw wasn't the bare beginnings of a baby.

It was puppies.

Charles gathered the puppies in his arms and set them before the fire in the den. They squirmed and gargled. He walked to the laundry room and opened the pantry which had been the baby closet since spring. He picked up a small knitted blanket. Charles returned to the hearth, knelt, arranged the yellow blanket into a nest, and transferred the puppies to the blanket-nest individually. One. Two. Three. Four. Five. Five puppies. Their eyes were sealed and they wriggled atop and between one another, their little mouths parting and closing in search of milk.

Charles walked back to the bedroom, where Maggie lay motionless, her legs still splayed. He gently cleaned her thighs with a wet dishtowel. He placed another towel between her legs and straightened them, then pulled down her nightgown and tucked the comforter around her chest. Her breaths were even. Charles kissed her forehead and extinguished the lamp.

He grabbed the washcloths from the bathroom and tossed them in the pot on the fire; the water was still boiling. The wind blew outside. It transferred through the snow-insulated cabin as a low thrum. Charles crossed the den to the bookshelf and picked a selection from the shelf Maggie had labeled "MOMMY'S CORNER" in blue glitter-glue on a piece of pink construction paper cut in the shape of a stork. He flipped to "D" in the index. "Daddy's Checklist. Decorating the Nursery. Delivery Options. Diaper Changing Essentials." He flipped to "P" in the index. "Packing for the Hospital. Pelvic Pressure. Pet and Animal Safety." Charles flipped to that. It turned out dogs could carry bacteria such as campylobacter and salmonella, which a pregnant woman ought to avoid, and that it was wise to accustom a dog to a newborn by bringing back a blanket carrying the baby's scent from the hospital. Boundaries had to be set for the dog once the newborn was home in the nursery. Charles returned to "P." "Placenta, Preeclampsia, Premature Birth." Charles flipped to that. Useless. Preemies were prone to underdeveloped lungs and feeding troubles, but according to the book, they were not prone to being puppies.

Charles replaced the book and returned to the fire. He wrung the boiled washcloths out on the rug and shook them to dissipate the heat. The puppies appeared to have fallen asleep. He picked up the least entangled puppy and wiped its face, its belly, its little legs and tail, cleansing the blood and mucus from its fur. It suckled the air and whined until he put it back in the nest. Charles carefully pulled another puppy from the pile and wiped it off. It was dappled gray, with white feet. He put it back in the nest. He cleaned the last three puppies, changing washcloths as they soiled, and watched the fire as the quivering pile of puppies fell into a quiet slumber.

The grandfather clock chimed. It was Christmas. Charles put the ham hock and potatoes back on the rack. He stirred the broth, now and then, and stared into the bricks of the hearth.

When Charles awoke, the fire was weak, just an intermittent flame and the ashen glow of logs carrying their last heat. His back crackled from sleeping on the hard floor. It was too dim to read the grandfather clock, but Charles saw two dark shapes about a foot away from the blanket-nest on opposite sides, and he grabbed them, terrified to feel how cool the puppies were. He realized they were crawling into the darkness in search of their mother. Charles edged closer to the fire, stoked it, and tucked the two puppies under his sweater, atop his belly. He hunched over and pushed slow, hot breaths through the sweater, massaging the puppies through the yarn. A tiny haunch extended, a little head shook side to side: they were okay. The other puppies voiced aggravation as Charles lifted them to tuck the voyagers at the warm bottom of the mass, but they settled quickly, and he fed some kindling and a hearty log to the fire.

Charles lit the lamp by the bookshelf and turned to the grandfather clock: quarter past five, in the morning, he assumed. Grabbing two washcloths from the floor, he pulled out the crusty, burnt Christmas Eve meal. A mewling from the nest. Charles jabbed the charred ham hock with his thumb, licked it. Definitely ruined. More mewling. He grabbed the lamp and crossed to the bedroom door.

Maggie was still buried beneath the comforter on her back, arms atop the blanket with her pale palms upturned. Her head fell to one side on the pillow, her lips barely parted; she would look peaceful, if she had ever been the type to sleep on her back, but she always slept on her belly with her elbows hitched out at awkward angles that threatened to oust Charles from the bed. He thought she looked clinical, exposed. Dead. Charles touched her lips. She rustled.

"Charles…"

"Shush. It's okay. You're okay." He rubbed her shoulder and stroked her arm. "You're okay, Maggie. How do you feel?"

"I feel awful. Is our baby okay?" Maggie opened her eyes and her mouth danced a quavering line between hope and desolation. "Can you tell? There was so much blood."

Charles stared at the comforter. Maggie was much better at getting stains out of the wash than he was. He wasn't sure if it was okay to put a down comforter in the washing machine. The machine wasn't working, but never mind that, was it okay to soak a blanket filled with feathers?

Maggie touched his arm. "I lost the baby, didn't I?"

"There isn't a baby. Get some rest, honey. You rest up. I love you." Charles fetched another muscle relaxant from the bathroom for Maggie, tucked her in. When her eyes shut, he closed the bedroom door.

His hand rested on the cool knob; blood crusted his nails. It would be different if Maggie had agreed to see the doctor when Charles first asked. And he hadn't just asked. He had begged her to go, but she replied that her body was the dominion of her husband and God, alone. Humbled by Maggie's pure convictions, flattered by those words, Charles had backed down, but he now understood how weak he had been. He hadn't protected his wife.

And what, now? A pillow pressed deep into the blanket-nest until nothing moved beneath his weight? A systematic wringing of soft little necks? Charles couldn't back down this time, couldn't fail as the protector and provider, so when he turned to the growing fire, and the five fuzzy shapes within the nest, he thought: food, clothing, shelter.

Charles scooped more snow into the water pot and set it above the flames. The mewling was louder. He pulled two pink onesies from the baby closet and some scissors from Maggie's craft box and cut off the leg and arm sleeves at the shoulders and thighs. He folded the remaining torso sections of the tiny outfits and laid them in the craft box. Charles fetched bottles and nipples from the baby closet and hesitated by the simmering water, fairly certain he was meant to sterilize them first but aware of a yipping near his right foot. He dropped the bottles in the pot and stepped over the nest to search the laundry room pantry for powdered formula, where he found that the box provided detailed instructions for mixing formula according to human nutritional standards, but lacked a conversion chart for his current needs. It seemed negligent.

And why on God's green earth does that seem so, Charles stopped to think. When Charles was a boy he had a little beagle mix named Bratwurst who survived on table scraps alone and never ate a kibble, and he was the happiest healthiest dog—

And Charles stopped thinking just as quickly. He stirred the powder into a jug of water and grabbed the five cutoff sleeves. The puppies' faces were tiny pink things, eyes glued shut, ears just miniscule flaps. They squeezed and looped into one another like fuzzy gray and white intestines, with one pup jet black. Charles picked that one up first. It was the runt—he carefully turned it in his palm—*she* was the runt. He guided her into one of the pink sleeves and set her in the nest. The next puppy had a smushed face and steely coloration about his head and tail, and he arched his back and cried and cried as Charles slid him into another sleeve. He rubbed the puppy's tummy as the others began to cry. The water was boiling. Charles fitted the rest of the puppies into their sleeves.

Their mouths wouldn't open wide enough to take the bottles' nipples in fully, so Charles had to cradle each puppy on its back in his hand and let the milk dribble past their thin lips. The meal quieted them, and they drowsed together in a warm pink lump.

Charles pried open the front door. Snow. He tore back the curtains in every room. Snow. He thought about dousing the fire and wriggling to the rooftop but the passage wasn't wide enough; he would only lodge himself and suffocate, and assuming he snapped his skeleton apart to fit through the chimney and somehow came out operable on the other side, the ATV and tractor would still be buried in that thick, ungodly pallet of snow, with no way to locate them or get them to the surface, besides. He opened the front door one more time. Snow.

He remembered playing outside during winter breaks as a child, digging deep in the snow and channeling through the compressed powder, carving intricate webs of frosted passages invisible to anyone on the surface, and how his mother used to call him back inside each day to peel away his wet, frigid clothing and warm his hands around bowls of soup or chili. And now, Charles saw the impenetrable white wall beyond the doors, the windows, envisioned the four-mile journey to the pass and the twelve-mile stretch to town, and there was no one, there would be no one, to call him to the surface.

"What are these?"

Charles had been on a vigil, feeding the puppies every couple hours, kneading them into releasing themselves atop open cloth diapers he'd spread in a mat on the floor. He had plucked a scant meal of burnt potatoes for himself and fallen asleep on the rug. He moved to stoke the fire.

"Charles—what are these?" Maggie stood in the middle of the room, her hair limp with sweat, the gray nightgown stiffened into wrinkles around her bloody groin. She wrung one hand about the opposite wrist and curled and uncurled her toes, awakening into her numbed body's sensations.

"They're puppies."

"Well…okay. Good." Maggie struggled to open the front door. Her hands were weak. She stared, and the snow glared back, as concrete and impassable as before save the laughable dents made by Charles to boil up water. "Well…" Maggie scratched the corner of her eye. She glanced at the puppies, swaddled in their nest and makeshift cozies. "They're cute. They're little, aren't they? Look like newborns. So you got the back open."

As Maggie walked to the kitchen, Charles stood and said, "No, Maggie," but she continued to the back door and tugged it open: white.

"You crawled out a window? What were in those pills, anyway?" Maggie returned to the den and carefully lay down by the fire, wincing and pressing a hand to her abdomen. She took a deep breath and reached out to stroke the black puppy's neck. "Puppies on Christmas. You're amazing." She smiled.

Charles sat by Maggie and put a hand on her knee. "They're not strong. We only got that powdered formula, and I don't know that it sits well." He paused. "I've been up with them most of the night. They're hungry little guys."

Maggie turned to Charles and asked, "Where's their mom?"

Charles shook his head.

"Well she got in somehow and she got out somehow, where'd you burrow out? The bathroom? Is there a way out the laundry room? Did you get to the ATV?"

"Snow's got us piled in. We're buried. There's no way out."

"But—" she waved a hand at the puppies, "there's a way *in*! Way out, way in."

Charles closed his eyes. "It's only been you and me, Maggie. It's only been a day." And he looked at the puppies. He looked at her stomach. "No way in or out."

Maggie stood, steadied herself against the wall, and clapped her hands. "C'mere girl." She whistled. "C'mere girl." She weaved window to window to door to window, just as Charles had done. She looked under the couch and bed and in the dryer and oven and even the toilet tank. "Where's the dog?" Maggie dug her nails into Charles's shoulders. "Where?"

"There's no dog. I didn't know how to tell you when it happened—"

"Charles."

"—and you were scared and all that blood, I couldn't tell you when they," he motioned weakly to her hips, "well, when they came out."

"You're not saying that."

"It's gonna be okay." He paused. "It's like you say, when God gives we receive, and we love. He works in mysterious ways, and He gave you these to give to us, and…they're healthy. I love you, it'll be all right."

Maggie clenched her nightgown in her hands and released it and touched her belly and snapped her hands back and then held them away like a poison. "I lost our baby, not my mind. Oh God I lost our baby—" Maggie sobbed.

Charles picked up the dappled puppy and held it out, "But you didn't. You didn't lose our babies."

When Maggie collapsed, Charles carried her to the bed and put a glass of water on the nightstand.

As the grandfather clock ticked away the final hours of Christmas, Charles constructed the bassinet by the fire. It had been dissembled into slats and legs, stored by the dryer to save space until the baby came. He tried to nail the pieces together quietly, shaking the bassinet to test its sturdiness before lining it with yarn blankets and depositing the swaddled puppies. They looked content in there—they wriggled less. Charles fiddled with an old fishing vest and, between awkwardly stabbing himself with a needle and stopping to reassess the logistics, succeeded in jerry-rigging a nursing vest. The malleable bottle liners dropped into the vest's many pockets to attach to sewn-in nipples poking through holes in the pockets' bottoms. With the puppies in a pile on the rug, he could lie on his side and guide them to the nipples. Their little paws kneaded the pockets and dinner was served.

They looked so fragile in the orange glow—their soft bellies, their tiny awkward legs, their blind, squirming movements. Charles had to make sure that the smallest, the black one, had her fill of milk each time. She tended to get jostled away from the teats. The puppies were back in the bassinet and Charles was just unbuttoning his vest when the bedroom door opened.

Hollow-eyed, Maggie looked at the bassinet, but Charles wasn't sure she really saw it. She had changed into her pink bathrobe.

"Maggie, you're up."

She walked to the kitchen, picked up one of the pitchers of cold water—Charles had been melting containers of snow throughout the day—and turned into the bathroom. Charles heard the water splash into the tub. She brought a kettle of water to the tub, then a mixing bowl of water.

Charles touched her arm as she returned for another pitcher. "Let me warm you up some bath water, Mags. Just a few minutes, let me get you a warm bath ready, that's all cold."

She put the pitcher down and returned to the bathroom. Uncertain, Charles put two big pots of water into the fire and checked the puppies, whose chests rose and fell in slow unison. He finally took a deep breath, picked up the lantern, and went into the hall. He felt Maggie's bathrobe under his feet as he stepped into the dark, chilly bathroom. There were only a couple of inches of water in the tub; she sat there naked, knees pulled to her breasts. Her skin looked shiny, her hair gooey. Charles saw an empty body wash bottle cast aside on the tile and realized Maggie had poured its entire contents on her head. She rubbed the gel up and down her arms, up and down, up and down. She hadn't wet her skin first. The gel spread around like jam.

Charles knelt by the tub with a cup from the sink and dunked it in the shallow bath. He tilted Maggie's head back and carefully poured water along her scalp line, letting it run through her hair. "Come on, help me rinse this. You got too much soap here." He poured cups and cups over her head and tried to massage the soap out with his other hand, but the water quickly turned to pure lather and her body was still sticky all over. "You're freezing, this ain't working, I'm getting the pots off the fire, you stay here."

As Charles wrapped towels around his hands and reached in to grab the first pot, he heard laughter. It was almost like the laugh she had when she looked out the window in spring and the fat squirrels were clinging to the chickadee feeder, rocking it around, shaking seeds to the ground to fatten themselves up even more. She'd laugh and say, "Poor chickadees," but what could be done? And it was kind of like the laugh she had the time she was knitting a cardigan for an older lady in her church group who'd fallen ill and she got through nearly the whole sweater and realized she had somehow counted ten more stitches per row into the left sleeve than the right sleeve, and Charles assured her you couldn't tell— you really couldn't tell—but Maggie kept imagining that poor old woman tugging and picking at the smaller sleeve wondering why she felt so lopsided, and on top of being sick? Maggie had no choice but to laugh as stitch by stitch and row by row she undid the entire sleeve, winding the yarn back into a ball as she tugged her work loose. It was almost like those laughs.

But it wasn't. It wasn't those laughs, and the difference iced

Charles's blood even with his hands plunged into the fire. Naked, legs dripping, the soap crusting on her breasts in white scabs, Maggie laughed and laughed as she returned to the bedroom, pills rattling in her hand.

On New Year's Eve, one by one, the puppies opened their eyes.

The dappled gray girl with the white feet was first. "Well look at you," Charles whispered. He was sitting in a rocker beside the bassinet with a bowl of stew in his lap, chewing hunks of beef and cabbage. He rubbed her ears with his thumb as she looked around with quiet cries. "A lot to see. Those are your brothers and sisters." Charles held up a spoonful of stew. "This is cow. It's good, but you can't have cow just yet. You'll like cow. And who are you."

Charles knew Maggie had to have left the bedroom during the past week, but he never saw her. She had to be sneaking out when he was asleep on the couch. There would be a pitcher of water missing from the kitchen, or a box of crackers. Sometimes he heard laughter, but not often. He was grateful for that. Other times, if he pressed his ear to the door, he heard her voice, low and rapid, but he couldn't make out her words. The relentless rhythm could be prayer, it could be nonsense, or madness: he didn't know. As the days passed he grew thirsty for contact in the buried cabin, and he hadn't named the puppies he was mothering through the hours. He tried to think of them in abstract terms but that wasn't working in the slightest as he cradled them and mixed formula and revolved about them in his isolation, so when that dappled puppy finally opened her eyes and blinked as Charles licked his stew spoon, a deep piece of his gut seemed to snap, and he was able to say, "You're Addison."

A few minutes later, one of the boy's eyes peeled open. "Welcome to the party, bud." His pewter fur gave way to a creamy face and belly. "Lot quieter than Addie. Sister's got a lot to say. What about you?" Charles set his bowl on the floor and put the puppy in his lap. "Little guy, you seem like a Fred. Wanna be Fred? Yeah, you'll be Fred." Charles picked up the boy with the steel-colored tail and head. "You're Raoul. Raoul. What kinda name is that." Charles laughed. "You'll grow into it. And you," he said, wiggling the paw of the girl with muted gray and brown stripes across her back, "you are Lindsey. Lindsey's a pretty name. Pretty name for a pretty girl."

That left only the black runt to name. Charles grimaced to think of her as the runt, but she was: so weak compared to her brothers and sisters. Charles ached watching her shiver when she accidentally rolled away from the others. She worried him. He nursed the puppies on the rug—Raoul opened his eyes. A couple of hours later, Lindsey followed suit.

Fresh logs crackling in the hearth, Charles checked the grandfather clock: ten 'til twelve. He couldn't be certain, hidden from the sun, locked in the lantern-light, but he thought it was about to become a new year. He waited five more minutes and knocked on the bedroom door.

"Maggie? I might've lost track, but," Charles swiped at a tear rolling down his cheek, "but, it's New Year's, I think."

He closed his eyes and flattened a palm against the door. Four years ago on this night Charles and Maggie had plans to go to a New Year's "black tie" gala in the village, but the truck's engine wouldn't turn. Charles had known how silly the event was going to be—the same handful of folks from church who always put on potlucks and bingos, most likely wearing the same dresses and jackets they put on for services each Sunday and just calling it "black tie." Maybe some streamers and punch. But Charles fidgeted and fussed with the truck engine for twenty full minutes in the freezing wind, willing it to kick over, because Maggie was inside and she'd had her hair in rollers the whole day so it would lay in soft, dark curls around the shoulders of the dress she'd bought just for New Year's. It was deep emerald, a velvety material that showed her curves. Charles thought she looked so sophisticated. The one thing he'd always thanked God for was giving him such a wonderful wife, and her beauty that night made him realize the whole Bible's worth of praises couldn't capture how lucky he was.

He gave up on the truck when he looked down and saw a gash on his finger, bleeding heartily; his hands had grown so numb that he hadn't realized he'd sliced himself against part of the engine.

"I tried, baby. Truck's not going anywhere tonight."

Maggie had shut the door behind him and said, "I figured as much. Good thing we got a bottle of wine and some records right here, huh?" She handed him a glass and said, "Let's dance."

And they danced. They rarely drank: a glass of wine on Thanksgiving, a drink at New Year's, so as the bottle emptied their desires grew warmer until they stripped off the fancy clothes and touched and licked and caressed one another on the rug by the fire like a couple married for six hours as opposed to six years. They had stumbled to bed naked and talked and giggled for an hour until they fell asleep, well before midnight.

Charles rubbed his palm against the door. One of the puppies whimpered. He thought it was Raoul.

"Did you hear me? It's New Year's. We got about three minutes to midnight." Charles wanted to sob. He wanted to scream. But he spoke quietly, evenly. "Maggie, you have to talk to me. You've gotta come out. Come on out, now, and have New Year's with me."

It was muffled, but she responded.

"Wh—Mags, what was that? What'd you say?"

"When he brings darkness, it becomes night, and all the beasts of the forest prowl."

"Maggie?" Charles pounded on the door. "Open this. Right now!"

"Test the spirits."

"Right now, Maggie!"

The door opened. She had properly cleaned herself: Charles knew because she stood completely nude before him. She grinned. "Many false prophets have gone out into the world, Charles."

Trembling, Charles picked up Maggie's bathrobe and draped it over her shoulders, trying to tuck her arms into the sleeves. "It's freezing in here."

Maggie struggled out of his arms and closed her eyes. "My frame was not hidden from you when I was made in the secret place."

"Stop it."

"When I was woven together in the depths of the earth, your eyes saw my unformed body."

"*Stop it.*"

Maggie fell back on the bed and grabbed one of her breasts, slowly running a finger between her legs. "She said to herself, 'I am the one! And there is none besides me!'" The grandfather clock chimed midnight and Maggie moaned, then laughed. "What a ruin she has become, a lair for wild beasts!"

Charles yanked her hand from between her legs and pressed the bathrobe over her body.

She lashed at his face and screamed, "All who pass by her *scoff* and shake their fists!"

His lungs froze and he slapped her. He slapped her right across the face, and when the madness didn't leave her eyes, he slapped her harder.

Maggie looked up at Charles, crouched atop her, and whispered, "It's cold, Charles. It's really cold."

"Come on under the blankets." He pushed a bag of oyster crackers off the comforter, and, with a moment's hesitation, shoved Maggie's Bible to the floor as well. "There you go, snuggle in. Warmer?"

Maggie nodded, clutching at her shoulders with trembling hands. "Did you make a resolution?"

Charles shook his head. His blood was exhaustion. His skin was exhaustion. There were no words. When Maggie pulled back the corner of the blanket and patted the mattress, her eyes were wet and scared and something closer to normal. He pulled off his jeans and sweater and climbed in beside her. His eyelids felt magnetically compelled to close; he knew he'd have to be up in a few hours to check on the puppies, but the fire was strong, and he was so tired. His wife was warm, and close, and he was so tired.

Maggie kissed his cheek, murmured, "Happy new year," and Charles was gone.

It was dark when Charles opened his eyes. That didn't tell him anything. It was always dark. For weeks the world had been shadow and fire and lantern-light. Maggie wasn't in bed. He kicked off the blankets and felt his skin tighten in the frosted air, pulled on his clothes and crept to the door.

The fire was almost dead, just glowing coals across the den. Charles heard scraping in the kitchen and turned the corner to find Maggie furiously working at the wall of snow blocking the back exit. She wore a puffy coat over an old pair of overalls and scraped and pawed at the snow as high as she could reach, madly diving into it with her mittened hands, pulling chunks to the floor where a puddle was spreading around her feet.

"You're gonna ruin the floor," Charles said. Maggie didn't stop to acknowledge him. Charles returned to the den to rebuild the fire and tend to the puppies, who were loud with hunger. He strapped on the nursing vest and plopped the puppies on the rug, taking care to ensure the runt got her fill, as always. Cradling the little black puppy, Charles decided to name her Dora. It was the name Maggie planned to give their first daughter, after her great-aunt Dorothy, who meant a great deal to her, but also because the name meant "gift." He heard Maggie grunt as she fought against the snow. Dora hadn't opened her eyes yet.

Charles took off the vest and left the puppies on the rug. He stood behind Maggie in the kitchen. "What are you trying to do?"

Maggie pawed out a few more handfuls of snow before laughing and saying, "To *do*? What's it look like I'm trying to do, Charles?" He could see her wrists between the coat and mittens each time she reached up; the skin was red and raw.

"It looks like you're trying to escape."

"That's a good word for it."

"Suicide's a good word, too. That's all it is. You get out there, how you planning to get anywhere? You think someone's waiting for you up there? Think you're a rabbit, just gonna hop across the snow and up to town? You're just making it damp and awful for us in here, can't you hear them crying? They were starving. Didn't you hear them?"

Maggie panted, "I heard them," and kicked the snow. She sank into the icy puddle at her feet. "Hear them all the time. I *feel* them."

Charles crouched. "It's two boys, and three girls." He paused to gauge Maggie's reaction, but her face was blank. "There's Addie. Fred. There's, she's beautiful, with these stripes…she's Lindsey. Will you please come meet them? Please?"

"I always said, I always *thought*, that no bad could come our way 'cause you'd beat it off with a shovel or run it over with a tractor, or something." Maggie smiled. "I believed it, I really did, that Beelzebub himself could come knocking and you, your *goodness*, would make it so he couldn't step in the door." Maggie pulled off her mittens. "But, it's been told, we can't give the devil a foothold. We can't give him that."

Charles had trouble speaking. "I don't understand."

Maggie looked him in the eye. "He warned Jerusalem. Did we miss it? Did He warn us?"

Charles pulled Maggie out of the doorway and latched the exit. "You need to get by the fire." He nodded at her overalls. "You'll catch a cold in those."

Maggie stayed crumpled on the ground. She said, "He shoots with deadly and destructive arrows of famine. He shoots to destroy." She stretched out, extending her arms, pointing her feet. "Dogs surround me. A pack of villains encircles me. They pierce my hands and my feet."

She pulled in her legs, clutching them to her chest. As Charles dragged Maggie to the bedroom to strip her, drug her, and put her to bed, she began to cry. Her words were too soft to hear, but Charles caught enough to know the verse plaguing her mind.

I will send famine and wild beasts against you, and they will leave you childless.

The grandfather clock had chimed three more days when Dora finally opened her eyes. It had chimed perhaps twelve more days, or twenty, when the puppies began to walk. They'd doubled in size, and their ears were open. The muscles grew in their legs, and in their throats: they learned to love the sounds of their voices barking in high pitches. Charles set up the playpen to give them room to romp. A detachable bracket suspended a mobile of colorful smiley faces above the playpen. Charles would wind up the mobile, and as the red and blue and yellow faces began to circle in time to the tinkling music, Raoul, Addie, Lindsey, and Fred darted about, yapping at the faces and clawing at the sides of the pen. Dora stood in the middle, teetering uncertainly on her tiny legs before plopping down time and again. Again, and again, Charles wound the mobile, delighted as the puppies ran and ran and ran in dizzy puppy circles before falling into woozy naps. Smiley faces. Smiley puppies. Smiley Charles.

Charles started soaking kibbles of hard cat food in saucers of formula to transition the puppies into eating solids. He apologized each time he fed them, feeling like a failure because cat food was the best he could do; Maggie always had a soft spot for the strays that hung out by the shed, so they'd kept a bucket of cat kibble in the house for years. He'd never cared for the cats. Mangy, whining, flea-bitten things, not that it was their fault.

But he was so proud of his puppies: only one month old, and already walking!

When the puppies tired themselves out, Charles often took the opportunity to nap. Other times, though, he lit a cigar and sat down to read about parenting. Unlike Maggie's friends, who passed along the onesies and bottles and books when they started trying for a baby, his friends had passed along a box of cigars and some old *Playboy* magazines, assuring him that once the children arrived, his wife would never put out again. Charles and Maggie had a good laugh over those skin mags; Maggie was beet red when he first showed her, but it only took some kissing and compliments to convince her to strike a few poses for him to enjoy. She didn't let him take pictures, of course, but he cherished the memory.

Now he sat reading about the unique challenges of raising multiples: feeding regimens, sleeping schedules, travel safety. Charles glanced at the plates of soggy kibble littering the floor, and the puppies drowsing in a comatose lump in the playpen. He tried to picture the world above the snow: was a smoke-belching hole, where the chimney poked through, the only indication that he existed? That they were all alive? He turned back to the book.

The individualized attention bit concerned him. All of the experts recommended finding ways to spend one-on-one time with each multiple in order to develop their unique personalities, and to form a stronger parental bond. Charles had been homogenous in his fathering thus far, but he could work on that. Maybe walk Fred while the others ate, or read to Addie while her siblings napped. He would figure it out.

Cigar perched between his lips, Charles took the book into the bathroom to do his business. The plumbing had been frozen since the blizzard hit, so Charles had worked the bathroom window open, scooped out some snow, and poured hot water down the side of the cabin to melt a chute where he could dump the contents of the chamber pot, which wasn't a chamber pot at all but a regular cooking pot that he relished the thought of someday destroying. Charles squatted and read a "Helpful Hint" enclosed in a little box: "Don't be ashamed if you can't tell your multiples apart at first—this is normal! Put a small dab of nail polish on each baby's toe and create a color key so you know who's 'Aqua Blue' and who's 'Sassy Silver!'"

Charles ashed his cigar in the sink with a self-satisfied flourish; he knew how to tell all five of his apart from day one. He never had to paint them. Who paints their kids? He took his time finishing the cigar and flipping through chapters, making a mental note to revisit the selections on teething and circumcision. As Charles jimmied the window open, he heard a squeaky yip: Lindsey. A throatier bark followed: that had to be Raoul. And then nervous whining, frantic yelps, and Charles forgot about the chamber pot and raced out of the bathroom, nearly stumbling over Addie in the hallway. He quickly snatched her up and hugged her, put a finger to his lips and shut her in the laundry room. From the hallway, he saw Lindsey cowering in the kitchen, a shivering ball of soft stripes with big brown eyes, and then he was in the den.

Maggie rocked on her knees before the fire, naked, her arms submerged to the elbows in the cat kibble bucket; the kibble was strewn all about the room, lodged in the floorboards, dotting the rug. Maggie's hair ran in long, black waves down her back. Her face was pale, and her blank eyes fixed to the bottom of the bucket, to the bottom of the water lapping her forearms, lapping as she rocked and whispered frantically.

"Even from *birth* the wicked go astray, even from the *womb* they are wayward and speak *lies*, and women *will* be saved through childbearing, if we do *not* give the devil a foothold, if we watch for those evildoers and mutilators of the flesh—"

Charles leapt on Maggie, slamming her head into the brick hearth. The bucket toppled, and the water washed across the floor. Charles gently turned the bucket and reached in. The body was sodden and dense, and her legs dangled inert, paws limp. Her little square head lolled as he laid her near the flames. He rubbed her side with two fingers, and water trickled from her lips. The tiny black chest didn't rise. She was soaking, freezing, dead.

Charles looked away from Dora's drowned body to the playpen. The netting. The other puppies had been able to climb the playpen's netted sides and jump out when Maggie reached in to grab one of them, but Dora wasn't strong enough to run yet. She hadn't learned to walk.

And she hadn't known to close her eyes.

Maggie didn't scream when she woke up tied to the rocking chair, her wrists and ankles bound to the armrests and glider posts, duct tape wound thick across her stomach. Charles had expected her to scream. He'd wanted her to scream.

For the next week he let the puppies run amok. Raoul tore the heads from pastel stuffed animals. Addie loved rattles. She'd toss them in the air and whip them back and forth, *shake shake shake*, until she was too tired to move, and then she'd wake up and *shake shake shake* some more. Lindsey and Fred were wrestlers, intent to gnaw each other's napes and growl and pounce all throughout the blended days and nights. Charles lounged on the couch reading fairy tales aloud, or he sprawled on the floor and let the puppies dance across his chest and face.

He gave Maggie water and fed her potatoes. She started whimpering on the second day, when she couldn't hold her waste in anymore. Charles didn't untie her. Maggie soaked in her mess, and Charles lit more cigars to amend the den's thick odor.

On the third day, Charles pressed the puppies' paws in finger paint from Maggie's craft box and guided them across sheets of paper. He pasted the sheets into the baby memory book he found on the "MOMMY'S CORNER" shelf, and held the book close to Maggie's face so she could see each of their little paw prints.

On the fourth day, Maggie begged for the Lord to intervene. Charles duct-taped her mouth.

On the fifth day, Charles boiled gallons of water and took a long, luxurious bath.

On the sixth day, Charles removed the tape from Maggie's mouth and let her have a sip of water. He replaced the tape.

On the seventh day, he moved the puppies to the bedroom, and when the grandfather clock struck twelve, Charles cut Maggie free. He wielded the butcher knife with a light, loose touch.

"Charles—"

He pressed the broad side of the blade to Maggie's lips and shook his head.

Charles stepped into the bedroom and latched the door. He doused the lantern, and in the darkness, he tried to remember his wife in an apron scrambling eggs, knitting scarves in the passenger seat of the truck, meticulously sorting coupons from the Sunday circular, but he couldn't overcome that vision of a ghoulish woman sticky with the residues of tape and vacated bowels, her hair a den of greasy black snakes shielding a face that Charles no longer recognized.

The government didn't finalize the death count until early summer; all told, they said, the blizzard claimed eleven thousand lives. The elderly and the poor crowded in the unheated apartments of the tri-state's big cities made up a small slice. Carbon monoxide poisoning peacefully swept away some suburban families as they slept. Would-be heroes died in attempts to rescue stranded motorists. But the bulk of the corpses came from deep in the Kentucky hills, from the forgotten Appalachian villages, the inaccessible hollers. It was a winter catastrophe the likes of which the States had never seen. The cities were chaos; resources couldn't be wasted on the scattered, hidden populations of the hills.

Charles found Maggie's body in mid-March, frozen and partially submerged in the last two feet of snow. She'd made it a quarter mile from the cabin. The tunnel she dug had collapsed before Charles awoke on the day of her escape, and he had closed the back door against the crumbling white chunks and latched the deadbolt. He reported her passing as a stir-crazy accidental suicide, and the sheriff nodded, and the coroner jotted "hypothermia" on yet another death certificate before signing off to have Maggie dumped in an icy plot beside the hundreds of other corpses pouring in from the surrounding hills.

Charles felt the years, their definition and passing, evolve with the breadth of his family's sorrows and joys—the outrage when Addie became pregnant just past her second birthday, and the complete dissipation of that anger when Charles greeted his dappled grandpuppies; the unrelenting heartache of losing Raoul before he turned ten, but the wonder of watching Raoul's own grandpuppies flourish, then his great-grandpuppies, darting about the yard with drool flying from their tiny, smushed faces.

It wasn't a bad life. If he couldn't speak of it, couldn't rationalize it, then that only proved the folly of words, he reasoned.

When Charles turned ninety and the succession of years began to erode his mind's inhibitions, he told the nurses in the home about the winter the snow fell so thick that it erased the cabins in the valleys, erased the gravestones and the churches. He held a dog close to his side, the dog the staff allowed him to keep as a therapy pet, stroking her jet-black ears as he silently prayed for his memories to survive, praying the love he felt and miracles he remembered wouldn't be lost to the insurmountable whiteness just over the horizon. Charles hugged the dog, and he told the nurses of a storm so vicious that God Himself was blinded, the winter so cold that God broke the rules of His creation and sent forth His precious creatures to be born in new ways, hopeful for His children, testing the faith of the little human creatures spiraling smoke and prayers unto the heavens.

Ron Rash

Something Rich and Strange

She follows the river's edge downstream, leaving behind her parents and younger brother who still eat their picnic lunch. It is Easter break and her father has taken time off from his job. They have followed the Appalachian Mountains south, stopping first in Gatlinburg, then the Smokies, and finally this river. She finds a place above a falls where the water looks shallow and slow. The river is a boundary between Georgia and South Carolina, and she wants to wade into the middle and place one foot in Georgia and one in South Carolina so she can tell her friends back in Nebraska she has been in two states at the same time.

She kicks off her sandals and enters, the water so much colder than she imagined, and quickly deeper, up to her kneecaps, the current surging under the smooth surface. She shivers. On the far shore a granite cliff casts this section of river into shadow. She glances back to where her parents and brother sit on the blanket. It is warm there, the sun full upon them. She thinks about going back but is almost halfway now.

She takes a step and the water rises higher on her knees. Four more steps, she tells herself. Just four more and I'll turn back. She takes another step and the bottom is no longer there and she is being shoved downstream and she does not panic because she has passed the Red Cross courses. The water shallows and her face breaks the surface and she breathes deep. She tries to turn her body so she won't hit her head on a rock and for the first time she's afraid and she's suddenly back underwater and hears the rush of water against her ears. She tries to hold her breath but her knee smashes against a boulder and she gasps in pain and water pours into her mouth. Then for a few moments the water pools and slows. She rises coughing up water, gasping air, her feet dragging the bottom like an anchor trying to snag waterlogged wood or rock jut and as the current quickens again she sees her family running along the shore and she knows they are shouting her name though she cannot hear them and as the current turns her she hears the falls and knows there is nothing that will keep her from it as the current quickens and quickens and another rock smashes against her knee but she hardly feels it as she snatches another breath and she feels the river fall and she falls with it as water whitens around her and she falls deep into the whiteness and as she rises her head scrapes against a rock ceiling and the water holds her there and she tells herself don't breathe but the need rises inside her beginning in the upper stomach then up through her chest and throat and as that need reaches her mouth her mouth and nose open and the lungs explode in pain and then the pain is gone as bright colors shatter around her like glass shards, and she remembers her sixth-grade science class, the gurgle of the aquarium at the back of the room, the smell of chalk dust that morning the teacher held a prism out the window so it might fill with color, and she has a final, beautiful thought—that she is now inside that prism and knows something even the teacher does not know, that the prism's colors are voices, voices that swirl around her head like a crown, and at that moment her arms and legs she did not even know were flailing cease and she becomes part of the river.

The search and rescue squad and the sheriff arrived at the falls late that afternoon. Two of the squad members were brothers, one in his early twenties, the other thirty. They had a carpentry business, building patios and decks for lawyers and doctors from Greenville and Columbia who owned second homes in the mountains. The third man, the diver, was in his early forties and taught biology at the county high school. The sheriff looked at his watch and figured they had two hours at most before the gorge darkened. Even so the diver did not hurry to put on his wet suit and air tanks. He smoked a cigarette and between puffs talked to the sheriff about the high school basketball team. They had worked together before and knew death punched no time clock.

When the diver was ready, a length of nylon rope was clasped tight under his arms. The older, stronger brother held the other end. The diver waded into the river, the rope trailing behind him like a leash. He dipped his mask in the water, put it on, and leaned forward. The three men onshore watched as the black fins propelled the diver into the hydraulic's ceaseless blizzard of whitewater. The men on the bank sat on rocks and waited. With his free hand, the older brother pointed upstream to a bend where he'd caught a five-pound trout last fall. The sheriff asked what he'd used for bait but didn't hear the answer because the mask bobbed up in the headwater's foam.

The brother tightened the slack and pulled but nothing gave until the others grabbed hold as well. They pulled the diver into the shallows and helped him onto shore. Between watery coughs he told them he'd found her in the undercut behind the hydraulic. She had been upright, her head and back and legs pressed against a rock slab. Only her hair moved, its long strands streaming upward. As the diver drifted close, he saw that her eyes were open. Their faces were inches apart when he slipped an arm around her waist. Then the hydraulic ripped free the mask and mouthpiece, grabbed the dive light spiraling it toward the darkness.

The diver told the men kneeling beside him that the girl's blue eyes had life in them. He could feel her heart beating against his chest and hear her whispering. Before or after your mask was torn off, the sheriff asked. The diver did not know, but swore that he'd never enter the river again.

The younger brother scoffed, while the older spoke of narcosis though the pool was no more than twenty feet deep. But the sheriff did not dismiss what the diver said. He too had seen strange and inexplicable things involving the dead but had never mentioned them to others and did not choose to now. We'll find another way, he said, but that river has to lower some before I allow anyone else in there.

The diver had trouble sleeping afterward. Every night when he closed his eyes, he saw the girl's wide blue eyes, the flowing golden hair. His wife slept beside him, her body curled into his chest. They had no children and now he was glad for that. He had seen a picture of the parents in the local paper. They had been on the shore, within thirty feet of the undercut that held their daughter, the expressions on their faces beyond grief.

On the third night, the diver fell into a deeper sleep and the girl came with him. They were in the undercut again but now the river was tepid and he could breathe. As he embraced her, she whispered that this world was better than the one above and she should never have been afraid. He emerged in his wife's embrace. It's just a bad dream, she kept saying until he quit gasping. His wife closed her eyes and was quickly asleep, but he could not, so went into the kitchen and graded lab tests until dawn.

The girl remained in the river. Volunteers cast grappling hooks from the banks and worked them like lures through the pool or stood in the shallows or on rocks and jabbed with long metal poles. Some of the old-timers suggested dynamite but the girl's parents would not hear of it. The sheriff said what they needed was a week without rain.

The diver slept little the next few nights. In class he placed the students in small groups and had them discuss assigned chapters among themselves. He knew they talked about the prom instead of pupae and chrysalides, but he didn't care. On the third afternoon, he skipped the teacher's meeting and sat alone in his classroom. The school, emptied of students, was quiet, the only sound the gurgle of the aquarium. He would never speak to anyone, not even his wife, about what happened in the classroom's stillness but that evening he told the sheriff he'd dive for the girl again.

Days passed. Rain came often, long rains that made every fold of ridge land a tributary and merged earth and water into a deep orange-yellow rush. Banks disappeared as the river reached out and dragged them under. But that was only surface. In the undercut all remained quiet and still, the girl's transformation unrushed, gentle. Crayfish and minnows unknitted flesh from bone, attentive to loosed threads.

Then the rain stopped and the river ran clear again. Boulders vanished for weeks reappeared. Sandbars and stick jams gathered in new configurations. The water warmed and caddis flies broke through the river's skin to make their brief flights before falling back into their element.

The sheriff called the diver and told him the river was low enough to try again. The next day they walked the half mile down the path to the falls. There were five of them this time, the sheriff, his deputy, the two brothers, and the diver. The sheriff insisted on two ropes, making sure they stayed taut. The water was clearer than last time and offered less resistance. The diver entered the abeyance as though parting a curtain, the river suddenly muted.

She was less of what she had been, the blue rubbed from her eyes, flesh freed from the chandelier of bone. He touched what had once been a hand. The river whispered to him that it would not be long now.

When he returned to shore, he told them her body was gone, not even a scrap of clothing or bone. He told them the last hard rain must have swept her downstream. The younger brother said the diver should go back and search the left and right side of the falls. He argued the body could still be there. The deputy suggested they lower an underwater camera into the pool.

The sheriff shook his head and said to let her be. The men walked up the trail, back toward their vehicles, their lives. The midday sun leaned close and dazzling. Dogwoods bloomed small white stars. The diver knew in the coming days the petals would find their way into the river, drifting onto sandbars and gliding the backs of pools, and the diver knew some would drift through the rapids and over the falls into the hydraulic. They would furl amid the last bones and like the last bones they would finally slip free.

Out from Under

And these signs shall follow them that believe; In my name shall they cast out devils; they shall speak with new tongues; They shall take up serpents; and if they drink any deadly thing, it shall not hurt them; they shall lay hands on the sick, and they shall recover.

—Mark 16:17-18

The snakes had become commonplace. As common as writing your name on a piece of paper. As common as watching Hailey Grace Walker faint during worship, convulsing on the hardwood floor, praising the Lord Jesus. Common.

Eli looked, from across the room, upon his brother who sat on the kitchen floor with his thin, six-year-old arms folded tightly. The left hand tucked under the right armpit, body rocking back and forth. The small boy had rolled into a ball and wept a harsh and throaty sob. Their father, mud on his boots and streaked across his forehead, kneeled and rubbed a circle between the boy's shoulder blades.

"What's wrong, sweetheart?"

He reached and took the boy's wrist.

"Lord have mercy," he said.

He picked up Andrew from under the arms and lifted him to the kitchen counter, the child's arm inflating like a grotesque balloon. "Eli," he said, "take that Bible there and turn to Mark. It's a rattler bite." He opened a drawer and found some towels while Eli grabbed the family Bible off the counter.

Flipping through the thin pages, "We taking him to the doctor?" Eli asked.

"No."

Eli looked up, though continued brushing through pages with thoughtless fingers.

"If we pray and have faith, God will be obligated to protect us. Don't need man's medicine."

"We ain't taking him to the doctor?"

"No."

"But—"

The tall man turned to his son. His eyes moved close to Eli's and nearly crossed in the closeness. "You mind me, boy," he said. "The Holy Ghost'll protect us. Turn that page to Mark."

Eli tried, but for the life of him, he could not find the gospel. The crinkling of onion paper seemed to scream until the Bible slipped from his hands and onto the floor, clapping as the pages came sloppily together. Eli froze, eyes on the book now at his feet.

"Pick it up," his father said, "it's after Matthew."

Their father had been going to church for several weeks on his own before he told his family that he'd been saved. He told them that Jesus had healed his drinking problem and that things would be different. True. The weeks after Jesus saved his soul, life had been easier. His father didn't yell like he used to. Or smell like he used to. Indeed, he told the family constantly about all the good Jesus had done for him, and before long, the whole family started going to church. To a church buried deep in the mountains amongst a thick forest of spruce-firs and rhododendrons, through paths of dirt speckled with granite lumps that grew from the ground like oversized tumors. To find forgiveness. A kind of salvation in the dark.

So, after Andrew's bite, the regular thing to do was to go to worship and pray with the church for Andrew's healing. Eli's mother decided to, instead, stay home with Andrew and to pray over him. Prayer: simple and precise. As simple as asking and receiving, but Eli wondered if this is the way the Lord worked, or just the way we'd like Him to work.

The sun fell behind the high horizon and the beautiful Sunday turned to black. The church was built of gray cinderblocks. A tiny box of a building: the ceiling low and the room smelling of sour wood—likely from water damage behind the paint. The pews and seats occupied much of the space, allowing little room to move

around, but they made do. A sloppy painting hung near the front
of the room with a Jesus that looked Eli desperately in the eye. An
upright piano with a finish that expired long ago sat in a corner
along with a few closed guitar cases. The men wore rough wool
suits and their elbows collided and bumped into one another. Eli
began to wonder how many more would be able to fit before it
would be difficult to breathe.

A man stood in the middle and was the gravity of the room. He
shook hands as people passed by. The pinky finger on his right hand
was missing. In its place, a flat nub of skin, scarred and scratched.
He wore a black suit, black tie, white shirt. His ears were long and
spotted. When his father greeted the man in the black suit, they met
with smiles and hardy handshakes and called each other "brother."
He called himself Brother Timothy. He extended his right hand
toward Eli with, "Good to see you again, Eli." Eli did not want to
shake the deformed hand, but he was getting older, thirteen, and
when a man held out his hand, you shook it. So, Eli reached out and
took this hand that felt dry and rough and incomplete with only
three thick fingers wrapping around the whole of his hand.

Eli and his father said their greetings and then moved to a spot
in the pews. Their seat creaked and rocked with their weight. Once
the pews filled, people sat in foldout chairs that lined the walls—
some, women with babies in their laps. More people entered the
church. Eli heard the occasional "glory" or "hallelujah." The
spiritual yelps of those so compelled by the Holy Spirit.

The flow of bodies slowed to an eventual stop, and as usual,
the air did indeed become more difficult to breathe. Brother
Timothy approached the podium and he spoke. "The Holy Ghost
is with us tonight. Praise be to God." He opened his Bible and
read a passage, Mark 16:17-18. "Yessir, the Lord is good, brothers
and sisters," he said. "May God bless and heal those of us who are
sick and struggling. Remember, the power of prayer is amazing. I
know Brother Lucius, who I was just talking to, said that he was
having some sort of headache and was having trouble seeing, God
bless him. He needs our prayers, so I ask all y'all to pray for him
tonight if you would, not to forget about him, and to give the

glory to God for our brother's healing. I'd like to also dedicate tonight's service to a sweet little boy named Andrew who was bit just the other day. Bit by a rattler, he was. And I'd like for all y'all to give an extra special prayer for him, because as you know it, children are blessings to us from the Lord, I firmly believe that. And I know we can heal him. We can heal him with the help of the Lord, hallelujah." The crowd mumbled their amens and then Brother Timothy stuffed a paper of notes back into his breast pocket and opened the floor to other requests.

A woman then raised her hand and complained of back pain. Another woman said her daughter was sick with an infection. A man asked the room to pray for a severe toothache. This went on and on. At times, someone might give a reason to praise God for working a miracle in their life. Prayer requests and praisings followed with enthusiasm and energy. In time, every person rose to his feet, adults, children, babies in arms. People wiped their foreheads with sleeves or handkerchiefs, but no one left, just crowded closer, raising hands and talking about Jesus.

Then, without cue, a man began clapping. And then another joined. Soon, much of the room pounded their hands together until the clapping found a rhythm. A tambourine shook. One man stood with eyes closed and started dancing. His dance was strange and out of sync with the beat. His limbs began to jerk and shake, like having a seizure on his feet. He reached over and grabbed a woman's shoulders and seemed to transfer his convulsions to her, and then she began shaking about the room much in the same way. A teenaged boy in the corner raised his hand above his head and spoke in tongues, kinds of words that Eli could never understand. More hands reached for the ceiling. A woman fell to her knees with fingers flattened together. Tears bloomed and then rolled like marbles from her eyes and onto her dress. The dancing man then dropped to the floor, his eyelids twitching, showing only the whites of his eyes from underneath.

The hammering of piano keys brought a new texture and vibrancy to the music. Singing became infectious and it was not long before the music turned deafening. A choir of voices without cohesion. Eli felt the rhythm under his skin, in his chest. It felt exciting, almost intoxicating. Almost like happiness. Visceral. His brain wanted to drown in the pleasant discord, but he did not allow it. It was too strange. Too bizarre. So instead, he rose from his pew and watched from afar and kept an eye on the happenings. His father, however, joined the clapping, bouncing his hips back and forth with a smile on his face. Every now and again someone might bump into Eli in midst of the excited dance. It was strong, vivid, tribal. His father no longer paid attention to his son. He moved on and joined the other members—it was the dance.

A deep-voiced woman shouted from inside the nest of people, "Praise be to God!"

Someone passed a wooden box to Brother Timothy, and Eli knew immediately what came next. The lid was the kind that slid open. Its construction was plain. The wood, clean yellow and jagged. Brother Timothy—the man dressed all in black—reached both hands inside and pulled out a wad of snakes entwined in a grotesque tangle. A man reached in and grabbed one and danced in awkward circles, chanting strange words. A woman reached and grabbed, then someone else did the same. Small children giggled and smiled, unbothered at the serpents writhing between the hands of the adults. Snakes flew across the room and landed on the wooden floorboards with meaty thuds. They were then picked up and passed to anyone willing.

A thud.

Pass.

Thud.

Pass.

One landed ten feet away from Eli's feet. It made a move in his direction, but his father scooped it up. He held the snake at its head and tail and he began to dance in circles with it. His eyes were wild and weird, mad. He held the snake above his head and mumbled strange words. There was an eccentric energy that followed him and his snake. A commanding energy, like triumph. His father passed the snake off to a young man that Eli did not know, and the dance grew more serious. There was a rattle. People backed out of the way, clearing room. Some shouted praises to the Lord, others shouted in tongues. Women clapping, children laughing. The energy of the movement. The sound of the rattle.

The dancing stopped of a sudden. Voices quieted as though suddenly muted. The tambourine was the last to stop—it was the rattle. Brother Timothy grabbed the snake from the floor, just behind the head and by the body, and passed it off and away from the young man. Eli heard a woman say, "Lord have mercy." He peeked through the crowd and could see two puncture marks in the meat of the young man's left hand below his pinky finger. His hand was rapidly swelling and looked less and less like a real hand and more like a plastic imitation.

The once lively room had dropped to a breathless silence, save for the hissing and rattling of angry snakes being shoved back into their wooden box. Brother Timothy rested a hand on the bitten man's shoulder and spoke. "It's okay everybody. It's all right. The Holy Ghost is with us. These snakes bite sometimes. You know it just as good as I do and sometimes we can't help it." He paused to look about the room. "If we pray for our brothers' healings, and we are true believers in Him, then God is obligated to answer our prayers. Did you hear what I said? *True* believers in Him, and God will take control." And then he erupted, "Praise be to God!" The crowd responded with shouts and praises.

The young man, bitten by the snake, looked down at his hand with an open mouth at a slight grin. Amazement. As though he were proud of it, as though his turn had finally arrived. Rosy blood escaped and rounded his wrist before dribbling to the wooden floorboards. His flesh would soon swell and then darken to purple and his fingers would turn shiny, like sausages. In time, one of his fingers would blacken and finally free itself from the other digits, like the umbilical cord releasing from an infant's belly. A sign that the child is free from its mother, now ready to enter fully into this strange and unusual world.

Eli's finger drew his name in the sawdusted table of the toolshed. He was not allowed, but inside he was. Darkness there, though blades of late-afternoon light seeped through the horizontal cracks of the boards. His hand hit a glass Pepsi-Cola bottle. It fell on its side and rolled off the table until hitting the ground without breaking. He heard a slight hissing, the sound of dead leaves being rustled by something small. He thought it was probably a mouse. His clothes, the spaces between his fingers and nails, all collected dust and dirt. Old lawn mower blades sat worn and rusted and tangled up in spiderwebs. His shoe shuffled the fine, silky dirt as he looked around. Something hard hit the skin covering his anklebone. Eli groaned at the pain and bit his lower lip and looked down at the cause. A block of wood. His father had been making things for the church since he found Jesus. Pieces of his carpentry lay everywhere. His ankle throbbed, but he could not tell if it bled or not. Reaching down, he felt dirt and warmth where the skin swelled. No blood. A thick flap hung to the side. The surrounding tissue bruised to a dark purple that hurt to touch.

The shed was very old, the wood weathered and paint chipping. Not unlike their house. When he was younger he asked his father if the house would fall on them. His father answered that God wouldn't let the house collapse because God protected them.

In a corner, there was a large box with a lid that slid open. He needed two hands to pick it up. It was light and felt empty. Its construction was plain. The wood, a clean yellow and jagged. He pinched the edge of the lid and wiggled it until it began to slide open. A dark substance that looked of feces was smeared on the inside. It smelled awful, rancid. Eli slid it shut quickly, and it closed with a clap. He felt the urge to vomit, the need for new air. Throwing the shed door open, he ran outside. A small brown mouse followed between his legs and out to the grass of the front yard. He thought he could smell vomit coming up, but it stayed down.

The smell.

He thought of his older brother, dead brother. He remembered being small and running to his older brother's room and seeing a blue arm hang out from under the bed. Fingers relaxed, pointing toward the ceiling. His mother pulled J.R.'s body out—the shoulder, loose and noodle-like. His twelve-year old frame slim and lean, healthy. Except for the pale color of his skin. Streams and chunks of vomit running over puffed cheeks. He remembered his mother reaching her fingers inside J.R.'s mouth to scoop the vomit out and how his older brother's head bobbed with the motion of her fingers. He remembered the miniature liquor bottles, scattered and emptied on the floor. He remembered when his father came stumbling down the hall, belt in hand, stink on his breath, and how he reached down and picked up Eli by the shirt and yelled, "What the damn hell are y'all screaming about?" Eli remembered his father's eyes as he looked over and saw the blue body on the floor and how he pushed his wife over and shook his dead son, occasionally slapping him in the face trying to bring him back to life. Sometimes at night Eli thought that he could see two eyes staring at him through the dark. The eyes were just pinholes in the blinds and the smells of vomit and liquor were but a memory of over seven years now.

He rinsed off his ankle with the water hose. It was cold.

Eli often wondered if he'd rather his father the way he used to be, or the father he had become. Sometimes he wondered if there was a difference between the two.

The infection had gotten worse. Eli figured that Andrew would soon die. The arm of the six-year old looked too large for his small body. He lay in his bed sweating. A wooden cross nailed above the bedpost. Eli pulled a layer of sheets back and fanned his brother's face. The area around the bite wound was now black, blue, red, yellow, infected. To Eli, it looked to be only a matter of time before the skin split from the swelling—impressive that it stretched as much as it had. A drop of sweat escaped Andrew's thin brow and traced the crease just before his ear then down to jaw and absorbed into his pillow.

Years before, their father had been bitten by a rattler. He was sick for a day until he came to the breakfast table and announced that Jesus had healed him. "Praise be to God." At a church bonfire, their mother stuck her hands into a pit of fire and came out unscathed. "Praise be to God." Last week during worship, Mrs.

Jennifer from down the street drank a vial of poison and didn't so much as get sick. "Praise be to God."

His father came in with his Bible curled under his right hand. "We'll heal him, son. Don't worry. Us and Jesus." He took a few steps forward, flipping through the pages. His father was very tall. Hair, jet black. His wrists were thin, but his hands were the size of baseball mitts. He held the book with one of his hands and put the other on Andrew's sweating forehead. His father took in a breath to speak, and three sharp knocks stopped him. He placed the Bible down on Andrew's nightstand and walked to the front door. Eli followed.

Deputy Skaggs stood at the front door, as he did from time to time. His father would say the deputy was a good young man, just doing his job and didn't mean any harm. The two greeted, referring to each other by their first names and were, as they always were, very cordial to the other.

"Got us a young man in the hospital last night, over a snakebite. Said he was hiking out in the woods, but I asked myself, who would go hiking at that late of hour?"

"Well sir, I hadn't got an answer for you."

"Heard tale y'all taking up serpents again. Praising the Lord while you're at it."

"Well Deputy, what I can tell you is that this town loves Jesus and that everyone praises Him different. I can't tell you why people say what they say, just as much as I can't say why people do what they do."

"You know if you get caught, we can pop a fine on you real quick or take you down to county for a while. And if minors is at risk we'll take you in for more than just a few days."

"Yessir."

The officer peeked his head over his shoulder and looked at Eli. "Everything okay, son?"

Eli stood, staring blankly at the officer.

"Yessir, everything here's just fine. My boy over there is sensitive about strangers is all."

The officer looked at Eli for a bit before turning back to his father, "All right then. Like I was saying, the Sheriff's got me doing door-to-doors today. Making sure everyone knows how the law is. You can get yourself locked up for handling around here. All that drinking poison and whatnot. Too many people don't come back from that sort of thing."

"I understand."

"You and your boy have a good day."

"We will, and God bless."

Deputy Skaggs walked off the front porch and back to his cruiser and drove down the dirt driveway onto the dirt road. His father shut and locked the door.

"Called Brother Timothy earlier," he said to Eli. "He'll be over shortly. Says he can help heal your brother." Eli doubted very much that his prayers were being listened to, like radio signals drifting off into space. Though he would not tell of his doubt or his fear that Jesus was not coming to help. Though Eli pressed his hands together anyway. He laced his fingers and bowed his head and then he prayed. And he prayed.

The kitchen was warm and quiet with the occasional click of spoon and pot or crinkling of a page turning. Light had only just broken over the horizon. The sun took longer to crawl over the ridgeline in the morning, though the air stayed cool and crisp. Eli's mother put a bowl of grits in front of him.

"Careful, it's hot," she said.

Eli scooped up a spoon-full, blew on it, and brought it to his mouth. Still too hot.

"Stir it to get the heat out," she said.

"Okay," he answered, steam billowing.

"Did you check on Andrew?" she asked.

"Yes, ma'am. He's the same."

"You know, it's his birthday soon."

"So. He's still sick." Eli spooned a small amount of grits into his mouth and swallowed it. "And, it don't make no difference anyhow. We'll just go to another church meeting. What's he got to get excited about?"

"Boy," his father looked up from his bible, "he's got Jesus to get excited about, that's what," he said pointing with his spoon.

Eli stared at his grits and kept stirring, steam still billowing. A few minutes passed. "Why don't we have a television set?" he asked.

His father answered, "Because."

"We used to have one."

"We're not getting a television set."

"My teacher says that Nixon and Kennedy are going to debate on television and that all us need to watch it."

He didn't answer.

"I thought I saw a snake go in the shed," Eli said.

"What were you doing in the shed?"

"I didn't," he lied, "I just thought I saw one go in."

"Boy, you ain't to go around chasing snakes, you understand me?"

"Yessir."

"And, I've told you before, you're not to go near that shed."

"Yessir."

"I mean it. This ain't no joke. You want to get bit too? You want to be hurting like your brother?"

"Well, then why do you get to play with snakes? You got bit once and came out okay."

His father reached across the table, and with a large hand, slapped Eli across the face. Hard. "You stay away from that shed, you understand me?"

Eli put a hand to his face and could feel warmth rise to the surface. He looked at the table with glared eyes, refusing the tears that were trying to push their way out.

He looked down at his father's clenched fist and said only, "Yessir."

A green suitcase lay open on Eli's bed and Eli filled it with clothes. There was no plan, his plan was only to do. Just do and nothing else. His father was off to see Brother Linley to spread the word that the family needed as many prayers as possible. His mother sat on the front porch, rocking back and forth, speaking in tongues. It was night. He knew he couldn't take Andrew with him, but he hoped he could at least go down the road and find someone to help, maybe that police officer, or just any place that had a telephone.

Once a few articles were packed in, he left enough room for other things he might need to keep him occupied. His eyes scanned the room. He found a copy of *Treasure Island*. A couple of bottles of Pepsi-Cola. All of which his parents did not know he had. He packed the things he valued and things that would bring him comfort during lonely nights. His eyes caught the leather binding with the golden words "Holy Bible" printed down the spine. He considered it for a moment before closing and latching his suitcase. He was leaving to get help, but he knew that even if he didn't find that help, he would not come back. He would hide, like a mouse in its hole, underneath and never surface.

Andrew's door stood ajar, though inside was black. The black looked of death. He was afraid to go in. He had this idea that if he did, death might pull him under too. His brother was underneath the covers, rising and falling heavily with a slight wheeze. Before he entered, he rested his suitcase against the splintered doorjamb. He could smell vomit. For a moment, he wondered if the smells of death and vomit were the same. He stepped slowly so that death couldn't hear his intrusion. He stopped a few feet away from the foot of Andrew's bed. "I'm sorry I'm leaving," he whispered, "but, I'm gonna go find you a doctor, I promise. And you'll get better, and we'll both be better and gone and away from here." He stood for a minute or so and looked at his brother one last time until he finally turned away toward the doorjamb, where their father stood with a green suitcase between two hands and then dropped the suitcase to the ground.

"Where you going?"

Eli's lip jumped up and down, but he wasn't going to cry.

"You're just going to leave us? Leave God? Your brother?"

He tried to say yes, but only the sound that came was of air shaking out of his nose. His father took two fast steps, grabbed him by the shirt and jammed his back into the wall behind. Eli heard a crack from his spine suddenly straightening.

"Just like that?" He let go, and Eli fell to the floor in a heap. Still, he did not cry. His father went to Andrew's side and pulled the sheets back. "Wake up, sweetheart." He put his hands under Andrew's armpits and sat him up. Andrew's face was tired, and his breath slightly wheezed. Their father reached over and lifted up the bitten arm. He flipped on a lamp to kill the dark, and there, like perfect symmetry, was perhaps a thing Eli hoped to never see. A sick sort of providence. The healthy arm of a six-year-old boy. The swelling, nearly gone. There was only the slightest sign of bruising. "See," his father said, "the Lord is good. It was His will to let us fix this, understand? You have to have faith, son."

A tear trekked its way down Eli's cheek.

Then another.

And then another.

He refused to but wept anyway. He was not leaving, and he reckoned that he never was. He wept out of anger, out of hate. Hate for his father and hate for the Lord. Eli imagined the Holy Ghost with fingers wrapped around his small body, face and legs. Suffocating him and never letting go. He was angry and not sure why. Everything was set in its rightful place and all would be okay.

Praise be to God.

Fred Venturini

Survey

The mall's pedestrian traffic was forceful and circulatory—to stand still and bagless was to be a clot against the steady veins of people streaming in and out of stores, going in empty-handed, coming out with stuffed bags, now oxygenated until the next sale or fashion fad rolled around. Chatter echoed throughout the two levels, a high and hollow sound in the mall's center, by the wishing well.

Frank just observed from a bench in the center of the mall, not wanting to chase his wife through a rapid barrage of designer stores. He hated sitting in the store's designer couches, always next to strangers, usually other men who were also caught up chasing the vapor trail of a shopping woman. He staked out an easy chair he could keep to himself, twirling his cellphone in his hands—Angie would call when she was done ravaging all the racks and dressing rooms the mall had to offer.

The mall bored him. He considered himself a poor consumer, tight with a dollar, not out of responsibility but of petulance. He checked the phone, impatient, willing it to buzz. The wait was akin to sitting in the lobby of a chain restaurant on a Friday night, hoping the oversized pager would rattle and flash—nothing but strangers and a lack of space. The waiting had a way of rubbing up against time, throttling each second down to a crawl.

After an hour, he decided to take a walk. He didn't move at the mall crowd's frantic pace. They were walking to get somewhere; he was in stroll mode, getting lapped by everyone from impatient teenagers to senior citizens walking for fitness. He caught a whiff of the chemicals in the wishing well water. Pennies corroded at the bottom, but not as many as there used to be. The debit card era had degraded the will to have a wish granted, apparently.

He decided the far right of the mall hallway was the wheels lane—stroller, wheelchair, walkers with tennis balls on the legs, which were close enough to qualify. Left of that was for the slow to middle movers—couples holding hands, husbands and boyfriends cut loose on their own, middle-aged folks in no hurry. The far left lane was for the determined consumers, the lifeblood of the economy, the women and girls and too-stylish boys walking like the place was burning down, bags flapping against their hips.

In perhaps the mall's most well-designed area, a cookie shop was set up next to a nutrition store. Coincidentally, the exact same ratio of fat-to-fit people were walking into each of them. Nothing could quite top the look of a fat guy coming out of the GNC with a bottle of vitamins and low-calorie meal replacement shakes, and locking eyes with a fit man his own age about to eat a cookie the size of a manhole cover.

A young girl stood against the movement of the crowd, pacing back and forth among the froth of people—eighteen, cheerleader fit, brown hair crafted to frame her face and eyes, tight sweater and tighter jeans, showing off the curling, perfect shape of her body. Frank could've dismissed her as just another piece of jailbait, but one look clipped him with déjà vu—she looked exactly like his first girlfriend. The feeling lapped him with the strength of time travel, vaulting him back twenty years when a tit was the holy grail. Ashley was her name, and a squeeze of her holy grails was all he got before she moved away.

But this couldn't be her. Maybe a daughter or niece, and of course time had to somehow blunt how clearly he could recall Ashley's features. Still, the girl was only pacing, looking frustrated. She caught his eyes and smiled. Frank flicked his eyes off of her and pretended to stretch and check his watch.

"Hey," she said, startling him with how quickly she had traversed the ground between them.

"Hello," Frank said. He scanned for onlookers, hoping that no one would be getting the wrong idea.

"I saw you looking at me," she said.

"It's not that, it's just that you look like a girl I used to know."

"Used to know? So I guess you don't remember me?"

Frank swallowed as the girl's smile lingered.

"I'm just kidding with you," she said, then giggled. This didn't relieve Frank—he had not forgotten the giggle from twenty years ago. "Hold on a second."

She reached into the fake plant next to them, and came away with a clipboard. Then, it cleared up for him—she was bait after all. An attractive young girl who hid her clipboard so that flirting guys and friendly gals wouldn't know, so they would talk to her and then not want to disappoint her when she asked.

With her biggest, flirty smile, she asked him, "Would you like to spend a few minutes taking a survey with us?"

"Why not," he said instantly, not even thinking it over. He wanted to stay around her until he could convince himself that his mind was playing a trick on him. She led him into a side hallway with restrooms, vending machines, and a couple of games where you could land a stuffed animal with a robot claw for a buck per try. He followed her through an unmarked administrative door into a tiny, sterile waiting room.

"Sit here for a moment," she said, "I'll be right back."

When a wispy old man in a suit led him into the rear offices, he realized that the girl had something else in common with Ashley— he would never see her again.

"We're so pleased you agreed to take this brief survey." The old man's suit hung from his bones, looking two sizes too big. He placed a single sheet of paper, face-down, on Frank's desk and handed him a sharpened pencil. "You'll find the answers to be rather self-explanatory. We urge you, for your own sake, please be honest in your responses. When you're complete," he said, "please take your results into Mr. Finnegan's office." He pointed to a tall door, and Frank noticed the old man's knuckles were twice the width of his fingers.

Frank took a breath and grabbed the pencil. The processing

area was a cubicle farm, a small one. Maybe a dozen. He heard nothing but the buzz of the fluorescent lights, even though the mall was just outside, bustling. No one else was in the cubicles. The old man had disappeared just as quickly as the Ashley look-alike. Before starting, he flipped open the cellular—no signal.

On the typed side of the paper, ten questions stared at him. Each one had a one through ten rating, with ten being "very satisfied" and one being "unacceptable."

How do you rate the quality of your marriage?

Strange. No product demos? No "have you ever used X brand?"

How do you rate your physical health? How do you rate your level of career fulfillment?

Frank marked answers like he was tearing off band-aids, quick and dirty, never letting the consideration of a question hover inside him for long, marking nothing with extreme satisfaction or extreme dislike, the answers hovering from four to seven. But he stopped cold on question eight: *How do you rate your relationship with your child?*

Not children, or something vague enough to apply to everyone, like "child(ren), if any," but *child.*

Rate the level of satisfaction with yourself, as a person. Please consider overall honesty, character, integrity, or perhaps pervading feelings of regret, anger, or frustration.

"What kind of fucking survey is this?" he said aloud, with no answer. He marked a response, a seven, wanting to get done and get out.

And finally: *What is the overall level of satisfaction with your life? Please feel free to expand on your response in the provided area, or on the back of the page, if necessary.* Another seven.

"Hey, I'm done," he said, standing, peeking over his cubicle wall like a prairie dog popping out of a hole. "Hello?" Frank took a lap around the processing area—empty desks cornered into cubicle walls, beige, the color of skin, the cloth stretched tight against brown, metal spines. The drop ceiling above him looked like off-white slices of coral reef, matching the drab, blank walls with no decor, no signs. Except one—an elongated, plastic plate on a door that read "Charles Finnegan."

He knocked twice out of courtesy, waited, and heard a muffled, "Come in, please."

The office was built from the same sterile palate as the rest of the place, but with a shining, wooden desk in the center, with black eyes and streaks swirled into the wood, making it look real and expensive. The desk was barren of paperwork, a blank surface except for the clasped hands of Mr. Finnegan—the huge hands of Mr. Finnegan, the interlaced fingers looking like a thick ball of gnarled oak. He looked tall, his face long, his ears pert, a freshly grown salt-and-pepper goatee barely dusted on his chin and lip. Bushy eyebrows clashed with his tan suit and skinny, bright red tie. Finnegan smiled a too-white smile full of teeth as thick as pinky fingers.

"Mr. Burris, we're so glad you took this opportunity." Finnegan stood and waved Frank into the folding chair opposite the desk. Neither man offered a handshake.

"Where did you get my name?" Frank said. "I thought this was anonymous?"

"What would give you that impression?"

"The fact that, well, most surveys are anonymous, but this wasn't like any survey I've ever taken." Frank tossed the survey onto the desk. The sheet of paper fluttered back and forth twice before landing, as if rocking to sleep. "And I don't know how you got my name, but if I detect one bit of bullshit coming out of this, I'll make things quite difficult for you and your little fleet of jailbait wenches."

"Now you see, that's your problem," Finnegan said, eyes square on the survey. "You are never forthright about your internal condition. You aren't angry. You're scared."

"Fuck you." Frank tried to walk out, thinking a hearty fuck you was the perfect punctuation on this unfortunate little exchange. The door was locked. Frank rattled the knob a few times and when it didn't open, he knew damn good and well that his internal condition was pure and absolute anger—it blotted his breath and vision as his hands clenched into fists. He wanted to punch something. Maybe even someone.

He turned, teeth and lips tight, the air heavy inside of him. Finnegan was standing, taller than perhaps any human had a right to be. The room looked smaller as he stood, his smile gone, dousing Frank's uprising before it turned violent.

"I'm afraid this won't do." Finnegan pointed to the piece of paper. "Sit down, Mr. Burris. We have to discuss the accuracy of your answers."

"What kind of shit do you think you're pulling here?" Frank said, his back tight against the door, wishing it would collapse behind him. "You need to unlock this door."

"Take this first response," Finnegan said. "You are quote, *very satisfied* with the quality of your marriage. This is not correct. This is not forthright."

"Why wouldn't it be? Who the fuck are you to judge?"

"I don't doubt that you love her, but love is not the same as satisfaction. Love has phases, satisfaction does not. My evidence to the contrary would be two instances of successful cheating out of an approximately two dozen serious attempts."

"What is this. This some kind of joke? Do you think you can fuck with me like this?"

"Only one person's being fucked with here," Finnegan said, "and it's me."

"Did Angie put you up to this?"

"You're approaching this with an unclear mind, Mr. Burris. Sit. Please, we have to get these answers correct if a proper evaluation is to be made."

"Who are you to evaluate my fucking marriage, you big-footed cocksucker." He found himself unpeeling from the wall. "Now open the door or I'm calling the police."

Finnegan melted into his own chair, managing to look genuinely casual. From the drawer of his desk, he withdrew an old-fashioned rotary phone, and slammed it down on the desk loud enough to make the bell *ting*.

"Call them up."

Neither man moved.

"Call the police. Report to them that on June twentieth of last year, you met a bartender after her shift. You drove into the country, looking for a place to park like you were sixteen again, but instead couldn't take the search any longer. You whipped the truck into park right there on a blacktop road. You tried to fuck her from behind with a vigor that bordered on sexual assault. She didn't say no, but she kept telling you, 'I don't know, I bet your wife is great, I don't know about this,' but you were insistent on getting your dick inside of her. Weren't you, Mr. Burris? Now, it's probably not a legal offense, you were both drunk and simply shaken by the prospect of the ordeal. You laid her on the open tailgate of your 1997 Silverado and lasted for about three pumps and came on the inside of her leg. On the way to drop her off, you said, 'I love my wife,' which was code for 'please don't tell anyone.' She said, 'I ain't no home-wrecker' which is code for 'I won't tell a soul as long as you leave me alone from now on' and you dropped her off and haven't been to that bar since."

The room only had another empty chair, squarely placed in front of Finnegan's desk. Frank was sitting in it by the time the story was done. Finnegan then took the phone with his frying-pan of a hand, and placed it back into his oversized desk drawer.

"You see Mr. Burris, you are satisfied with safety, with the idea of being married. But we have our doubts about the ultimate level of your marital satisfaction."

"Does she know?" Frank asked. "Did you tell her?"

"I'm going to give you another chance," Finnegan said. He tore the survey into small pieces of paper and let them scatter onto the floor. "You see, I couldn't find one answer that was even close to honest or accurate on this baseline survey. We're going to give you another survey. Perhaps you'll find this one more specific, and easier to answer honestly. Now the idea of being honest with yourself might be a new concept, so we'll practice first. Would you be disappointed with your son if he turned out to be gay?"

Frank took a deep breath. Aaron was ten. He cried too much and hated sports. He had the soft, blue eyes of his mother, and a knack for finding her clothes and running around in them. This behavior could be typical for most boys, Frank told himself, girding against the possibility of homosexuality.

"Yes."

"Good," Finnegan said. "Now if I were to tell you that he was indeed gay, that I knew it beyond all certainty, would you love him as much?"

The thought of not loving his son felt real inside him, pushed deep into his center, repelled by his pulsating hatred for homosexuals.

"Yes, I'd still love him."

"I didn't ask if you would love him. I asked if you would love him as much. As much as you'd love him straight."

"Love has phases," Frank said. "That's my answer."

"Now that's not an honest answer. That's a silly, defensive, soft answer meant to protect you from the honest truth that you would not love your son, that you would be more satisfied with your life if he were straight and masculine."

Finnegan opened a drawer again. He had another piece of paper, and slid it, face down, in front of Frank.

"I'm afraid that due to your inability to accurately evaluate your own level of satisfaction with your life, we're going to have to implement a precaution that these answers are as honest as possible."

Finnegan took the pencil and pressed the point into the flesh of his middle finger. He smiled, rose, and walked across the room. Blank walls. No frames or photos or portraits, but drilled into the wall to the left of Frank was a hand-operated pencil sharpener.

"If you answer dishonestly," Finnegan said, grinding the pencil lightly in the sharpener, "one of my most convincing subordinates will find your wife in the mall, and professionally coerce her into a secluded area, and rape her. Harshly, in fact."

He placed the pencil on the desk. "Your silence indicates that you may be honest about your fear for once, and understand the serious nature of this possibility?"

"You son of a bitch," Frank said. "I should rip your fucking throat out right this second."

"Yet you are too frightened. The truth that I've confronted you with is too much to marginalize with violence, with risks. Correct? Let me ask you again—do you want your wife raped?"

"No," Frank said. "I love my wife."

"Then finish," Finnegan said. "Be honest with yourself and your life, and we can work to close your case to your benefit."

Frank stared into Finnegan's chest, paralyzed by the prospect of answering the question at the top of the page.

Tell us about your fantasy that your wife has died and left you a settlement—why this intrigues you, and why you never allow yourself to linger on this thought for long?

He continued to skim the page: *Do you like being a father, and what would you do if Angie became pregnant with a second child? How would you feel?*

The third question was the worst of the batch: *If given a choice of your wife or son, which one would you prefer dead? Meaning, would you rather be a single dad or in a childless marriage? Would you rather have both of them dead if you were forced to lose one, freeing you to start from scratch?*

And finally: *Tell us, in detail, about why you are so dissatisfied with your life—even though you deny this dissatisfaction.*

"Those get to the very heart of it, don't they?" Finnegan said in a breathless, excited whisper. "I always enjoy the transformation in our clients. Don't worry, Mr. Burris—they always look as somber as you at this point, but the truth will begin to set them free. We will make this honesty worth your while." He gestured toward the survey again.

Frank stared at the curious arrangement of questions, then gazed into Finnegan's pleased face.

"You sit there and try to convince me to write an essay about not loving my wife, about wishing she were dead—yet you threaten me with violence against her. So which is it, you fucking hypocrite?" He flipped the pencil into Finnegan's chest, who looked to inhale the sum of his frustration, let it burn in his lungs for a moment, then exhaled it out, slowly, and grinned again, calmly picking up the pencil.

"The nature of the threat is intentional, Mr. Burris. Please consider that my subordinate will ejaculate inside of her, leaving the possibility that you'll have to hold her hand through an abortion or raise the bastard son of an assailant. Instead of imagining your wife's ordeal as the threat, imagine what the situation will put you through—her lost time at work, the emotional fragility, the destruction of your quarterly bout of dutiful, marital sex. Now, when considering your first question, do we believe we are leveraging a loved one against you? Or could it be that the thought of living with a post-rape wife, who has been sexually attacked, who is traumatized, and must rely on you for constant support during her time of recovery, vulnerability, and therapy scares you more than her actual desecration? But here I am hinting at the truth you must be careful to discover on your own."

He handed Frank the pencil. After staring at the questions for a long, long time, he finally began constructing his answers, stopping twice to sharpen his pencil, stopping once more to get additional pieces of paper that Finnegan was happy to provide.

Finnegan was right. The frustrations flooded out of him. He allowed his complaints and grievances with life to become real on the page. He didn't want his wife dead. He didn't hate her. He cared for her, he was just bored. He wanted new, exciting women in his life, a new one every week. No, he didn't want another child. Hell, he didn't want the first one, and certainly not a gay one. Children made him feel old, shackled, broke, and inadequate— especially if he was raising a faggot. He honestly felt his job was satisfactory—low stress, medium pay, room for advancement, easy duties. Sure, he crunched numbers, but numbers were absolute. They were right or wrong and easy to track. He felt complete at the end of each work day. But he should be something more, something important. He didn't know what—but when a sad song would come on the radio, he would be inspired to be more, craving a measure of fame and adoration. But he had no talent, no passion—why did he feel like less? Why did a wife and child feel like leaden anchors sewed to his very flesh? He worked out the dilemma on the page—wanting to rise, having ambition to complete his life and be known, perhaps even adored. Could he do something to inspire? Change the lives of others? Make a difference in any way possible? He couldn't tell, but he couldn't explore himself while wedged into domestic oblivion.

I don't hate my family, he wrote. *I do love them, but part of me would be happy they are gone, God help me, if something were to happen. I would hate myself for feeling it, but I would be happy and satisfied to have my life to myself again, even though I would grieve them and miss them terribly. I cannot deny the truth you already seem to know.*

When it was over, Frank watched while Finnegan leafed through the pages.

"Can I go now?" Frank asked.

"This is quite good," Finnegan said. "Helpful. I didn't think you could admit to all these feelings. Laid bare on the page, we're all animals, aren't we? Do you ever wonder why we can't allow ourselves such raw evaluations? We brush them aside."

"What do I have to do to leave? I'm tired. Angie will be looking for me by now. You got what you wanted."

Finnegan stuffed the survey into one of his drawers then stood up. He stretched, the bones crackling like a fresh fire. "Off you go, then."

"I suppose you aren't going to tell me what all this was about."

"It's about you, Mr. Burris. It's about taking steps to improve your life experience, to enhance your satisfaction and expectations. We'll evaluate your answers as a panel and determine the best course of action."

Exhausted Frank just shook his head and headed for the door, but stopped short of opening it. "Action?"

"Of course. We will remedy the sources of your dissatisfaction, and you will experience an enhanced quality of life. This is what we do."

The door opened, pushing Frank away. The old man grabbed him by the arm, his grip betraying his age. "This way," he said. "And good day to you," Finnegan added.

On a Monday after work, Frank came home to his favorite meal, linguine with meat sauce, and a double helping of garlic bread. Angie had a glow, that good news glow that made her cheeks red without makeup, her chest flushed just above the swell of her breasts. He noticed things about her he hadn't before in these last couple weeks—the way her skin would glide under his fingertips, the smell of her fresh out of the shower, the way her hair would spread out on the pillow before he turned out the light. She noticed something different about him as well. She had mentioned his heightened sense of affection, his improved gentleness with Aaron. "The dinner is to celebrate something," she said, then kissed him, her lips parting to bring his mouth deeper into hers, a holy grail kiss enhanced by the feel of her dress loose against the flesh of her hips.

"I'm pregnant," she said. "Six weeks."

Six weeks. The day at the mall. After his ordeal with Finnegan, they got home and she modeled her new clothing purchases. The high of shopping combined with his stress turned into a freak arousal between the two of them, and they engaged in a bout of sex they hadn't experienced in years.

After she told him the news, Frank began to cry. He pressed his head into her shoulder and she held him, his body loose against her, the words of his survey stuck inside of him, lodged, scratching against his every thought. Of course Angie took this for joy, and rubbed his back. She cried with him. They sat on the couch. In the kitchen, where she met him, he had put down his briefcase and the mail. Tucked between a sporting goods flyer and the utility bill was a postcard without a return address, and an emblem with an F and R entwined in twisting, steel letters. Underneath it, in the same font, "Finnegan Renovations" and the slogan "Helping you find joy."

Congratulations! Your improvement plan has been approved and is on its way! After its imminent, guaranteed, and unavoidable arrival, we will contact you to schedule grief therapy appointments and help you become acclimated to your new, joyous life as chosen by you! We appreciate the opportunity to serve your needs.

That evening, Frank went to the mall, alone. The door in the hallway, the one that the Ashley girl had led him through was still there. Inside, he found an empty space with naked cords hanging from the vacant tiles of the drop ceiling, the walls with spackle patches and spray painted, random numbers denoting work orders. A janitor stepped in and told him it was under construction and off limits, that a university extension was setting up shop, and that no one had occupied the office for months.

He brought a penny with him, from Aaron's piggy bank. On the way out, he tossed the coin into the wishing well, then walked out into the dying light of the fading day, wondering when they would come, wondering if he could convince them that life is like love—there are phases and a man can change.

Blake Kimzey

The Boxer and the Bear

The animal hitting me in the mouth was from northern Arkansas, a big burly black bear out of hibernation. We tumbled from the bar. It was time to go, I knew that much. I stood unsteady on the sidewalk and felt the cold cutting through my shredded jacket. The bear reared up on his hind legs and pawed at the thick winter air in front of him. I shouldn't have picked the fight. Little Rock was covered in arctic blast. The snow pink, aglow with bar lights. Before the bear killed me my older brother Chris separated us. He stood between us, arms outstretched like a referee about to call two wrestlers to the mat. But the fight was over. From high above I must have looked like a pussy trying to fight the biggest dick in Arkansas.

"Goddamnit," Chris said. "It's fucking darts."

"He started it," I said. "Reset the game play with his pointer claw. Just up and hit the button. Why I don't play electronic darts. Not with money on the line."

The bear didn't say anything. I wanted to knock his block off. He just growled and huffed air out his nostrils and looked agitated and circled on the sidewalk making a ring of paw prints.

"That's enough," Chris said. "Get your ass to the van before he tears you to pieces."

My avian bones wanted to snap in the cold. Through my split eye I could see the fat bouncer making eyes with the bear. They looked like brothers. The bear bundled in a corduroy coat and scuffed cowboy boots, steam rising off his dark black head, the fur thick and frozen and brittle. The fat bouncer stood in a Carhartt jacket and steeltoe boots. He had his arms crossed, guarding the door to Joe's Tavern. He stood serious like secret service for a Nevadan bunny ranch. I laughed at him guarding no prize at all. My torso stung. I choked out a splatter of blood. It made a bright red constellation on the snow.

"Fucking bear," I said, but didn't look up. A red strand hung like syrup from my chin. I was sad and angry and stoned. Five days earlier our baby brother Dan had stood on the train tracks in Fayetteville and let a three-engine locomotive with a hundred cars in tow run him over cold. The funeral was closed casket, the Baptist in him lost forever.

"Hey!" Chris yelled. "Knock that shit off. You aren't big enough to kick my ass, let alone his. And he's a mess I can't clean up."

"Juice spill, aisle four," I said, and laughed. "Clean up, aisle four." I had been a grocery stocker in high school. Cheerleaders had called me a stalker.

Chris grabbed me by the collar. We stood nose-to-nose and unsteady, lolling on that root-ruined sidewalk.

"Hey," I said. "That fucking hurts."

"No it doesn't," Chris said. His breath was hot yeast. He tapped at my temple and then pointed at the bear. "You need to think."

"I am," I said. I wanted to kill the bear and find a taxidermist that could set him on his hind haunches and situate him in the corner of my living room, his eyes forever glazed. I spit a yellow tooth in the direction of the frozen gutter. The street was slush and tire tracks. I didn't feel a damn thing and figured this beating for mileage. I had snorted a weak line of heroin in the bathroom. Chris held the creased tinfoil and then I did the same for him. We were small in stature. You could have fit six of us in the stall, four if Dan had been there. The drug and pints of Pabst sat heavy in my blood and I had to shit. At least I didn't have to drive.

"Fucking worthless," Chris said, hollering at the fat bouncer. "You know you've got a smaller flashlight than a mall cop?"

"Yeah, bitch," I said.

"You need to get a hold of that bear before he kills someone," Chris said. "It's a matter of time."

"Pack up your pussies and move along," the fat bouncer said.

We moved along. I looked up. The night sky was clearing, black and luminous above the winter haze. Chris put his arm around my shoulder. I looked back at the bear. He was back on all fours like an animal and had his nose in the snow. He'd probably found some bar piss leaking from the bricks. He didn't seem to mind the night and the chill closing in. Chris shot the bird, but not toward the bouncer. He shot the bird into the night sky and to me it was all a blur.

Tawny Leech

The Quillman Girl

It's dusk by the time Jasper and I get to the carnival and the neons are just beginning to flicker on all the rides and the crane flies haven't even had time to swarm them yet. The place is dead. I know it's a weeknight, but it's summer and there're only a dozen people here. Doesn't feel right. When I was a kid, the Sesser homecoming was what I looked forward to: the sweet smell of funnel cakes, licking the cotton candy off my fingers so grime didn't get stuck to them when I clung to the lap bars of the rides, watching the big mechanical taffy puller and wondering what would happen if I got my arm caught in it, if it'd twist me up like taffy; and seeing people I didn't recognize because they didn't go to the church school; and all those lights, some that chased each other, some that blinked and all of them bright.

I saved my birthday money every November so I could buy a wristband and ride all the rides as many times as I wanted all night long. It was the one place I got to interact with the *secular world*, as the teachers at church school called it, and I liked watching the girls. They seemed so different from me in their tight shorts and make-up and teased hair, and I didn't understand why my mom would let me go with no questions asked, by myself, and stay until after dark, not knowing I followed these girls around, watching their hips sway and their hands graze the butts of their boyfriends, so naturally that it seemed accidental but I knew it wasn't, and then their boyfriends would grab them by the small part of their waists and pull the girls hard against them and I wanted that, but my mom always said *no* when I asked her if I could be friends with them.

* * *

Jasper wants to ride the old, rusty kiddy motorcycles, so I let him.
Give him three tickets to hand to the carnie operating the ride, but
Jasper's too shy to do it. Won't even look at him. Can't blame him
really, the guy's whole face is covered in piercings, three just on
his mouth, one at each corner and then another that goes kind of
catty wonk in the middle of his upper lip, like maybe he sneezed
right when the guy was about to put it through his nostril or
something, and they're all made out of those thick metal bars, the
ones with the glass balls on the ends swirled with hot pink and
green that hold the piercings in place, and you know it hurt real
bad when he had it done because it's not a little hole for an earring
to go through, it's a hole for a metal rod, and he probably didn't
get it done at the jewelry store in the mall, where I got my ears
pierced when I was little, and they probably didn't use that cute
piercing gun that's covered in purple glitter and makes that *ting*
sound when the trigger is pulled.

He probably did it himself in the bathroom of his trailer,
laughing at his reflection laughing at him, letting the blood drip
from his chin and pool in the moldy plastic sink. That's why Jasper
doesn't want to look at him. He knows this guy's a savage. In fact,
I'm scared of him too when he looks at me. And he does. And he
keeps looking. And then he spreads his lips, smiling, and I hear
those glass balls bounce across his fuzzy, yellow teeth.

"Hi there, ma'am," he says.

What his breath must smell like: like ashes, like electricity, like
burning flesh. And his skin is thick and dark and tough, except
around his mouth. That part's powder white like chalk and I have
no idea why.

"Jasper, honey, hand that man your tickets and get on a
motorcycle."

Jasper nods his head and does what I tell him. Hops on a green
one. His favorite color. Thinks it's lucky.

It's a simple ride that screeches as it goes round in slow circles,
and Jasper loves it. I watch him, not taking my eyes off him for even
a second because I feel that carnie looking at me and I don't want to

encourage it, the staring, because it makes me feel naked and dirty, because now I'm aware of how thin my white t-shirt is and I remember that my bra is gray, easily seen under the white cotton, and almost a cup size too small and revealing, and I regret wearing jean shorts and I can't keep myself from imagining him climbing on top of me in my bed with the clean sheets I just put on it and wanting him to get off me but not being able to wiggle out from under him and nobody coming to help me when I yell and I feel disgusting and want to squat down and pull my shirt over my legs and rock myself until I feel better, like I did so often when I was a kid, and then when I found out I was pregnant and again five months later when my mom sneered at me when I modeled for her the long, white skirt and pink cotton t-shirt I was wearing to church that Sunday and she said, "Great, Little Girl. You're starting to look pregnant."

Jasper waves like a beauty queen as he passes by on his motorcycle, so I wave back and smile, but he's already past and slowly circling around the track and away from me, and when I chance a glance at the carnie, he's watching him and then he looks at me and smiles, and so I decide to run next to Jasper, make it a race. I put my arms out in front of me, make the *vroom* sound that tickles my lips and rev my pretend motorcycle. Jasper leans forward in his seat, his elbows jutting out like wings, and snarls at me like he thinks a motorcycle rider would, looking at me and then forward again, because after all he's a cautious driver and needs to keep his eyes on the road.

As I trot along beside the green motorcycle, I'm startled to notice that there's a little boy, younger than Jas, maybe three, grubby and tan, on the motorcycle behind him. He wants to play, too, smiles real big when I look at him, so I slow down for just a second and run next to him before stopping on the opposite side of the ride. The carnie can't see me here. When I stop running, the grubby little boy looks over his shoulder and watches me, his eyes big and blue and shining like the carnival lights, but as he gets farther away that smile fades and he cranes his neck so he can keep his eyes on me like he's scared I might go somewhere, might leave him.

The ride finally grinds to a stop and Jasper jumps down from the bike and looks around, confused as to where he's supposed to exit. It's the same place where he entered, which is right by the carnie, so I walk over to the gate and holler for him.

"This way, buddy," I say and turn sideways to put myself between him and that man.

Jasper sees me and smiles and runs toward the gate, the grubby little boy tagging along right behind him, tugging on his pants because they're a couple sizes too big.

When Jasper gets to me he wraps his arms around my hips and holds me tight and I wish he wouldn't because now the carnie knows what I look like being touched, and, I think, he can pretend that Jas and I are his family, watching us, his woman and child, enjoying his carnival.

That thought doesn't bother me as much as it probably should.

Something about it feels familiar, and for a moment I stand still and imagine that life with him, my own skin thick and dark from endless hours in the sun and my child dirty and living off nothing but cheap carnival food and how easy it'd be, but I look at Jasper and see that he's clean like the sheets on my bed, and that feeling goes away and I'm relieved and excited.

That grubby boy just watches Jasper and me, his head cocked to the side.

"What do you want to ride next, kiddo?" I say to Jas.

"That one." And he points to a big ride, the one with seats that look like umbrellas, the Paratrooper. It's one of my favorites, and it goes around sort of like a Ferris wheel but faster and the seats dangle so that when the ride goes up the seats swing wide and you feel like you might fall, and you're afraid for a second, but then as it makes its way around and back down toward the ground it tickles your stomach so much you can't help but smile.

"Come on back when you want another ride," the carnie calls out. Then he adds, "Little Girl," the name my mother has always called me and I freeze and all around me the rides whiz and whirl in their little circles, the Scrambler, the Rock-O-Plane, the Zipper, never stopping; but I can't move. *Little Girl.*

The grubby boy darts past, taking Jasper's hand in his, leading him to the entrance of the Paratrooper, both of them laughing and skipping. After a moment, I'm able to follow.

The summer I was fifteen, my mother sat at the kitchen table doing her Bible study, head bowed, highlighting quotes with colored pencils when I came in to ask her if she didn't mind taking me to the carnival.

Without even looking at me she said, "You can take your bike to town tonight, but you have to be home by 8:30 and not a minute late." She looked up at me finally. "Do you understand? Not a minute late or you will be grounded for the rest of the summer and I mean no going anywhere, no phone calls, no radio, *absolutely* no television, you won't have friends over. Nothing. Do you understand me, Little Girl?"

"Okay," I said and smiled. She didn't like that I was so excited.

"I said, 'Do you understand?'"

"Yes."

"Say you understand, Little Girl."

"I understand." And I bounced on my toes, waiting to hear if there would be more rules to follow before I tried to hug her. She didn't like to be hugged unless you could time it just right, which I had figured out was after she gave me rules.

Walking out the door, I felt happy and strong and like maybe I had super powers now, even though my mom said super powers were of the Devil. I thought I could see really far away. In the baseball field all the way across our big back lot and through the tall shrubs I watched the players standing with their hands on their knees, waiting for the ball, I heard the *ping* when the batter whacked it into the outfield and number ten on the red team ran to it and launched it to first base.

I jumped off the porch, thinking maybe I could fly, and over the top of the fence I spied the Quillman girl, our neighbor who I wasn't allowed to talk to. She was tall and thin, her shoulder length blonde hair parted to one side, hoping to disguise her dark roots that had started to show weeks ago, which my mom said looked trashy, but I thought she was beautiful. She bounced as she walked down the long driveway and hopped into someone's old green Camaro, the driver honking even as she approached the car, and then I closed my eyes and took a deep breath through my nose and the air was sweet and thick with honeysuckle.

My bike was locked up in our shed. The shed was dark and always full of wasps that I had to dodge while I got my bike untangled from the garden hose that it always somehow got caught up in. I unlocked the door and ducked as the first red wasp dive-bombed me and then I ran in and yanked my bike out without bothering to untangle it and a bunch of gardening tools went over with a loud clatter.

I knew she'd be mad, say something about my being too selfish to bother picking them up or ungrateful for the nice things the Lord had provided for us. But I just wanted to get going before she changed her mind because I was starting to feel like I was being tested on something and my heart beat faster and my hands got sweaty like they did when I was called on in math class and I just wanted to go.

I hopped on my bike and wobbled a little as I started down the driveway and to the road and I skidded through the loose gravel at the threshold of the drive, which I didn't usually do, and I thought I might fall down and bloody my knees and the blood would soak through my jeans, and it scared me. As I rounded the first curve, I looked over my shoulder at my house.

I knew she was in there, still doing her Bible study, babbling in tongues for my safety, and I pictured her clutching her colored pencils, her nails digging into the wood, leaving half-moon marks like the ones on the backs of my arms, or maybe she got up and was anointing my door with vegetable oil again, still babbling, and I thought maybe I was supposed to go back home so she wouldn't worry and get mad, but maybe she wanted to be alone and that's why she let me go and my hands started shaking and the tears started running down my cheeks and I pedaled faster because I knew that the carnival with its sweet smells of sugar and sweat and the girls in their tight, pretty clothes – I just *knew* it would make me feel happy.

* * *

It was eight o'clock and I was next in line on the Paratrooper. I had timed them all. Most ran for two minutes, sometimes three or four if there was a lady with big boobs wearing a low-cut shirt on the ride. Sometimes, if I spotted a good one, one who knew the right way to flirt with the carnie while she was waiting in line, maybe slap his arm when he teased her about what kind of cigarettes she smoked or made fun of her favorite football team, which she would claim to not really know anything about, it was just the team her boyfriend rooted for, and then the carnie would get real close to her and whisper something and she'd bite her bottom lip and say something back, I'd follow her the whole night, but there weren't any like that here this time.

I rode by myself, knowing I was pushing my curfew, but I had to have one last go before I went home. When the carnie opened the gate, I showed him my wristband, even though he didn't care. It was too late for him to care.

The umbrella I got in was pearly pink and dingy, the sparkly finish coated in gunk and dirt. A wad of pale bubblegum stuck to the top of the blue umbrella in front of me where a young couple was being seated. I grabbed the lap bar myself and pulled it closed and locked it. When the carnie came by to check, I said, "It's okay. I've got it." He yanked on it anyway and it rattled loosely under his hand. He grunted and moved on.

I was the only lone rider. The other two occupied gondolas held giggling couples who bothered me a little because they weren't paying attention to the ride, just giggling and squeaking and touching each other. I forgot about the others once the ride started and the wind whipped past my face and the lights below glowed and blinked and raced and I closed my eyes and still saw them. This was my last ride of the night, the last ride of the year.

We had made one go-around when the whole carnival suddenly lit up, blazing brighter than before, brighter than I'd ever seen it and I thought it was coming alive and then there was a deafening popping sound, and then the midway went dark and everything stopped.

The couple in front of me shrieked and the man yelled, "What the fuck!" as our ride ground to a halt and other voices rose around me in the dark. I was stuck at the top.

I had to get home or Mom would kill me, I thought, but the ride didn't come back on. I panicked and wondered if I could climb down, even moved around a bit like I was going to, but then I looked to the ground and it was dark and far away, hundreds of feet it seemed, though it couldn't have been more than a few yards. And below me were the rough, hushed voices of the carnies scurrying around, the weak beams of their flashlights sweeping the ground. What was going on?

I thought of my mother's babbling voice and I wondered if she knew this was going to happen. If this was my test and if I passed I would receive the gift of tongues. At first, I wanted to stifle it, but my mother's babbling voice emerged from my mouth. I sounded stupid, but I was glad, because that voice helped me know that I wasn't dead, alone up there in the air. I prayed.

For twenty minutes I sat up there sniffling and crying and babbling, no idea what was happening, before the lights flickered on again, but weaker than they had been before, and my seat lurched forward. When the carnie freed me, I bolted from the ride.

I got on my bike and headed for home, riding fast and breathing hard, and in the air I smelled something strong. It wasn't a skunk but it made me gag like a skunk does when I rode my bike past a dead one on the side of the road and when I breathed it in through my mouth, I could taste it and it was bitter on my tongue. I spat.

It was nearly nine when I finally got home. Almost a half hour late. I knew what my mom would do when I walked through the door: she would pretend I wasn't there, letting me ponder what I'd done and wonder what my punishment would be.

Instead, she was waiting for me. And when I walked through the door, she grabbed me up and hugged me, tighter than she ever had and I struggled to breathe. "I thought it was you," she said, again and again. I had no idea what she meant. "I thought it was you. I thought it was you."

* * *

That night, the phone rang and I lay there and listened to my mom tell her prayer-warrior friend, Rita, about the Quillman girl who had stepped on a live wire at the carnival that night, the ground damp, her feet inexplicably bare. Two hundred and twenty volts burned straight through her. "Still clutching her cigarettes," my mom said, describing what she'd heard from the ladies on the prayer chain. "Yep, they said she was coming out of one of the carnie's trailers after doing God knows what in there with him and stepped right on it. Died right there on the spot. Never saw it coming."

I slipped out from under my blankets and moved to the end of my bed. The moonlight was shining around the edges of my blinds. I pushed the curtains to the side and looked out the window at the Quillmans' house expecting to see something: an ambulance, grieving friends, hysterical women holding each other; but it was dark in the house. It looked the way it had looked every other time I peered out my window at it, hoping to catch a glimpse of the Quillman girl. I liked to pretend we were friends. That I was her little sister. Her secret keeper. Not a single light was on in her house.

I let the curtain fall back in place and returned to my pillow and closed my eyes and I dreamt about the Quillman girl, roots showing and beautiful in death and smiling, clutching her cigarettes, and happy with her life, even at its end.

The grubby little boy, he takes my hand in his and guides me toward the ride he and Jasper want to go on, moving quickly and knowledgably, being mindful of the carnival goers, which there seem to be more of now, careful not to cut them off or alarm them, and they are oblivious to us, laughing and pointing and holding onto each other's arms. Jas lags behind until I call for him to catch up. He does, and I grab his hand, but he has a hard time keeping up. I have to yank him by the arm to keep him moving. His eyes dance from one ride to the next, giant machines whirling bright against the night sky, all of them packed with people now and running full tilt, and then to a dart game where the prize is a giant stuffed panda bear nearly as big as a house, and he smiles and pulls against me.

He tries to slow down when we pass a food cart stuffed with bags of colorful cotton candy hanging from the ceiling, stacked in piles on the counters, mounds of it from the floor to the ceiling, and the cooks inside keep making the stuff even though no one's buying and they make it so fast that it's falling out of the serving window and onto the ground and Jasper reaches out to grab one of the sacks of spun sugar, but I won't let him take it, and all of the carnies—so many now for such a small carnival—stop what they're doing as we hurry by and smile enthusiastically at me.

We're going faster, the grubby little boy still pulling me along by the hand, and the lights whiz past and I'm afraid so I try to pull my hand from the boy's, but I can't. His grip is shockingly strong for such a little guy. And as we pass by the rides, the carnies call to him fondly, as though they know him. Have always known him: "Josh, come here!" and "Hey, Josh. I got something for you, pal." It's like they're all trying to be his favorite uncle for some reason. But he doesn't stop, just looks at them and shakes his head, annoyed maybe that he even has to respond, or solemnly, like an old man. I can't tell.

And then I hear a woman's voice. It's tender, but still louder than the shouting of the men. Josh slows at the sound of it and looks around, wonderingly and cautiously, trying to locate the source of the voice, but the woman is nowhere to be seen. He releases my hand, and I feel both untethered and terribly afraid, like I might turn into smoke and be blown away by the spinning of the rides and bustling of people, drifting away from the carnival, away from the little grubby boy and the carnies; away from Jasper.

The carnies circle insistently around us now that we're separated from Josh, all of them noisily trying to get my attention, teasing Jasper with trinkets, cheap plastic rings, Chinese finger traps, and sweet glistening treats. He reaches for them all, his clean, chubby hands outstretched, but I pull him closer to me. As the men close in around us, their bodies thick and solid as tree trunks, I hear the woman's voice again.

"Josh," she says, and she steps out of the shadows from between two semi-truck trailers. She's beautiful, slender, blond, wearing a long, thin ruffle and lace dress and she's braless and the dress drapes delicately over her body, her chest exposed and it's not vulgar, but graceful. She leans down toward her little grubby boy, puts her face close to his, close enough for a kiss. "Joshie," she whispers, and he stares at her with his amazing bright blue eyes. "Where you been? Hillbilly's been hollerin' for you."

A man steps out of the shadows as well and puts his arm around the woman's small waist and looks at me. It's the carnie from the motorcycle ride, and he smiles at me with his chalk white mouth as he pulls the woman closer to him and puts his hand low on her hip. The carnies make deferential noises. This man is their king.

"I know who you are," I want to say to the woman, but my voice won't come. It's stuck in my chest and hurts. "You're the Quillman girl. And you're dead."

She says nothing. Maybe she doesn't know who she is anymore. Maybe, being dead all these years, she has forgotten.

I lean over to pick Jasper up, so I know he's close and safe, and the Quillman girl likewise picks Josh up in her arms and squeezes him, and Josh nuzzles her neck, and she smells his hair and sways a little. Her feet—which I only now notice are bare—move gracefully, soundlessly, weightlessly over the ground. Everything about her is dainty and fluid and I wish that I could be that way. I wish I could move like that.

I could go with them, I know. Jasper and me could go and we would be welcome. Him and Josh would be friends. Both of us belonging to him, to Hillbilly. His chalky white mouth all over me every night, just as surely as it is all over the Quillman girl every night. Lovers. The three of us.

Jasper's grip gets tighter around my neck. Choking me a little. Only moments ago he felt so slight, but now the weight of him, and he's struggling against me, keeps me rooted to the ground.

My mother's voice, the babbling of tongues, the gift I never did receive, rises up in my throat, and I choke it down. I will not pray in front of these people. I will not be my mother before these people.

"My baby," the Quillman girl whispers, and Josh laughs a satisfied little bubble of laughter, and they all three drift away into the shadows from which they came, Josh still in her arms and Hillbilly's rough hand squeezing her hip tight, Josh and his mother dancing, and then they're all gone.

An Ugly Monkey

I was drunk when I came out of St. Mark's, but that seemed okay because I was drunk when I went in. I'd thought about going to confession, but when I saw the booths and Jesus on the cross and the Holy Virgin, I couldn't bring myself to do it. It was dark in there, hot and humid to suffocation, and I was sweating hard. The sad little crucifix I'd bought last week was just a lump in my pocket. Hell, I'm not even Catholic, not since I was a kid, so what good could any of this possibly do? Margaret wasn't taking my calls and I had my doubts about anyone else listening either. It seemed the best idea was just to go on home.

Outside it was cooler. I was walking down 34th Street, minding my own business. From the shadows between Tony's Lounge and The Szechwan Palace slides this greasy little fellow in a white polyester suit, and he's hissing at me. You know, "Pssst, pssssst," like in a movie. I kept on going, because I had enough troubles of my own and I figured this probably meant more. But then he said it and I stopped. I had to.

"Hey meester, wanna buy a menkey?"

He said it just like that, just like Peter Lorre. At first I couldn't figure out what he meant.

"A menkey?"

"Yes, a very fine menkey. See?" He made kissing sounds with his lips and from behind him somewhere scampered this big, ugly monkey. God yes it was ugly, probably the ugliest monkey I've ever seen. Maybe the ugliest monkey that ever was. Its fur was gone in big patches and its exposed skin blotched white and red.

There were open sores here and there on its chest and one of its eyes was brown and, so help me God, the other was blue. Just as blue as the sky. It wore lurid green Bermuda shorts with orange stripes down the sides. The thing stood about three feet tall and clamped between its teeth was a cigar, smoked about half-way down. Quick as shit it climbed up the guy's leg and then had its arm around his neck and he was holding it like a kid. The monkey took a puff from its cigar and blew smoke rings into the air.

"It's magic, sir. Four wishes, four—"

"Get away from me with that damned monkey," I said.

"But sir—"

"I mean now." I turned back the way I was heading and moved on out of there. I didn't even look back but after a block I stopped at the crosswalk and felt something grab my leg. I looked down and there it stood, ugly and smoking, and I swear it smiled at me.

"Get the hell away from me," I hollered, and kicked at it. It dodged under my foot and rolled between my legs. Then it hit me square in the balls, and hard. I went double and fell to my knees. I thought for a minute I was going to puke, but I held on. The thing paced back and forth beside me, making those monkey sounds like in the Tarzan movies. Then it stopped and scampered up the side of my body and put its arm around me and kissed me right on top of my head.

Okay, it was just a dumb animal, and it was lost, and its instincts made it protect itself—and now maybe it was sorry. I didn't exactly forgive it, but I was willing to not try kicking it again. I figured White Polyester would be right after us, running down the street, looking for this thing, but he still hadn't shown by the time I was able to stand, so I walked back to the alley where I'd seen him. The monkey followed right behind me. When we got to the alley, the guy wasn't there.

"Eeep," said the monkey. "Eeep eeep eeep."

I tried everything to get the monkey not to follow me. I yelled at it. I cussed it. I almost kicked it, but I figured that wasn't such a good idea. So what could I do? Hell, when a man's lonely and going crazy with it, he sometimes forgets his better judgment. Or maybe he just gives in easy. I went on home and the monkey went with me.

It was a third floor walk-up and the monkey kept right with me as I slogged up the stairs. When we finally made it to my room I opened the door and it ran inside. I got my emergency pint from the shelf over the sink and poured a glass of whiskey. I needed it. There were big yellow bananas in the cabinet, from where Margaret was over the other night, the last time I'd seen her, and I figured I might give the critter one after I had my drink. They weren't doing me any good. I just couldn't see eating them after what happened. And of course, there was the crucifix. She'd left that behind, too, and maybe that's why I wandered into the church. I'd been carrying the crucifix in my pocket for days and every now and then I brought it out and held it to my face and took a deep breath. I did this now and shoved it back into my jacket. I was ready for that drink.

But the monkey had other plans and they didn't include either crucifix or bananas. Before I could even get the glass to my lips, it grabbed the bottle from the table. It took a drink and then another and before I knew it the bottle was empty. Great. Just what I needed, a big drunken monkey with a skin disease. With the booze gone the thing got mad. It started waving the empty bottle and screaming.

I downed my sorry little glass and the monkey glared at me. It made a noise from the back of its throat and showed me its teeth. They were big all right—long, sharp and yellow. It made the noise again and closed its eyes then opened them wide. Its eyes sparkled. The brown eye had the look of a dark, polished marble. It was so brown that it was almost black, almost dark enough to be empty, like the mouth of a cave or the gateway to hell. The blue one was sunshine summer skies and ocean waves and, in spite of the monkey's overall hideousness, I felt drawn to it. I might have walked over and petted this thing, but it still looked mad enough to kill. Then I looked close and it was as if the blue eye were becoming huge, like a baseball or cantaloupe. It swelled, became the entire room and I fell into it and it wasn't that monkey crouched in the corner, but Margaret, big titties and all. It had been more than a week and I felt myself getting hard. It was Margaret and Mary and a crucifix held between her thighs winking and my balls sang go! go! and I went. I was on the floor fumbling my belt with one hand and fondling giant breasts with the other—I even got my fingers into the warm wet goo of cunt—when Margaret or Mary leaned close and bit me hard on the leg. The pain was magnificent. At once it was no longer a woman, but the monkey, and I jumped back and scurried crab-like across the floor.

My God my God I've fucked the thing, I thought. No, not fucked it, not quite, but so close, close enough to feel it hot and slick, close enough to smell. I stood and straightened my clothes and moved my erection so that it didn't catch in my underwear. I couldn't bring myself to look straight at the monkey.

And then it farted. God, what a fart. It was loud and long and rotten. The gas from that creature's belly smelled of hell and disease and everything sick. It was like a cloud from a death house, putrid bodies and shit so bad even the flies wouldn't bite. The very stench of it slapped at me and I staggered into the wall. I held my breath, made it to the window, flung it open and hung my head out. I gagged and tried to hold on, but up came the whiskey. I watched as it splattered on the sidewalk. Shit, I thought. Shit. I must have hung out that window for five minutes, shaking, until finally the smell began to let up.

When I turned back to the room, the monkey was on my couch, innocent and serene. Its legs dangled toward the floor and its arms stretched out almost the length of the sofa. I watched as it opened its fly and jammed a hairy finger up its ass. What now? The monkey brought the finger up to its nose and took a deep breath. It shook its head and cried out and waved the bottle again.

"Oh Jesus," I said.

Was I going insane? I didn't know what to do with the damn thing. I didn't have any more liquor, so I called up my pal, Frank. I didn't tell him what was going on, but I asked if he'd bring some whiskey over right away. He was there in twenty minutes and he brought his girlfriend, Stella. Even though he was going a little bald, Frank was a ladies' man and always had a woman in tow. Lately it was Stella. She was a looker and wore the clothes to prove it.

"Lord God Almighty," said Frank as he walked into the apartment. "Who shit?"

Before I could answer, Stella saw the monkey and the monkey saw Stella. This woman was one of those freaks of nature who get an overabundance in one area but shortchanged in others. While she curved to big and small perfection in all the right places, with the legs, tits and ass of a 1940s movie queen and the face of a $200 whore, Stella was also the only person I've ever known without a sense of smell. She couldn't smell a damn thing. Ordinarily, this would seem to be a handicap, but with monkey fart residue hanging oily on the air, it now worked to her advantage. She was also nearsighted and much too vain for glasses, so I guess she couldn't tell at first what the thing on the couch was. I'll be damned if I knew, either.

"Oh, a doggie. Nice doggie," said Stella.

The monkey sprang across the room and ran its hands up her short red dress and groped her panties. Stella screamed and jumped up and down, bouncing and jiggling and hitting the thing on the head with her purse.

"Oh, Frankie! Frankie, get it off!" She was almost hysterical, and who could blame her? Frank was right there and he did what anybody would do. He tried to kick the monkey away. The little bastard was preoccupied with Stella, so he didn't react quite in time. He tried to duck, but Frank's kick got him pretty square in the ribs. Frank had played some ball in school and it was just like a Saturday back on the field, one more punt for the team. The monkey rolled under the table with a big squawk, then tumbled back toward Frank and, from the floor, planted him a solid kick right in the nuts. Frank went to his knees and I guess the monkey saw the whiskey he was carrying, because he grabbed the bottle and shot across the room. Frank fell over and lay there moaning. Stella climbed up on a chair screaming and jumping up and down, holding the hem of her dress tight around her lovely thighs. With each jump her breasts rose and fell in heart stopping rhythm and her dress rode a little higher on her legs. You might fault the little monster's manners, but you couldn't question his taste. The monkey stood in the far corner. He'd opened the bottle and now he was drinking in perfect contentment. I sat down on the couch and tried not to stare at Stella. I didn't say a word.

After a while, Frank was able to sit up.

"Jesus Christ, Gordon, what the hell is that that thing?"

"What the hell do you think it is, genius? It's a God damned monkey." Stella and Frank stared at the monkey and the monkey stared back.

"Eeep!" it said. "Eeep! Eeep!"

"I think it's a chimp," said Stella.

Frank gave Stella a dirty look.

"Well, what the fuck are you doing with a monkey? Anyway, it doesn't matter. I'm gonna kill that little son of a bitch." Frank got slowly to his feet and picked up an ashtray and made as if to move toward the monkey. The monkey put the bottle on the floor, still holding it by the neck, and gazed at Frank.

"I don't think I'd do that if I were you, Frank. He's pretty quick."

I told them the whole story of how I came to have the monkey in my apartment, stopping short of it changing into Margaret or— and?—the Holy Virgin, and the rest of that business.

"Four wishes?" said Frank. "Whoever heard of four wishes? It's always three."

"Don't be a moron," I said. "There aren't any wishes and there's no such thing as a magic monkey."

Frank gave me a dirty look.

"I'm just saying the old guy got the story wrong, okay?"

"Whatever."

"He is kinda cute, though, ain't he?" said Stella.

"Stella, that is without a doubt the ugliest monkey that has ever lived. I think it's got the mange."

"Look who's talking, baldy," she said.

Frank ran his hand across his thinning hair and shut up. It was plain that Stella had hurt his feelings, and I didn't see any call for that. Loyalty, that's what counts. She knew Frank was touchy about his scalp, so she went right for it. Loyalty is a rare bird.

"Come here, little guy. Come to Stella." She waggled a finger at the beast. It was pretty loaded by now and it did well to stagger over to her.

"Bobo," she said. "I think we should call it Bobo."

"Eeeep eeeep," said the monkey. It sat down beside Stella and patted her foot.

"Good Bobo," she said. "Nice Bobo."

Bobo rested his head on Stella's foot and gazed up. It looked like he had a pretty good view up her skirt, but Stella didn't seem to notice. It didn't matter, however, because in a few seconds he was out cold, passed-out stinko drunk. Frank retrieved the bottle.

"Hey," said Stella, "it looks like he's got something in his pocket."

I almost said he probably had something in his pants, all right, when Stella reached down and pulled a card from the awful green of Bobo's shorts.

"Listen to this: 'My name is Emil. Please do not give me cigars or whiskey.'" There was another name on the card, The Great Silvera. Stella shook her head and looked at me accusingly. "You shouldn't let Bobo drink," she hissed. She reached down and stroked his fur. "The poor thing must be old. Look at how his hair's falling out."

Frank had been sulking on the couch ever since Stella's crack about his hair, but now he piped up again.

"Hey Gordo," he said. "You got any more of those bananas left?"

I nodded and caught Stella blushing.

"Hey, honey," said Frank. "Go in the kitchen and get the monkey some bananas. I bet he'll wake up hungry." When she was gone Frank leaned over to me and winked.

"How'd Margaret like the bananas?"

Frank managed a porno store, and I guess he saw all kinds of things in the magazines and videos he sold. He was the one who suggested Margaret would go for the fruit. All women love that kind of stuff, he said. The crucifix had been my idea, after Frank's, but I didn't see any reason to bring that up.

"She's gone, Frank. I don't think she liked them much."

Frank sat back and nodded knowingly.

"Another frigid bitch," he said. "No offense, Gord." Then he ground his right fist into his left palm.

"So this Silvera guy must be the one who dumped the monkey on you. Let's go find him and kick his ass. Nobody whacks me in the balls and—"

"Frank," I said, "it wasn't Silvera who whacked you. If you want revenge, your boy's right over there."

Frank considered this for a moment and then glared at Bobo or Emil or whoever this monkey was.

"Don't even think about it, Frank." It was Stella, back with the bananas. There were seven left from a bunch of eight. "At least if you're planning on going around with me anymore." You could tell Stella meant it, but I'll be damned if I knew why she had such affection for this creature that a couple of minutes earlier had been a second away from raping the bejesus out of her.

"You know, Stella, sometimes I wish you weren't such a good lay. Then I wouldn't be so willing to put up with your shit," grumbled Frank.

Stella grabbed a banana and peeled it fast and bit off the top half. It was a ferocious bite and she chewed hard and swallowed. There was a mean look in her eye.

"And I wish you'd quit thinking about all those other women and just concentrate on me! You think I don't know about those whores you run around with? I do! I do!"

As I said, Frank was quite a ladies' man, and I guess it was hard for him to stick with just one woman.

About that time the monkey woke up. First he fluttered up the brown eye, and then the blue one just shot open.

"Eeep! Eeep! Eeep!" The monkey looked first at Frank and then at Stella. He shook all over and did a somersault.

"Well," I said, "what I wish is that this damned thing would just disappear." Frank and I toasted to that and Stella gave us both the evil eye.

"Hey," she said. "Where's Bobo?"

Sure enough, the monkey was gone. I'd left the window open and the wind was blowing the curtain into the room. We all went and looked out the window. We were on the third floor, but there was a drain pipe that he could have grabbed onto and shinnied down. Anyhow, there was definitely no monkey.

Fortunately, he left the bottle behind. We drank it off and tried to figure the whole thing out, all except the business of my unfortunate hallucination. I still kept that to myself. We even tried calling The Great Silvera, but couldn't find a listing. By the time the whiskey was gone, we were all laughing about it, and even getting hit in the balls seemed funny to Frank and me. Frank and Stella made up and were hanging all over each other, and it was no surprise that when the whiskey was gone, they left too. After that I didn't see Frank or Stella for a while.

In the days that followed, I found myself going by the Catholic church every now and again. There was something about the place that attracted me, but I can't say just what. I was never able to go to confession, even though I was pretty sure I should. I couldn't even pray. The crucifix was always in my pocket, even though when I brought it to my face it now smelled only of wood. After a while I stopped visiting the church or lingering by the alley between Tony's and the Chinese place on my way home. It was a couple of weeks later that I ran into Frank at a bar. He looked awful.

"It's Stella," he said. "She used to be so great in bed. She had moves like you wouldn't believe. And now, and now. . . ." His voice trailed off. I was about to suggest he dump her and find some new talent, but it was obvious from the pain in his face that there wasn't another girl in the world. For some reason I felt guilty, but not much. We sat and drank and didn't talk.

Frank left a half hour before closing. It was Friday night and I decided to give Margaret one more try. I walked to the back of the bar where the pay phone was. Before I dialed I mumbled a wish out loud. It was the best I could do. It rang ten times. I let it go a couple more for luck. No answer. Then I thought about Stella. I thought about her jumping up and down. I thought about that jiggle and those amazing thighs. I remembered Margaret and Mary and that crucifix and my balls sang. Even hideous Bobo flashing back into memory and biting couldn't cool me off. There was no way Frank had made it to Stella's place yet. She answered on the third ring. She sounded glad to hear from me and said she'd slip out before Frank made it home and meet me at my apartment. What the hell. Bad pussy's better than none at all, especially if it's human. I hung up and got one for the road. Maybe

she'd like the Polish sausage I'd been saving for Sunday dinner.
Dead Jesus on the cross in the warm wet dark.

Whoever heard of four wishes, indeed?

Scavengers

On the game show, Margaret veered from the script and did not say, "Yes, I'm married to my wonderful husband, Donny." In response to the exuberant host's note-carded question—"And it says here you've been married for eight years?"—Margaret looked straight at the camera and said, "No, Chip, you're mistaken." Then, unable to stop herself, she practically shouted, "Everything I win is all mine!"

Then they were on to the next contestant, married for thirteen years to his beautiful wife Barbara, and the next, a chubby red-headed girl who collected insects and had come "all the way from Kansas City." By the time the show aired a week later, Margaret couldn't bear to watch herself lose to the insect girl, and even worse, she had decided not to leave Donny after all.

Back home in Mississippi he was a dental hygienist, and he hadn't gone with her to the taping because he had to hose out the mouths of root canal patients. "Why not just go ahead and be a dentist?" she had asked him on their first date, and he said, "You go ahead and be a dentist." Not that she could make fun of him now, because he had a job and she didn't.

"Everything I win is all mine," Donny called from the living room, where he was watching the program even though she told him not to. "That's funny."

The game show, the game show, the game show! She lay in bed after Donny had gone to work and tried to will herself back there, back to California and the studio lot and the palm trees, the green room and the make-up people and the studio audience who had seemed to genuinely care so much about her. When she asked for a D and there was no D on the board, a loud AWWW echoed around her, and she felt cradled in support and goodwill. Maybe that's what church was supposed to be like, but at church she'd always felt itchy and only read the bulletin to find typos. Our Lard in Heaven, Here my Prayer! That was the best one.

On the phone to her mother in Memphis, she said, "They were so nice backstage, after I lost. Chip shook my hand, and his assistant Julianna gave me a hug."

"What was that about not being married?" her mother said.

"I was joking. We're encouraged to joke."

"Oh," said her mother, who watched nothing but infomercials.

"If we're funny, we might get invited back." No one had told her this, but it sounded plausible. "Or maybe some talent scout will watch and think, Oh, I need this person in my reality show."

"Who needs a reality show?" her mother said. "Real life is real enough."

"True," said Margaret. "It's plenty real all right."

Would it hurt or help her chances if there were children? She set up the camera in her living room, in front of the open window that revealed the springtime lawn of the front yard. The magnolia tree hid the trashy house across the street, with the rusty swing set and dilapidated picnic table in the yard. Margaret and Donny had been meaning to move for five years now but hadn't gotten around to it.

If she wanted to be on that show where they swapped wives, she would need children. It was called *Wife Swap*, but really it was about putting the Redneck Woman in a household full of little liberal Poindexters, and the Professor Wife in a trailer filled with shotgun-carrying hillbilly children. That didn't seem fun to Margaret. She didn't know if she could survive in the wild or eat bugs, but maybe she could. *Would you rather live with a bunch of hillbilly children or eat bugs?* she Twittered. She liked Twittering, she liked having followers. There were over 500 of them now, and she didn't know who any of them were. After she lost on the game show, she Twittered, *O the agony of defeat*, which wasn't clever but it expressed how she felt, and GrlPwr3 wrote, *You rock n dont forget it!!!!!!* Many of her followers did not spell correctly, but she didn't let it bother her much.

BUGZ DEFIANTLY, Twittered MelDel, and no one wrote back for a while so Margaret decided she might as well make a tape for a program where the winner gets to work for Donald Trump. She knew she had no chance of winning, but she could be a spit-fire and say outrageous things, and sometimes that was more important than winning.

When she had told Donny about her video audition idea, he said, "Or you could apply for jobs."

"I will, I will," she said. They lived in a university town in Mississippi, and if you weren't a dental hygienist, like Donny, you had to work at the university. Which Margaret had, until a month ago.

It wasn't such a great job anyway, administrative assistant for an engineering professor. The professor was a woman, and she was always talking about her kids and how smart they were. When Margaret said, "You should go on *Wife Swap*," the woman looked alarmed and then asked Margaret to fax some documents to Austin. Margaret had lost her job because she spent too much time on her computer filling out applications for game shows, Twittering, checking to see if anyone had Friended her, and trying to figure out who was Ignoring her.

She was wondering if she should change her clothes for the video—it was eighty degrees, but she looked better in a turtleneck—when the doorbell rang. A college-aged girl in a pink sorority sweatshirt stood on the front steps smiling at her. She had a thick blonde ponytail and her teeth looked like she'd never needed a root canal. "Hiya," she drawled. "My name is Delores, and this is going to sound weird, but I'm on a scavenger hunt, and I'm wondering if you have a pair of red mittens I can borrow."

"Red mittens," said Margaret. She saw the girl giving the camera a curious glance. "I'm making a tape. Wait here."

She had to dig all the way in the back of the storage closet, behind Donny's old climbing boots and camouflage jacket, from when he used to hunt. There were no mittens in the Winter Clothes box, because it never got cold enough in central Mississippi for mittens. They were in the Stuff box, sent to her by her mother last Christmas with a note saying, "Just some of your little things I didn't have the heart to throw out. Cute!!" Enclosed were Margaret's third grade composition book, a photo of her dressed as a cat for Halloween, her ballet shoes, and a pair of tiny red mittens. She pulled a black turtleneck out of the Winter Clothes box, too, might as well.

"I hope they weren't supposed to be grown-up mittens," Margaret told Delores.

"These are perfect," she said, beaming. "Thank you so much. I really want to win this thing."

"Losing is no fun," Margaret agreed.

Donny came home smelling of mint and rubber gloves. "You're not gonna leave me," he said to her. "Because you love me too much." He smacked her ass. He was right, of course. If only he would just give in about the babies. She was thirty-eight years old.

"If you're not going to man up and get the job done, then I'll find someone who will," she told him. She had heard a wife say this on a talk show, and the husband had burst into tears and promised to man up.

But Donny held her chin in his hands and said, "It's your hormones talking. Give it another couple of years."

"But I can't help it! It's a biological imperative!" She sniffled.

"So is death," he said, and kissed her.

The next afternoon, Delores was back, but she didn't return the mittens. "It turns out," she said, "this scavenger hunt is kind of an ongoing thing. I didn't wake you, did I?"

Margaret had put a bathrobe over her bathing suit before answering the door. "No, of course not," she said. "I was just making a tape where I'm supposed to be at the beach." She had been standing on a yellow seat cushion, wondering if it would look like a surfboard from the right angle. There was a show called

Beach Hut that filmed in Malibu, and all she had to do was prove she was fun in the sun.

The girl was wearing the same pink sweatshirt. Margaret noticed now that the letters were too faded to read, not that she knew anything about sororities anyway. "So, what I need now is a postcard from a European country. Would you happen to have one of those?" She arched her eyebrow at Margaret the way investigators did on TV when they were tricking the criminal into confessing.

"Right," said Margaret. "I wish."

Delores seemed pleased with this response for some reason. "Excellent!" she said. "A cork from a bottle of Spanish wine?"

"A can of Budweiser is more like it," Margaret said, and then cleared her throat because she had already had two tallboys today, and it was barely four o'clock. She thought it might make her seem fun on her audition tape.

"Okay, well what about a white cupcake-shaped ceramic music box that says You're Very Special across it in pink script and plays 'Eidelweiss.'"

Margaret felt her heart lurch a little. "Oh my," she said. "I have one of those."

It was in a box up in the crawl space. "I appreciate you going to all this trouble!" Delores called from below while Margaret pawed carefully through the pink fiberglass. Why oh why had she and Donny not gotten rid of all this junk? There was even a box of *National Geographic*s.

Margaret handed down a battered Thom McCann shoebox. "This is sort of where old Christmas presents go to die," she said, as she made her way down the ladder.

On the living room carpet, they pulled out the contents of the box—a Hallmark ornament of a cat on a Christmas tree, a pair of shiny fake-gold candlesticks, and the music box. "My mother gave this to me when I was way too old for it," Margaret said. "What thirty-year-old woman wants a music box?"

"It's pretty," said Delores, holding it as if it might break. Margaret thought of saying, "Just keep it!" but then what if her mother came to visit and wondered where it was? She was always threatening to visit.

"This is some scavenger hunt," Margaret said.

"I worry that we're drifting apart," Margaret told Donny. "So drift more towards me."

"I'm not doing Facebook," he said. "And you need real friends."

She pretended not to hear him. "We could try out for a reality show together," she suggested, and when he didn't say anything she said, "I just want some of the finer things in life, that's all I want. We're not going to get them with good old fashioned hard work, so why not be on TV?"

"What fine things do you want?"

"Trips to Europe. Spanish wine. I want dresses that come from a store that doesn't have the word *mart* in its name."

"This is all because you're mad about the babies," Donny said. "When we got married, you didn't want babies, and in another couple of years you'll come back to your senses. We just need to stick it out until then. We have fun together, just you and me."

"We go out for tacos on Fridays," she said, and he said, "See?"

She had no idea who it was babbling on the other end of the phone, but eventually she figured out it was the insect girl from the game show—or Amanda, as she was apparently called. "I was thinking about you," said Amanda. "I'm in town. Can you see me?"

They had exchanged phone numbers and fake hugs in the green room after the show, but Margaret hadn't expected they would actually keep in touch.

"I thought you lived all the way in Kansas City," she said.

"I do, but I'm staying at the Comfort Suites. I need to see you!" She sounded a little crazy. Margaret was almost finished recording a tape expressing her desire to live in a house full of ranting lunatics, serving as the "calm voice of reason, or if that's not fun enough, to encourage my housemates to do incredibly stupid things."

"Sure," she said to Amanda.

* * *

Amanda's hair was flatter and greasier than it was on the game show, but she looked just as happy as she had after solving the puzzle and winning twenty-five grand. "I had a fight with my boyfriend, but he's going to marry me because now I'm rich." She smiled; apparently, this didn't bother her. "But he said I had to get rid of some of my very prized possessions. And I thought of you! I don't know why, you were just nice. And I don't have a ton of friends."

Margaret sat on the edge of the king-sized bed and bounced a little in anticipation. "That's very kind of you," she said. "I'm sure I couldn't take anything valuable," she added, because of course she knew she could.

Amanda was standing next to a cloth-draped object beside the ice bucket, grinning like she had when the confetti fell from the ceiling at the TV studio. She pulled the cloth off to reveal what looked like a shoebox-sized clear plastic aquarium. Only instead of fish, there was dirt. And more dirt. And two oblong creatures moving around in the dirt.

"Good God," said Margaret. "I saw someone eat those on a reality show once." She was on her knees, staring.

"They're scarabs," Amanda said. "They're beautiful and sacred."

"Oh, they are!" cried Margaret. They seemed to glow, their brown bodies shining like jewels, their wings a glimmering, iridescent gold.

"There's some cow poo in there," Amanda said. "Just so you know."

"They're dung beetles," said Donny. "They spend their days rolling up balls of shit. But that's cool. At least they're keeping busy, being productive members of society." He gave her a look that suggested she could learn a thing or two from the dung beetles.

"They're scarabs," she said. "Egyptians worshipped them because they roll the sun across the sky."

"I can see that," said Donny.

* * *

She took a picture of the two beetles in their cage and posted them on Facebook. The reactions were immature: *Ick, Gross,* and the like. "They are beautiful and sacred!" she wrote. "Maybe you can't tell so much from the pix, but trust me." Sometimes instead of making videos or Twittering, she would just stare at them as they rolled their big balls of dung; she liked to carry their cage from room to room with her. She read about them online and found herself hoping that they would lay eggs (or that at least one of them would) and that she would have a whole cage full of glimmering creatures and smooth round balls. Sometimes instead of going to bed, she would stay in the living room (Donny didn't want them in the bedroom) and put them on the top of the TV and stare at them. They had little faces, and she was almost sure the black glittering eyes were smiling at her.

One Friday afternoon, Donny said he needed to get away, clear his head. "To the cabin," he said, but there wasn't really a cabin, just a rundown shack out in the Alabama woods where his family used to stay during hunting season. "You could come with me," he offered, but they both knew she wouldn't. He had taken her there once, and when Donny said, "I can skin a squirrel, you want to watch?" she had threatened to leave. There was no cell phone reception or even dial-up out there. Not even dial-up! Before he left, Donny said, "Good luck with your audition tapes. I'll be back on Sunday night." Then he sighed and left without kissing her goodbye.

"I know you're probably surprised to see me yet again," said Delores. "But I need something else, if you don't mind."

"What if I do mind?" Margaret said. "Just kidding." Although she really wasn't. She had asked some of her Facebook friends if they'd heard of any "on-going scavenger hunts" and several people—including her old boss, the engineering professor—wrote to tell her it was clearly a scam, and to expect to be robbed.

Delores frowned. "I need a stuffed white bunny wearing a homemade gingham apron. Also, a blue hot water bottle, and a soft white towel that was never used. Check the top of Donny's closet—his mother sent you those for Christmas and you forgot about them. Dig around while you're in there and grab me a Gnome diary, but rip out the first three pages because you wrote in them when you were fourteen."

It wasn't as if Margaret *decided* to get these things, or even knew where to find them—but suddenly she was moving through the house, rooting through drawers and closets—the towel and the old diary right where Delores said they would be.

Please don't take the scarabs, she thought, as she handed over everything. Just not the scarabs. I love those damn bugs, she realized, and tried not to cry at how pathetic she was.

"And go ahead and email me those videos of yourself," Delores said, "while you're at it."

"Is this a robbery?" Margaret asked at last, when she'd hit *send* and put the pile of objects at Delores' sandaled, red-toenailed feet.

"Does a robber give you presents?" Delores said, and produced a box from seemingly nowhere. "For your trouble," she said. "I shoplifted it for you." And she handed Margaret a pregnancy test.

Donny had gone out to the wilderness to get away from her, and now she couldn't even call to tell him the good news! Or was it good? It was news. At first she thought: *It's a miracle,* and then she realized that she'd been so obsessed with audition tapes and scarabs that she hadn't taken her pills in almost a month.

Before she left, Delores had asked for something to carry her things in.

"*My* things," Margaret corrected, tossing everything into a Wal-Mart bag. "I don't think this is a scavenger hunt at all!"

"These aren't for me," said Delores. "They're for my baby. The mittens and blanket and hot water bottle are to keep her warm when I take her to the north, the music box is so she'll know how much I love her, the bunny is to keep her laughing, and the diary is so she can get out her feelings on paper when she's going through those awkward teenaged years. The towel is just because everyone needs a towel. The videos are so if she ever finds out about you, I can show them to her and she can realize how much better off she is with me, because you're a lunatic. I'll come back tomorrow for that box of scrapbooking stuff you bought at Wal-Mart last year and never got around to using. I think I'll like to scrapbook." She smiled. "When she grows up, she's going to send me postcards from Europe and drink expensive Spanish wine, and marry a minor prince. You'll probably see her in fashion magazines."

"She'll have the finer things in life," Margaret said miserably. "But why do you want *my* baby?"

"Ask your mother if she remembers an old sorority sister named Delores who wanted to come to her baby shower and she said no, you're just a dumb mooch, and then I said, 'I curse your baby girl, and I will take her firstborn as my own.' Ask her if she remembers *that*."

"Oh, her," said Margaret's mother. "Delores was always eating our food and never replacing it. Did you see her? How does she look?"

"It turns out she's a never-aging sorority girl scavenger-fairy," Margaret said. "She looks good."

"Well, what on earth did she want?"

Margaret stared at the two pink lines on the pregnancy test. "Just to say hi," she said to her mother, who evidently didn't have the best memory in the world.

As a child, Margaret had held her parents' dinner guests hostage with her rendition of "The Good Ship Lollipop," because she had seen Cindy Brady do it. But otherwise, she had been content with her parents' attention, then her boyfriends', then Donny's. She hadn't realized she craved another, tinier audience until mid-way through her thirty-seventh year, when she woke up one morning sobbing and not knowing why. Only gradually as the day went on—the typing of memos, the answering of phone calls, the lonely lunch at her desk—did she understand what was wrong with her, what she wanted. *Is it unreasonable to want this?* she had Twittered, and pretty much everyone said it wasn't. *You go get what you want, gurl*, said someone called RacyLacy.

* * *

When Margaret had asked Delores, "How on earth did you even find me?" Delores laughed and said, "Credit check, Google, YouTube, Facebook, Twitter. I couldn't have not-found you if I'd tried."

Food, trees, shelter, water, fire. What more could a growing child need? It was worth a shot anyway.

She took the lid off the plastic cage and tipped it over, telling the scarabs, "The world is full of shit. Go and enjoy." Then she got in her car and headed up the street to refuel for possibly the very last time. Who needed a car in the wilderness? She wondered what would happen when Delores came back and found no one home—the front door wide open and a note taped to it: *Take everything!* Maybe other scavengers would already be there, carting out the computer, video recorder, the big screen TV, the credit cards, the iPhones—staring bewildered at the open box of funny-smelling dirt on the floor. By then the scarabs would already be safely away, rolling, rolling, rolling the sun across the world while the humans filled their arms with all they could hold.

Rebel Yell

"Lamar," said Ray over the phone, his voice urgent. "I've got something I think you'd be interested in."

"I'll be in New York next month," I said. "How about we meet up then?"

"This can't wait," he insisted. "You need to come to Appomattox. I've got something good for you."

I hadn't heard from Ray Miller for three months, but with that call, I was on the road to Virginia. We had an odd relationship. A professional one, if you want to call it that. Maybe I'd finally get to see where he lived—in all the years I'd known him, he'd never once invited me to his home.

Not that I blamed him.

Ray was someone I liked to think of as one of my special agents in my burgeoning "found art" enterprise. As the sole executor of such, you might say my specialty was capitalizing on tips about art that was not just valuable, but also often significant in other ways, such as a knife used to stab Rasputin in one of the many assassination attempts against him. Art with a rich history.

I would, in turn, sell these items to wealthy patrons, the type who liked to keep their names out of the papers and who pursued art almost like a fetish. Some collected guns, others Russian crystal vases, pre-unification German pottery, or lampshades covered in human skin. I depended on my agents to let me know about these lucrative, ill-guarded, or black/gray market art objects of value. Then with my expertise at lock-picking and social engineering, I "found" these pieces of enameled jewelry, gilded salt cellars, chalices, and carved bones, and passed them on to ready buyers.

Unloading these items was easy. For the buyers I serviced, the less paperwork, the better. Often all that was needed was a phone call to someone on my list, a mention of the item, and my price. The deal was made. My regular buyers trusted me, and I in turn looked out for them, despite their eccentricities.

Ray ran a company that installed museum lighting—all those tiny fixtures, with bulbs that cost four-figures each, which made the illuminated pieces of art look priceless. He and I had a working relationship now going on to seven years.

Some installations he worked on were in public galleries, some in private homes. When running electrical wiring and mounting lamp hardware, he'd also pick up on how the security systems were installed and where the sensors and alarms were placed. He was also one of the first to know about new items of value on display, and their exact locations.

Ray was a good agent—it was in his best interests to help me maximize the value of the items I collected, while minimizing the security risk. He deserved every percentage point of his cut from the resulting sale of each item that found its way into my van and into the hands of my buyers.

Found art was win-win, for those who lived on the edge.

On the phone Ray had promised me something that would make the drive from Texas to Virginia worthwhile. I knew he wouldn't have called about some clay bowl or Babylonian statue smuggled out of Iraq, for example. Since 2004, the market had been saturated by government workers and contractors bringing that shit back in their luggage.

And he knew never to even mention liberated religious iconography, like crosses, no matter how delicate the silver filigree, ornate the enameling, or lifelike the impaled Jesus looked. I'd dealt so many crucifixes over the years that you'd think buyers were stockpiling them as a hedge against some sort of vampire invasion. But I'd grown increasingly ill of just holding the things.

No, Ray knew I especially liked to deal in blades, precious metals, and gemstones. In particular, I had an affinity for items that stabbed and cut—knives, daggers, and swords. There was something primal about holding an edged weapon. Some people stared into campfires. I lost myself on the blade as I held it in my hands.

I felt the edge and the edge was me.

I lived on it.

My favorite weapon in my own collection was a katana made in the early 1500s by the swordsmith Muramasa, whose craziness was said to have seeped out of his skin and folded into the steel of each blade that he made. Once a Muramasa blade was drawn, it is said that it could not be re-sheathed without the blade first tasting blood—the owner's if no other victim was available.

I didn't really believe that kind of talk. But when I found that Muramasa blade in Kyoto, thanks to a tip from my Milanese agent, I immediately coveted it, and I couldn't help but try to acquire it. I never did draw the blade from its scabbard, but when the former owner wrestled me to the ground as I tried to slip away with it, I flung his body off me to find he had been impaled by the sword.

Maybe there was something to the legend after all, but that's when I became a believer. That's when I felt a constant longing for the sword, to hold the blade in my hands. That's when I felt I knew the soul of Muramasa.

Now, as I crossed into Virginia from Kentucky, driving up I-81, I felt a tingling that made the hairs on the back of my neck stand up. It wasn't because of the weathered slopes of the Blue Ridge Mountains, waves of unspoiled green on either side of the interstate from trees bursting with new leaves after an early spring. Maybe I was apprehensive because of the intrigue behind Ray's call, but that really didn't seem quite right either.

The sun dipped below the edge of the mountains. I was tired of driving. The map said I was close to Appomattox, so I pulled off the road to a hotel in Lynchburg, near what looked like a university campus. The next morning, looking out the window, I saw that the side of the neighboring mountain had been shorn of trees and covered with colored rocks to form a glaring logo: LU. It looked hideous. Could probably have been seen from space.

A pamphlet left in the room advertised times for worship services at Thomas Road Baptist Church, founded by Jerry Falwell, on the Liberty University campus. It seemed ironic that it was a church that scarred nature to broadcast itself to an uncaring world that did not want or need to hear its message. I certainly didn't.

Somewhere down the hall I heard knocking on the doors— awful early for the maids to be coming by.

I looked again at the map. Ray was to meet me in Appomattox at the Huddle House restaurant, which he described as being like a Waffle House, only less upscale.

There was a firm knock on my door. I opened it.

A young man in a crisp white shirt, a navy sport coat, and tan trousers stood clutching a book. Behind him waited an older lady dressed in her Sunday finest—it was a Tuesday—and several layers of lipstick, mascara, and foundation.

"Good morning sir," said the young man, with enough energy to wake the dead. "How are you today?" He had perfect hair.

"How can I help you?" I said.

He held up a Bible, a gold cross embossed on a cover of black leather. "Are you worried about your soul?" His teeth seemed unnaturally white. "Would you mind if I talked to you about Jesus?"

"My soul is just fine, thanks," I said.

When I shut the door, harder than I had meant, a framed picture on the wall tilted to an odd angle. In the picture, a man, also with unusually white teeth and dressed in clerical black, spread his arms wide. In the background were buildings on the Liberty University campus. Beyond, the city of Lynchburg itself fell away beneath the shadow of his smile.

I would have blinked and driven right by Appomattox if I hadn't seen the sign commemorating the city where the Civil War ended: "Where Our Nation Reunited." The Huddle House restaurant sat wedged between three automobile parts-supply stores. Why such a small town needed so many stores for oil and gaskets wasn't clear.

The smell of grease and sausage gravy assaulted my nose when I walked in. A few men in worn t-shirts and jeans sat on stools at the counter. They were picking at plates of eggs, biscuits, and grits, watching a plump waitress leaning against the counter, who in turn looked with glazed eyes at the cars and trucks as they passed by the window.

I'd seen that waitress, or someone just like her, before in my travels across the South. She had been in every diner, budget motel, and discount store I'd ever visited. She always seemed to be waiting, waiting for something to happen. I didn't know what she was waiting for and I doubted she knew herself.

Ray sat in a booth in the rear of the restaurant. A large plastic glass of water with ice sat untouched on the table in front of him, condensation pooling around the base and soaking into a paper napkin.

"What's going on, Ray?" I said, slipping in to the seat across from him.

Ray shifted uneasily.

"I don't have much time, Lamar," he said, motioning for the waitress. "I'm going out of town after I talk with you. I'll be back tomorrow night."

The waitress took our orders.

"Okay," I said. "What you got?" Ray definitely looked nervous.

"I'm on a job here locally," he said. "First time that's happened. Anyway, they're opening up a local branch of the Museum of the Confederacy in town. Not everything will fit in their main museum in Richmond."

Ray's New York accent always got worse when he was nervous. Right now, it was strong. "Seen any good pieces there?" I said. "I didn't think the Confederate army had anything much of value."

He paused until the waitress set down my coffee and left.

"What's the one thing they did have?" he said.

I shrugged. "Maybe some embossed weapons, fancy dress uniforms? Cannons?"

"The Confederate army," he said, dropping his voice, "had something the Union army could never match. They had Robert E. Lee."

"Yes," I said, "but what's that got to do with us? He's dead and buried."

Ray continued as if he hadn't heard me. "During the Civil War, the country's best generals, classmates at the military academy, commanded armies fighting against each other. Robert E. Lee was practically worshipped by his troops—they loved him, despite being starved and beat to hell. To end the war, Lee surrendered his army to Grant in a ceremony held in the study of someone's home in Appomattox."

"Common knowledge," I said.

"Lee's chapel and tomb are in Lexington," he said.

"Fine," I said. "Lee's buried in Lexington. So?" I looked for the waitress. My food hadn't shown up.

Ray was practically whispering at this point. "Evidently there was an old building, long fallen into ruin, on the site of the new museum here, just up the road. During excavation, they found a kind of tunnel or catacomb deep in the ground."

"What was in the catacomb?"

"I don't know for sure," he said. "I got a glimpse of a set of maps. They showed where they were excavating, and a tunnel, and rectangular shapes."

At this Ray stopped, and I saw a ghost of recognition in his eyes when he realized he had my full attention.

The waitress set down my plate of eggs, bacon, and toast, but I pointed my fork at Ray. "What are we talking about?" I said.

"I couldn't tell from the blueprint. There have always been rumors around these parts that Lee's body isn't actually in Lexington. Some group, maybe the most obsessed of his former soldiers, was said to have absconded with it before Lee's casket could be sealed beneath the chapel." Ray's hand shook as he reached for his water. "It was kept out of the papers. Nobody knew where they had hidden the body. Some say they actually worshipped Lee. Some say they were waiting for the day when technology was advanced enough to bring Lee back to life, so the South could rise again, under his command."

My food steamed between us. I put down my fork. "The only people down here still talking about a Confederate comeback are old men in white sheets and Civil Rights activists agitating for support." I laughed. "You really think people stole Robert E. Lee's corpse and brought it to Appomattox for a Second Coming?"

The look on Ray's face told me that was exactly what he believed.

"And I thought the people in Lynchburg were unhinged," I said.

"Fine." Ray looked offended, but given the amount of money we had made each other over the years, his pride took a backseat in business-related matters. His accent softened, but he spoke resolutely, as if trying to push through some inner turmoil. "If you want something quick and easy, Lee's sword is on display in the museum, though I've heard it's a fake."

"Where's the real one?" I asked. At the mention of Lee's sword, I could almost feel my Muramasa blade in my hands. Perhaps holding Lee's sword would give me insight into Lee's soul as well.

I grabbed my glass of water and took a long drink, to cover the quickening I felt.

"Like Lee's body, no one knows," he said. He pushed away from the table. "Lamar, I'll be back tomorrow night—I can get you into the building with my keycard."

"Ray," I said, my hand on his arm. I tried not to show my interest in the project, in the sword. "I appreciate you giving me a call."

He hesitated.

"Where did you say you were going?" I asked.

"Hollow Lake," he said, looking, well, it pained me to say he looked disturbed. "Never been there," he continued. "I'm meeting a potential client. Probably some eccentric who wants lighting for his collection of Faberge eggs." He laughed nervously.

"Don't forget to give me that address." I winked, but he didn't seem to catch it.

He also didn't see me tailing him, though I kept my distance anyway. After only two turns we were on a winding country road—residential suburb on one side, rolling pastures on the other, with unobstructed views of the Blue Ridge mountains in the distance. After a few miles, we turned onto Country Club Road.

I hadn't thought Appomattox was big enough to support a country club.

The income bracket of the folks living on that road seemed a step above the surrounding neighborhoods. Fields dotted with black and white cows lay next to stately red brick homes with Hummers in the driveways. By contrast, Ray turned his van into the driveway of an industrial-styled home, with sharp angles, metal railings, and concrete. My guess was that Ray, a transplant from New York, fit in with his neighbors about as much as his artsy house fit in with theirs.

I drove on.

After nightfall, back in my hotel room, I made sketches of the museum based on my observations of the building and grounds I'd seen after my reconnaissance. I checked and rechecked my equipment, clothes, and other items I depended on during such operations. Years of experience had taught me a lot, especially to keep up with latest trends and technologies in the security field. More security was going digital these days, so regular attendance at the DEFCON hacker's convention in Las Vegas was critical for staying current. Also, right outside Vegas there were world-class firearms classes and shooting ranges, even if they weren't all legal.

Security, as they say, came in many forms.

This one DEFCON I had attended had booked the entire west wing of the Rio hotel and casino. The admission badge was a bronzed medallion—each person's was different—cut with hieroglyphic icons and runes and numbers and shapes. From the program, any of a number of workshops and presentations could be attended, on hacking, decrypting, coding, decoding, making, and breaking. There were contests too, and the main hall sported a complex symbol painted onto the atrium floor. It was in code, and the key to decrypting it was partly contained in the admission medallion.

I had walked by a group of kids peering over the lids of their laptops. One gave some sort of signal, and they all turned away from me, smoothly and quickly, as they silently closed their laptops.

I learned that "Spot the Fed" was built into their DNA, though it was definitely a false alarm in my case. Deals and discussions were made in the labyrinthine corridors dividing the presentation rooms. No cameras. No recordings. You couldn't look too clean, otherwise you'd be too suspicious. Everything was about breaking the code, making the con.

Kind of like the Penn and Teller show I had caught later that night, also at the Rio—you could never describe exactly what you just saw, but you had to admit that it blew you away.

Ray never made it back from Hollow Lake. I waited an extra day, just to be sure, but grew restless and couldn't take pacing in my room and staring at the LU mountain anymore. The hotel, or maybe its proximity to Liberty University, was making my dreams dimly lit and my nerves raw.

It was decided. Rural location, in and out job—couldn't have asked for an easier mark. Plus, I was done with Lynchburg and its creepy vibe. Like holding a crucifix, just being there was making me ill.

I decided to go it alone.

After parking in the outer lot of the Country Club after midnight, I walked up the road to Ray's house. The neighborhood was quiet, the pasture stretching out like a black void. Unlike his neighbors, Ray's property was covered in trees, so I had no worries about being seen. Only the crunch of gravel and leaves as I slipped through the shadows announced my presence.

Using a set of handmade lock picks some kid at DEFCON had made out of an old band-saw blade, which I instantly had paid for in cash when I saw the rich patina on the metal, I smoothly picked Ray's backdoor.

Once inside, I made my way through the dim spaces. The house was sparsely furnished with Scandinavian leather sofas and Italian Baroque carved wooden tables. A Chinese terracotta warrior guarded Ray's office, my payment to Ray for one particularly lucrative finding. The statue glared in the ghastly light of the moon coming in through a window.

On Ray's desk I found invoices from lighting vendors, boxes of bulbs in various sizes, and folders from his business. Nowhere did I see any blueprints. However, hanging on a chain from an arm lamp I found a keycard for the museum.

Thank you, Ray.

About twenty minutes later, I pulled my car off the side of the road. The air smelled faintly of compost and the stars glimmered above. I cinched my backpack. Instinct flared and I turned, just in time to watch a fox glide like a ghost across the road, disappearing into the night.

I did the same.

Breaking into the museum was more difficult than I had expected. My precision pellet gun defeated the scant perimeter security lighting, though Ray's keycard was useless. The reader also required a thumb scan, an almost unheard-of level of security for a museum displaying Civil War artifacts. This discovery unconsciously made my eyes squint, and my breathing sharp.

I wondered if maybe I should have waited for Ray.

I finally gained access to the main gallery through a hole cut into a window's glass after firing a circuit another DEFCON kid had assured me would disable the electronic security sensors, using some sort of electromagnetic pulse. Ray had said the museum people had only recently discovered the crypt, or whatever it was, so they probably hadn't had time to implement full security measures. The keycard and thumbprint scanner was likely the first, and only, security layer they had time to install.

Nevertheless, though I didn't hear any alarms, I knew I couldn't trust my luck to that kid's promises. I couldn't risk taking too long, so I set to my task.

I hurried as quietly as I could through the galleries, noting mounted flags from the various states of the Confederacy, as well as glass display cases of soldiers' uniforms, weapons, maps, quill pens, boots, and other artifacts from the Civil War. My trained eye took an inventory of the items of worth, including a display case of General Lee's uniform and, according to Ray, fake surrender sword.

In the back of the museum I found a locked door. The lock was simple, and a firm rake of the pins opened the door to the administration offices. I quickly scouted cubicles, a lounge, and a small kitchen. In a section of the building with no windows, I discovered a metal stairwell.

I crept down one flight of stairs to the landing of the basement floor, my flashlight cutting small windows through the darkness. The first room was empty, save for a desk and chair. The following rooms appeared to be designed to hold excess museum pieces, with shelving, racks, and mannequins. Ray had mentioned that the Museum of the Confederacy in Richmond only had enough space to display ten percent of their holdings. It seemed likely that much of the inventory would be coming here.

At the far end of the otherwise empty floor I passed through a small archway and found another set of stairs. My shoes scraped pale chips of rock and dried clumps of cement—the archway was a recent, rough addition. As I passed through, the hairs on my arm prickled, as if the atmosphere in the small stone antechamber was ionized.

Cautiously, I descended the worn stone steps. The stairwell curved down sharply, and there was no handrail. The passageway was narrow, not much wider than myself. Despite the cool flow of air down the stairwell, my skin felt clammy and my breathing became shallow.

I dropped my backpack on the steps so that I wouldn't get wedged in a tight space.

The flashlight kept me from making a misstep on the stairs, but only being able to see a small circle of light at a time made the hewn walls of the stairwell seem constantly changing, as if they were organic rather than rock.

Once down the stairwell, I found the floor uneven, and I moved carefully, my shoes crunching something brittle. Wary of holes or pits, before putting my foot down I tapped it to make sure something solid was indeed there.

With my hands in front of me, I inched slowly through the blackness. I felt like an astronaut floating in space at the end of my tether, on the brink of the universe.

The air was cold, like ice that penetrated my skin. Yet strangely I couldn't see my breath. The batteries in my flashlight were new, but somehow the light seemed dimmer, as if the darkness itself absorbed the radiance.

I felt a draft flowing back up the stairs. The air current had been rushing in when I had entered; now it was flowing out. No, now it was coming in again.

That was what was making it seem so cold—the constant flow of chilled air, in and out, as if death itself was breathing.

I stopped. My hand found a wall, and my fingers brushed over a surface with smooth knobs, like river stones. The entire wall seemed composed of these protrusions, and I leaned in closer to get a better look.

The light from my flashlight had become so dim that I could have been in a fog, or perhaps even a dream.

I pulled at one of the protrusions on the wall and slid something out. I held it in front of my flashlight. From having seen many museum displays of skeletons over the years I knew what a human thigh bone looked like, though I had never actually held one in my hands before.

It felt heavy. I expected the shaft to be smooth, but there were rough gouges there, and my finger traced out strange shapes carved into the bone.

I dropped the femur—I realized the wall was made of stacks of bones, piled end on, like firewood.

Taking a step back, something cracked beneath my heel and I looked down.

At first, I thought the floor was covered with little sticks. Kneeling, I found that the floor was made of finger bones. Thousands of finger bones, piled who knew how deep.

I took another step and toppled backwards, striking my head against something hard.

Dazed, I tried to catch my breath. The air seemed thin and my hand came away wet from the back of my head where I had hit it against a vertical stone, rectangular and smooth.

On the top of the stone I felt a carven shape—a statue. Like a blind man reading someone's face with his fingers, I tried to make out what was on top of the slab.

The object was a sarcophagus; the shape was a man lying in repose.

A trickle of blood ran down my neck and broke my reverie. Stepping forward, grinding finger bones into powder as I went, I found two more stone coffins. The largest had a stone stand beside the man lying on the slab; on it was a sword. The gold fittings on the scabbard and hilt glistened when illuminated by my feeble flashlight.

I felt a strange attraction to the sword, as I had felt with my Muramasa blade, and I knew that General Robert E. Lee's sword far above in the museum was indeed a fake.

I wanted to see this sword's edge, to feel it, naked in my hands.

I took another moment to steady myself. My head throbbed. My vision blurred and I felt nauseous. There was a maddening ringing in my ears, a syllable of sound that emanated from within my head.

I tried to wet my lips, but my tongue provided no relief.

It was cold. So cold. In the room that breathed.

I balanced the flashlight on the lid of the sarcophagus. Carefully, I reached up with both hands and gently lifted the sword from its stand.

The sarcophagus lid shifted and my flashlight tumbled to the floor and went out.

I felt a hand, firm, on my shoulder.

Falling, I sank into beckoning bones.

I dread that my thoughts may never come back, though I fear more for my memory.

That should have been the end, but He gave me a new beginning.

The Muramasa blade is drawn and rests, thirsty, on my lap.

Screaming, I wait for my General.

Contrivance of a String Bean Marblewood

We got so bored living in Kentucky. The sensation of a sneeze was the highlight of our day. Nothing occurred there. Yawning contests and television festivals. Destination: Wal-Mart.

People crapped. Every once in a while, an idea came for us. An idea came for Robert, who insisted on being called Jesus. He got the idea from the house he had just bought, one that no one else wanted. The workers had given up before they finished building it. I guess they got bored.

The house had a staircase that didn't go anywhere and doors where there were no rooms. Some of the rooms were higher than the others. Some of the rooms were only half painted, and the kitchen was essentially a hole. Architecturally, pragmatically, any which way, the house made no sense.

"You are cordially invited to my Surrealist Party. Come dressed as something other than yourself, preferably something other than this realm of consciousness. Arrive any time between 7:24 and Madisonville. Leave old vocabulary behind."

So there came Nally dressed as Kelly Ripa with her face torn off. There came Justin and Julie wearing sheet music blouses, feeding each other aged tenderloin. Julie pushed Justin in a wheelchair because he had trouble walking in his fins.

Jesus installed red light bulbs in each room. He made a big bundle out of the white light bulbs by wrapping them in saran wrap. He hung this bundle of bulbs on his front porch. He wrote "Possums are contagious" in ketchup on his living room wall. He served cottage cheese, bratwurst, sliced white grapes, clams, wine,

Dark Eyes vodka, and weird drugs, but he hid the weird drugs all over the house. He placed his guests' coats in the bathtub. He adhered a sign on the toilet that read "Work in progress. Contribute but do not flush." He didn't play any complete songs, just a mix tape with bits and pieces of hundreds of highly varied selections. Within a minute, we heard a snippet of "Linus and Lucy," a sampling of one of Jello Biafra's spoken word albums, the chorus of the Beatles' "Carry That Weight," a verse of the *Welcome Back, Kotter* theme, and a disturbing, slowed-down version of Olivia Newton-John's "Physical."

Jesus was dressed as an old-timey prostitute. He wound up his long, straight hair in pink curlers, wore leg braces, and draped a bunch of wet spaghetti noodles over his groin. He greeted guests by saying "Body of Christ" or "And they were on a five-inch and they sucked."

There came Carmen carrying a pool cue with a peach at the end of it. She wore a high school band uniform and sunglasses. There came John wearing a sexy salmon-colored robe and fringe-laced roller-blades. He duct-taped his fingers to his palms so that only his middle fingers could function. He kept asking everyone to chew on his middle fingers.

Jill, dressed as a disabled samurai, became upset when she felt a large centipede crawling on her face. Jesus had gone to the pet store and bought a bunch of exotic insects such as a Goliath beetle, a boll weevil, a hawkmoth, a daddy long-legs, a dragonfly, a walkingstick, a praying mantis, an earwig, a scorpion fly, and some other creepy bugs which I was not able to identify. He let the insects loose shortly before his guests arrived. Once all the insects died, the party was to conclude.

Jesus had invited one beautiful girl that no one knew (not even Jesus). All night she sat in a corner by herself. She wore an elegant white dress and her skin was frosty blue. When spoken to, her only reply was, "Talk to me about car crashes or strong work ethic."

I went all out. I wore Hammer pants and loaded the pockets with sandwich meats. I didn't wear a shirt and wrote "Are you mad at me?" on my chest with lipstick. I tied neckties around both arms and taped a syringe to my chin. I borrowed a monkey skeleton and hung it on my back. I begged people not to have sex with me.

"Who do you want to favor in the electric last year?"

"Regret."

"You're correct. But how do you persuade me so?"

"With webs of children."

"Please don't make love to me."

"I'll pull the lining of my teeth off. An on-going strip of enamel. I'll just peel it off completely."

"Amen."

"You do it to me every time, Grandma."

"A fellow has to pass the time."

There came Jr. dressed as himself. He thought theme parties were lame. Jesus told him to get the fuck out if he wasn't going to dress inappropriately. So Jr. took off his camouflage T-shirt and wore his shirt as pants. He wore his pants on his head and went topless, though he covered his nipples the rest of the evening.

There came Kenny dressed as a tampon with a Hitler mustache. There came Jamie as a Pink Lady from *Grease*. She had a kaleidoscope for one arm and carried a pug named Winston in the other.

Jesus had us write down a brief summary of a dream we had the previous night. We put the dreams in a coffee pot and then Jason, who was dressed as a plague-ridden UPS man, drew sketches based on the dreams. Each of Jesus' guests went home with a picture of his or her dream. I went home with a picture of me driving a car from the backseat right before violently colliding with a beached whale.

There came J.T. with a violin strapped to his chin. He wore only a loin cloth and spoke only with his violin. There came Barnrat dressed as Salvador Dali. Jesus said, "You'll have to do better than that." Barnrat replied, "Ah, but wait," and proceeded to collapse onto all fours. Barnrat spent the remainder of the evening crawling on the dirty floor singing Dolly Parton songs in the voice of a horror-stricken baby girl.

Jesus had just finished teaching us the A-bomb Dance when our parents and grade school teachers began to arrive. Jesus had told these adults that it was a surprise party, not a surrealist party. Some of us had found out in advance and told our parents and grade school teachers not to come. Some of us, such as Mutilated Kelly Ripa and Salvador Dali Parton, were shocked to see our moms and dads. Bubonic UPS Man was surprised to see his dad and his dad's twin brother. The Loin-Clothed Fiddler was embarrassed for his seventh-grade math teacher to see him like that.

The insects were slowly being squashed away. Because there was no furniture or anything else in most of the rooms, splattered insect remains were noticeable on the floors and ceilings. After the parents and teachers had been there for a while, the Goliath beetle, the dragon-fly, the praying mantis, and a few cockroach-like specimens were the only insects that I saw appearing regularly.

We were playing pin the flesh on the soldier when the beautiful girl that no one knew suddenly shrieked, "You've got it all wrong!"

Sweet mouths know too much. Clean up the future and kiss the rope. Empty fingers fumble, soaked in panic; the attic almost forgot. Mother runs through the window dirty. Mother will soil herself. Clear the tablet, pounding people back, the weight of the wood is just an excursion. Recklessly we sit on the machine, tongue in her mouth, at last complete.

Then Cal Ripken, Jr. arrived. He wore his Orioles uniform and brandished a baseball bat, just as he had been told to do. Ripken was in the area because he was starting a minor league baseball team called the Evansville Waves in nearby Evansville, Indiana. Taking advantage of Ripken's altruistic, good guy persona, Jesus told the all-time record-holder for consecutive games played that this was a party to benefit mentally ill twenty-somethings. Jesus said that the mentally ill twenty-somethings would be in attendance and that they all had one thing in common: They loved them some Cal Ripken.

Now that everyone had arrived except for the bishop of our diocese who hadn't replied to Jesus' invitation, the party reached a deliriously fevered pitch. Everyone entertained everyone. People screamed happily and strangers were innocently and playfully molesting one another. Most of the people mingled with ease. Cal Ripken mostly talked to that beautiful dead girl in the corner, which made me jealous. Eventually, the praying mantis was the only living insect.

That night, liberation almost entirely filled the red air in Jesus' disaster area of a home. No one in the history of humanity had ever been in these situations. Never in the history of human speech had these conversations occurred. Some of the parents and teachers adapted. Some were visibly uncomfortable.

My least favorite grade school teacher, whom I believe caused my phobia of reading aloud, cursed profusely at the praying mantis before crushing it with her purse. Jesus witnessed this and screamed at her, "Why did you do it, honky-tonk?!"

Then Jesus made all of us leave.

On the way out, I must have gotten on Cal Ripken's bad side when I shared with him my thoughts on bunting and teased him about that gorgeous dead girl he had been talking to. Ripken maimed me.

Helena Bell

Entropy

(1) I build. I am building. I am built.

(2) A house may be considered in a variety of ways. It is a collection of rooms (three bedrooms, two baths, a small closet off the kitchen, living room, dining room, sun porch, terrace, attic, basement) which can be deconstructed further into their composite parts: ropes, pine boards, the siding of old windmills, brick from a local kiln.

There are parts that existed within the house before it became a house: dirt and clay and stone.

The house rises and falls with each addition and revision. It is not unlike a sentence, or a body, or a polynomial equation. The façade may be reminiscent of a particular style from a previous era: colonial, neoclassical, Greek revival and such references may be purposeful or accidental. To observe a house is to observe a story in various stages of construction, and it is only to movement that the eye is drawn. A house is nothing without the people that live inside it.

(3) He calls himself Peter. He talks to himself as he works, sometimes sings, and from this I know he loves a woman named Mary.

I do not know if she is alive or dead, but when Peter sleeps he talks to her and her children under his breath and my eaves pull at their nails in strain to hear him:

Mary, there is more energy in the spaces between spaces. We are matter and dark, winding down and becoming more lukewarm. An infinite series of infinite series is the depth I feel for you as you pull me irrevocably towards stasis. Forever we will move backward and forward through time. Even as I feel him holding you, I am letting go.

(4) Peter counts his steps when he walks. There are eight stairs from the garden to the front porch. There are seventeen from the first floor to the second. There are nine rungs on the ladder, which drops down from the attic. These numbers are accidental but when he discovers it he decides to count more things: the height and width of each room, the switches and outlets, even the pattern of his doorways.

He adjusts each frame such that each is slightly smaller than the one before it and if one were to begin in the basement and follow each opening until the last, you would feel as if the world is spiraling off into a sudden and inevitable end. He makes other adjustments too: each line of windows a palindrome of increasing then decreasing size, a prime number of tiles on the bathroom floors, a wood grain inlay of a nautilus shell at the center of each threshold.

(5) When the last wall is walled, Peter invites his mother to inspect my corners and staircases. She holds tissues at the windows to check for drafts, sniffs the paint, and slams around in the attic in thick brown shoes to see where I am strong and weak and somewhere in-between. She does not speak, only mutters like Peter, and I do not like her. As she kicks at the doorways, questions my structure, I imagine cracking myself open and swallowing her whole. Yet, she loves Peter as I love Peter and so I remain quiet and meek.

"Mary was a bitch," she says. "The house works."

(6) My first winter I am not properly heated. The wind pushes snow and ice up to the edge of my foundation where I can feel it hardening like stone. I take it into me: molding, packing, filling the seams and running them over with dirt and the fur of a dead rabbit. I puff and puff, shaking icicles from the gutters and snow from the chimney. I think of Mary. I imagine how her voice must sound: strong and hard edged, and I whisper things I think she would say to Peter in a perfect world.

Slowly, Peter shivers less and less beneath his blanket.

The radio hums its low hum and though Peter cannot hear us, we all hum: the wool rugs, the ceiling medallions, the copper wires. We all help him sleep.

Many years later, I feel Peter die.

(7) There are five stages to human decomposition. Or there is one stage. Or there are a thousand stages. To number them is to enforce a consistency of proportion and pattern on a process for ease of human observation. Better to say a body dies. It falls apart. Better still to say a body dies, and becomes home to things that were outside of itself. It takes them in, and adapts to their needs and consumption. A body is merely an iteration, and will go through many more iterations.

An iteration may be examined on a micro or macro scale. An atom inside a cell inside an alveolus. A body inside a house inside a universe. One imagines that if one had enough distance that the whole of them could be lined up beside each other and appear as orderly and exact as a set of Russian nesting dolls. A universe inside a universe inside a universe.

Or alone, spinning among the dark.

Easier to imagine that there must be an order: a taxonomy of greater and smaller; like and unlike; cause; effect; a finite set of recognizable desires, decisions, and reactions as familiar and predictable as well-worn grooves on the kitchen linoleum;

and a new family will always choose to enter a house through the front door.

(8) I tell myself a story:

John and Mary fell in love and got married. They had three children meeting the socially dictated standards of aesthetic and character.

Mary met Peter, fell in love and left her husband John. Mary and Peter were happy for a short time and enjoyed such hobbies as sailing, photography, and collecting seashells. One night Peter gave Mary a picture frame made of small measled cowries. He had spent a long time collecting the shells and polishing them until they shined. As she held it, Mary thought long and hard about the how and the why of endings. She has ended many relationships before now, and believes she will end many more to come. Her explanations to Peter were eloquent but succinct. There was no beauty in the destruction, only a hollow ringing and the fear that nothing else would follow.

When she finished, a shell broke off and it was so small in her hand, she wondered how it was ever alive.

(9) Mary's three children grew up, married, and had children of their own. One day they received a letter stating that a man named Peter had died and named them his heirs. The oldest one said they should disclaim the house, and the box of personal effects. There might be some money in the savings account, and that is easier to split between the three of them.

The youngest said nothing, but lived in the city and had no desire to move.

The middle child was a woman named Madge.

(10) The woman Madge and her husband have an older daughter named Joyce who twirls in the attic room when no one is looking. With a little brush and pails of mismatched paint, she colors the walls pink, then yellow, then green pastel. Sometimes, though she does not know it, she stomps around in the same way Peter's mother used to and pauses to critique the same slanted window frames and question their integrity.

The woman and the man call her Joyce, but she tells me she prefers to be called Consuela as no one ever took a girl named Joyce seriously.

"It's okay," she says, "I'm not built right either."

I take her secrets into me and build for her. Build and build and build.

(11) When next I see her she is wearing a back brace; it wraps around her chest and bursts from the front of her shirt extending a metal hand to her chin. Now she can neither run nor climb like her sister and cousins and instead hides in a secret room only she can find: I have given it walls of feather mattresses and old broomsticks, a ceiling made of mosquito netting left overnight in the rain.

"Two years," she tells me. "I just have to wear it for two years. Then I'll be perfect."

Consuela grows in fits and spurts. Dark blue lines appear on her thighs, her stomach, her breasts. Though her parents say she no longer has to wear the brace, sometimes she does, pulling it tighter and tighter until it cuts into her flesh and she bleeds. She tries to curl her body around itself, to make it small and malleable as she squeezes her shoulders and hips into a dress that is too small for her, too small even for her younger sister. Eventually the seams rip, and her body and flesh unfurl in reverse order, only faster and there is nothing I can do but watch.

When she plays with her sister and cousins at hide and seek, I bend the walls and slant hallways so Consuela can sneak without ever being seen. When she emerges, victorious, from our secret closet she is happy for precisely 3.4 seconds as she twirls and twirls.

"But I *looked* there," her sister says.

"You didn't look hard enough," Consuela says, although she is wrong.

> Her sister looked,
> and looked,
> and looked,
> seeing nothing but dark shadows and the dust of a
> dead man's suit.

(12) Consuela grows and grows. Her sister marries, her cousins marry. Consuela is like a sequoia: impossibly tall and grand and I wish she would measure herself this way and no other.

The night of her niece's first birthday party she sits in the closet I have made for her and begs to disappear forever.

And I build.

(13) A quiet settles. Sheets are laid over furniture; a door is closed, and then locked. It is during this stage that air and water settle with gravity. They find the porous places and worm their way through the wood. Within a few months the joints swell and creak and no one notices except to say that such is the way with old homes. A thermostat breaks and the house will be too cold in winter, too warm in summer. Space heaters are purchased; they rarely work.

Renovations are planned, and then forgotten. They take on

their own shapes and float through the house like ghosts. They are with the family at dinner, sitting on chairs and wondering about the taste of salt.

Slowly the house fills with moths, termites, and other small things. Discoloration of carpet and drapes occurs, darkening of the cabinets and pipes. Tap water tastes faintly of rust.

Windows stick and one winter, gases heavier than air billow and pool on the bedroom floor. One by one, the inhabitants of the house fall asleep and pass on.

Finally the workmen come. Nails are lifted, then the wide slat pine and subfloor. Joists are supported, examined, treated with chemicals. A sill needs to be replaced. Glass bottles are lifted from the dirt and set aside along with newspaper clippings and old photographs. A new stairwell is built to the attic. Somewhere a woman suggests a scrapbook with copies of building permits and old plans. The idea is weighed, considered, but fades into the whine of an electric drill.

(14) A woman named Sarah is peeling eggs in the kitchen while her daughter and son explore their new home. Each time she grasps an egg from the cooling saucepan she wonders if it will break in her hand, the white and yolk spilling across the water.

The eggs are firm, but yielding. When she knocks them against the counter there is the faintest crack like snow underfoot. She rolls the egg under her hand, feeling the fissures race across the face of the shell. Crack. Roll. Crack. Roll. She observes that the process is not like a marriage; is not unlike a marriage. She observes that there is a finite number of parts to an egg: the shell, albumen, whites, yolk. A finite number of weak points. A finite number of the members of her family.

Behind her, her husband paces and offers reason after reason why they should not stay, why they should move to another house closer to town.

"I grew up here," she says.

Around her the entropy of the universe is increasing, and one day there will be a complete disorder of all the particles in it. She cracks the egg, rolls it in her hand. The shell is cold but the egg beneath it is still warm.

Sarah's husband paces, opens the closet door and closes it again.

"I always feel like something else is here. Watching me."

The peeled eggs go in a bowl, the discarded pieces on a napkin before being thrown into the garbage. One has come out beautifully fractured: a mosaic of shell and membrane like the tiled glass behind the stove.

"I grew up here," she says again. "It's perfectly safe."

(15) Sarah and her husband have a daughter they call Joyce. Joyce tells me she is named for an aunt who disappeared years ago and of whom no one speaks.

She tells ghost stories and monster stories; she tells her friends that some day snakes and spiders made of the bones of the dead will burst forth from the walls of the house like a flood.

One night, in perfect timing with her tales, as she flicks a light bulb on and off for effect, I loose a deep shudder from roof to basement sending bats and other furred things scurrying from their hiding places and the children scream

     and scream

     and scream.

Joyce and her friends do not return to the attic for a long time.

(16) Joyce is in love with her best friend's boyfriend. She doesn't say anything, but when they are walking up the new stairs to the attic, brushing aside cobwebs and boxes of ornaments, I see how her eyes follow him in the quickening dark. She doesn't notice, but his eyes follow her too. Katherine, the best friend, notices nothing and leans against a trunk before asking if anyone knows a good story.

"How about a ghost story," the boyfriend asks and looks to Joyce because he longs to hear her voice. I can tell he is only with Katherine to be close to Joyce, and Joyce is only close to Katherine to be with him.

"Did you hear about Martha?" Katherine asks. "I heard she got knocked up by that college guy she was seeing."

Joyce and the boyfriend gaze at each other, as if both realizing for the first time how Katherine is a mere receptacle and conveyor of gossip, of flash, of ephemeral moments meaning nothing against the weight of well-worn structures. Joyce is a cathedral. She is turrets and basilica and Brunelleschi's dome. When Katherine closes her eyes, her features blank as if everything which defines her has been shut off. Between Joyce and the boyfriend, the air hums with the heat of oil filled lanterns.

Once there was a lovely girl
who lived in a lovely house
which granted lovely wishes.

—

"I think I want to go home," Katherine says, and she and the boyfriend leave. I never see them again.

(17) Many years later, Joyce picks me.

She and Victor move in on a Tuesday, the day of their wedding when the curve of Joyce's stomach is a bare hint of twins. They smile and smile and smile, receiving their guests one by one and accepting soup tureens and linen napkins. No one asks, but Joyce is prepared to explain how she and Victor eloped months ago. This ceremony is superfluous. Redundant.

No one asks, but Joyce is ready. She is ready. All they need to do is ask and she will tell them how she has been married, and happy, for months.

Upstairs, I have squeezed the attic walls and stretched the roof tiles. There will be two cribs, two changing beds, two rocking horses, one blue and one pink. There will be two bookcases, each filled with the favorite books of Joyce and Victor's respective childhoods.

I am ready.

(18) A house is uncertain if it should be measured qualitatively (the magnanimity of its dormers; the robin egg blue of its porch ceiling) or quantitatively (the number of its inhabitants; the size of its weddings and funerals and Thanksgiving dinners;

the length of its nails, equally spaced to reduce redundancy;
two by fours;

the pulse of wires, of pipes, of plumbing and ducts, of shed skin and recycled breaths, the tangle of lamp cord and the shock of exposed brick against plaster).

I could count the number of rotten floorboards ripped up, windows re-sashed, appliances replaced.

I could wonder if I am still the same house, the lost parts of myself no more vital than fingernails or epidermis. Or a new house: a child, a great grandchild, a genetic variant, one in a long line of houses which will be built and destroyed and built again.

(19) Mary is born healthy, but her brother is not. Joyce takes her home and lets her sleep in the bed every night while Victor repaints the attic.

Later, he moves boxes to the upstairs of the garage filled with his favorite books, blue bears, a bag of changing cloths, and the head of a broken rocking horse.

(20) Mary tells her mother that the attic is shrinking, that once it took her 10 steps to walk from one window to the next, that now it is 8, that tomorrow it could be six.

"You are growing too fast to keep up with," she says. "Like your father. How is he?"

"He says it is warm in California, like a furnace. He looks forward to seeing me this summer."

Joyce tells her daughter a story like she used to tell her friends: of ghosts and unfillable voids, of dead things and furred things and things from which one cannot escape. This time I do not shudder; I do not shriek to send them both scurrying from the room; Joyce is so frail and the sun is so bright.

(21) Mary gathers tape measurers and black felt pens from the drawers. She carries sheaves of drafting paper to each floor, each bedroom and closet. She compares drawings and plans; she looks at old family pictures and builds models out of deconstructed dollhouses.

Beginning in the basement she ascends in a spiral, marking each doorway and window. She counts. She compares. She walks the circuit again; she runs it; she streaks through the house until she is dust covered and panting, and finally she begins to cry.

I creak and creak but she will not stop, not until Joyce comes and pulls her daughter into her lap and begins to hum softly to all of us.

"He left," Mary says. "I thought he loved us."

Joyce gestures to the window and to the city skyline beyond. "They all say that," she says. "But look, there are so many of them."

(22) Mary goes off to school, then college. One Christmas she notes how her mother's hands have turned so pale and asks how often her mother goes out.

"Now and then," Joyce says, and drops her hands below the table. "Tell me about school."

"How often?" Mary asks.

"I have the house," Joyce says.

"It's too big for just one person."

"Once you said it was shrinking. Perhaps it adapts itself to us. A perfect fit." Joyce smiles as if it is a joke between them.

Mary does not smile; she stares at the wall, considering.

(23) While Joyce sleeps, Mary sneaks up to the attic and finds the box with her old drawings and models, the legal pad of measurements and steps. She lists each doorway according to its width and when finally she has the order of it she walks the circuit from basement to attic once more. When she reaches the slanted sill and looks out at the world beyond she sighs.

"It's not me," she says. "It's you."

(24) Mary packs her mother's bags. She fills boxes with china, with yarn, with multi-colored vases and moves her into an apartment downtown. On Saturdays, Mary comes alone with mops and brooms and microfiber cloths. Sometimes there is a young man with her who brushes the hair away from her face. Together they sweep the front porch and polish the windows and place a 'For Sale' sign in the front yard.

Sometimes I shirk from Mary's gaze; sometimes I meet her head on, banging the shutters against the wind in time with her heartbeat. I groan under footsteps, plaintive and insistent.

> Still she shines,
> and shines,
> I admire her persistence greatly,
> she sells.

(25) A man comes with his daughter. The mother has died and

the girl has bad dreams he hopes will be smoothed away by country air. The little girl peeks in the corners and runs barefoot atop the linoleum, sliding headfirst into the stainless steel counter. They do not buy me.

(26) A family of six walks back and forth, back and forth, counting the bedrooms again and again as if observation will cause them to increase in number.

"You can always tear it down and build something else," Mary says. "The property spans a full acre."

(27) A single young woman, fresh faced and looking to invest, rings the doorbell. When Mary opens the door, I know this is the one who will pick me.

(28) Mary sits on the front porch with a cigarette and Diet Coke. The inspection has gone poorly and I know she blames me.

Joyce, *Joyce!* says good-bye to the coroner who holds the paper bag of skull and bones loosely in his hand as if uncertain what to do with them.

(29) This is a story I tell myself:

Once there was a universe and a body and a great between.

Once there was a story, which ended in the middle and began again and ended and began.

Once there was a man named Peter who was a physicist who despised all use of scientific concept as metaphor or simile who loved a woman named Mary who herself loved and was loved by many men and who had three children who had children of their own and some of whom I saw and some of whom I never saw and some of whom I hid away from the world.

(30) "No one will buy this house now," Joyce says but with a lilt as if asking permission. She is hopeful; she wants me back.

(31) Once there was a man named Peter who divided his life into days and then minutes and then seconds in order to examine the small pulse of his pain and to later stand back to see the beautiful curve it made into the distance.

(32) If I could speak, I would tell Mary I was built for her with love and hope and unwavering devotion. I will try harder, try better. I would tell her the match in her hand, the insurance papers mean

nothing to me. If she will not have me, I will dissemble myself brick by brick and move to a location of her choosing. I would tell her how I held Peter and Joyce and I will hold her too, an unending line of those who are not loved as they should be loved.

(33) Once there was a house which could neither feel nor observe the end of the universe, but could mimic the fine cracks made in the peeling of eggs. And the division helped as much as the listening helped: first the pain, and then order, and then the symmetry.

(34) I age while you stand still, Mary. I forgive you for loving another, for abandoning me, but know I will always be here for you. I am constant and changing and tied to you. You, who are all so cold, while

    I burn.

    I burn.

    I burn.

The Undertaking

When Hiram Ephram was nineteen, his father died, which made Hiram the new mortician of the mining and logging town of Shook Rag, deep in the Georgia mountains. They'd just finished supper and his father went outside to the woodshed for an armload of kindling, and likely a smoke or two. When his father hadn't returned in an hour, Hiram went out and found him slumped over sideways on a well-seasoned stack of birch, his pipe still smoldering in one hand, his eyes filled with snow. The next morning Hiram's mother told him, Well, Hiram, you've worked with your daddy long enough to know what needs done.

He asked if it would be better, more proper, to take his father down the pass to Garrity.

She shook her head and said, Proper, be damned. We'll take care of our own, son.

So that's what Hiram did. And when his mother died less than a year later, he did the same for her.

When Hiram was twenty-two, he asked Josephine Turner to marry him. She said no. When he asked her why not, she told him that she wouldn't be able to sleep in a house where the dead lay. Half a year later he proposed to her again and again she said no. The third time he offered the ring, she asked him if she would ever have to see any of the bodies.

The only body you'll ever have to view is mine, dear, he said, and that one only when you want to. She accepted.

Collin was born on a Tuesday, an easy birth but an uneasy child.

Hiram once told Josie that the holler had never really been one until Collin had come along and filled it with his cries. On a still day, as the ice dripped steadily from the eaves of the town, he heard his son's lusty wailing from the front door of the sheriff's office. By the time Hiram had reached the gate to his house he could hear Josie's voice, low and steady, singing the old lullabies that she'd known as a child:

Lay your head down now and rest, little one
 Let my voice be the last sound you hear
And I'll light a small candle to put you to bed
In the dark you'll have nothing to fear…

When Collin was thirteen, Hiram took him into the mortuary for the first time. Collin's skin turned the color of new milk as his father explained the use of the trocar, and his pulse beat fast and thready in the side of his neck when Hiram showed him how to change the blade on the scalpel. A body lay under a sheet on the table in the center of the room and Collin brushed against it once and jumped as if he'd been goosed. He squealed out loud and when his father spoke to him he could only stare at the floor.

Hiram said, It's no good, is it?

No, sir, Collin said. It's not.

Hiram nodded. Well, that's alright then. Go tell your mother I said to give you some lunch.

Collin looked as if eating might be the last thing in the world he felt like doing, but he ran from the room without looking back.

Hiram sighed and went back to work. He remembered his first time in this room with his father, and how the smell of the room and the thought of the things he would have to do had made the room spin around his ears and he'd gotten sick in the sink. After he'd been sick, he'd felt better. Not much, but he'd cleaned the sink with disinfectant and then gone back to help his father.

As Hiram pulled the sheet from the body and began his work, he wished that Collin had been just a little stronger, or maybe just a little weaker.

* * *

When Collin turned seventeen he went to work at the mine. Josie pleaded with him not to do it. You'll fall down a seam and be lost. It's too dangerous, Collin. Stay and work with your father. At the mention of his father's work, Collin's lip curled in a sneer. I'd rather be dead myself than do what he does, he said.

Josie asked Hiram to speak with Collin. Talk some sense into him. Please, Hiram, make him see it's too dangerous. You know. You've seen.

And he had. He'd seen the bodies of over a dozen men who had met their deaths under the earth. He knew exactly what Collin was getting into. But he had the sense that Collin knew, too. He felt the boy had the right to make up his own mind. So he said nothing. And when he asked Josie to pass the salt that night, she threw the shaker against the wall where it shattered then ran up the stairs to bed. Hiram sat alone at the table and finished his supper.

Hiram's best friend, Lew, was a talker, which suited Hiram just fine especially since Josie wasn't much speaking to him. Under the cloudless Georgia sky, Hiram and Lew stood waist deep in the water and cast their lines. Lew fidgeted and waded to the bank for drink and smoke; Hiram was still as a stump. Lew talked about the weather, the women he'd known, the jobs he'd had, the fish that he'd just now almost caught. Hiram noticed his friend's blood-shot eyes and scabbed knuckles but didn't know how to bring it up without sounding prudish. He'd heard the rumors around town about Lew's wife, Abigail, taking up with a logger from Trent and he wanted to tell Lew he was sorry about the whole mess, but that just wasn't the kind of thing you could tell another man without making him sore about it. Neither of them mentioned the new cast on her arm. And when she left without so much as a goodbye in the middle of the night a few months later, the gossips in town likely had much to say about it, but Hiram never brought it up. Not once.

* * *

Lew came over for suppers after that. Neither Josie nor Hiram minded the extra plate. Josie seemed happy to have another mouth to feed again. She didn't mention that they couldn't really afford it. Things were tight enough that she'd cut up one of her momma's quilts to make new socks for Collin. She was stitching one evening after Lew had left. Her hands fast and sure.

Workin' in that mine, she said, the boots'll cut into his feet something awful.

I offered him a better shake, Hiram said.

Her hands slowed and then stopped. Talk to him, Josie replied. You're his father. Say something. You have to say something to him, Hiram. When he didn't reply, her hands picked up their rhythm again, her fingers fast and nimble with the needle. Under and over, under and over, and the thread dragged along in its wake. She pulled the fabric tight over the wooden darning egg. Stitched again.

I don't like the thought of him down in the black any more'n you do, Hiram said.

The next morning when he came down to breakfast he found cold toast and cold coffee and no sign of either Josie or Collin. He drank the coffee and thought maybe he'd have a talk with Collin after all. After lunch, maybe. He headed to the mudroom for his boots but stopped when he heard voices outside the kitchen door.

It's not so bad as everyone makes out.

Not so bad, is it? Why does your father stay so busy then? Between the mine and the logging, your father's put half a dozen men in the ground just in the last year.

I'll be careful, Ma.

Careful's got nothing to do with it. Your father wouldn't say boo to a goose, but I'll have my say, Collin Ephram. You're not to work in the mines.

I'm sorry, Ma. But I am.

The backdoor slammed. I'll talk to the boy later, Hiram thought. But Collin didn't come home that night. And when Hiram went to bed and reached for Josie, he learned that there was something in his home far, far colder than any cup of coffee.

* * *

Collin's dead set on it, is he? Lew passed the bottle to Hiram as they stood in the fast moving water. Hiram sipped it and passed it back. Lew said maybe a few months down in a three foot seam with less than an hour of daylight will change the boy's mind and boys don't always want to be what their daddies want 'em to be and ain't it a shame and pass me that bottle while you're near the bank, would you, Hi?

Lew came for suppers and sat late on the porch carving a knuckle of yew or oak that would eventually have a place between his yellowed teeth. He clamped and puffed on the pipe in his mouth as he carved and cussed at the one in his hand. Hiram poured the hooch and they drank until the moon rose and the lightning bugs lit the pines on the slopes of Cotter's Peak.

One night after pouring about three fingers of good cold shine in his gut, Lew said, It's my fault about Abigail, you know. If I hadn't been drinking, she might still be here now. Hiram looked at Lew and thought he looked older than his fifty-three years that night, his skin loose on his jaw and neck, his thin hair blown in a haystack by the March wind. Lew had been drinking more and fishing less. He'd stopped carving. No more were the sweet wood shavings that had settled in nightly drifts on Hiram's porch.

You think so, Hiram said.

I do, Lew replied, and you know I'm right to think it.

Hiram knew well enough not to argue with Lew when he'd had a skinful and left it alone but he thought that time and fate had been unkind to his friend, and that the man could use some small measure of joy in his threadbare life. So the next day he took Lew to the hole and gave him his three favorite flies and he didn't give a damn if Lew lost them to the water or a catfish or dropped them in the dirt on the way home. Hiram's flies had always been better than Lew's and they both knew it. Hiram was just all around better at keeping things pulled up tight.

Lew tied the first fly—coppergoldbrown and quail feather shiny—and made his cast and let out a holler when he reeled in the first fish of the day.

Lew didn't show up for supper the next night, or the night after that. Hiram went to Lew's house. There was no answer when he knocked. He said one word, though he would not remember doing so later. In a voice not even Josie would have recognized he whispered—Daddy? The door was unlocked and he went in. Lew was sitting in the chair closest to the hearth, an empty bottle on the floor at his feet. Hiram had spent time enough with the dead to know their stillness, but he reached out to touch him anyway. Cold as stove wood.

He found a few little carvings of animals, no bigger than his thumb, on the mantel over the fireplace and put them in his pocket. He took the pipes, the box of tackle, and Lew's fishing pole. He looked a while longer, running his hands over the scarred wood of the trestle table, the one straight-backed chair. Then he stopped by the sheriff's office. Then he went home and put the little animals on the desk in the parlor. Fox, bear, coyote, rabbit, something that looked like it yearned to be a mountain lion.

Hiram Ephram took the heavy apron from its hook on the blackwood door. His hands wrestled at the small of his back until the knot was right, then he walked to the table at the center of the room and picked up the soap.

He soaped Lew's hands and face, his feet and legs, always working toward the heart as his father had taught him. The drip in the sink was a metronome to his work.

Plink.

Move the head side to side and place it on the block. Pick up the hands, rub loose the stiffness in the wrists, fingers, elbows. *Plink.*

Now the feet and ankles and knees. There was a scar on one shin. Hiram wondered how he'd gotten it. Understood that now he'd never know. He rinsed the body then the light caught the bright-dark glimmer of the scalpel and he tilted the head to the left. A tiny incision; less to stitch and wax later. He inserted the feeder tube and opened the valve on the gravity feed bottle that held the embalming fluid. *Plink.*

When the fluid had run its course, he angled the needle in the opposite direction and ran the fluid up the carotid artery and into the head. He stitched the incision on the side of the neck, aspirated the abdomen, purse-stitched the hole left by the trocar. *Plink.*

He looked at the trail of cotton thread that hung from the incision just above Lew's navel. He snipped off the excess and held the piece of string up before his eyes. He thought of all of the flies he'd tied and cast and lost to the water and wished he'd given more of them to Lew. *Plink.*

As he stared at the piece of string, Lew spoke from the table beside him.

My wife never left, he said.

Hiram jerked away from the table and dropped the string as if he'd been snake bit. Lew's face was still, his chest neither rose nor fell. He was dead, still just as dead as he'd been when the sheriff had helped bring his body in. Hiram had just about decided he'd imagined it when Lew spoke again.

She told me she was going to leave me and I grabbed her by the neck and I just... Hiram stared at Lew's face, at his unmoving lips. The voice came from everywhere, from nowhere.

I buried her near the ridge on Cotter's Peak. And then I said she'd left me and everyone believed it. Why wouldn't they? But you know what, Hi? I loved that woman. Right to the end.

Hiram walked to the door and his shaking hands fumbled at the strings of the apron but eventually he was free and he hung it on the peg and went out to the parlor to find a drink. He could usually take it or leave it, but right now he felt as if he'd never needed one so badly in his life.

I'm tired. Anyone could imagine things in this kind of situation I'll bet. It's only natural.

By the time he finished his drink he felt a little silly. His grieving mind had simply filled up the silence with the voice he was most accustomed to. He went back to the mortuary and finished working on Lew. It was a good job and Hiram thought Lew would have approved of the suit he'd chosen for him. *Plink.*

As he turned off the light to leave, Lew spoke again from the darkness.

I loved that woman, Hi. I kept her wedding ring. Put it in my tackle box with my sinkers. I loved her right to the damn end.

Hiram closed the door.

After Lew was buried, Hiram found himself going to the hole more often than he had before. He stood on the bank but he didn't fish. Not anymore. He stared across the gully at Cotter's Peak and he wondered if there was a midnight-shallow grave somewhere along the ridge.

Summer came, and with it came Tera McLeod. She was only a few years younger than Collin… She'd taken a tumble on the slippery rocks of Ewan's quarry and her once-pretty face was now a crazy geography of lumps and ledges, mossy scrapes and deep cuts. She lay on Hiram's mortuary table nude, with her toes turned inward. *Plink.*

Her breasts were still so young and firm though cold and pale. There was a dark-bright spot of lividity on her left breast and Hiram massaged it briskly with the soap. Won't show anyway. *Plink.*

He went to fetch the water to rinse her body and she spoke from behind him:

I was gonna go with Bobby Killian to the dance but I don't guess that's gonna happen now.

Hiram dropped his pail in the sink and it rang like a bell. Walked back to the table and looked down at her.

I suppose he'll take Amy, instead, she said and then she sighed, the sound of an autumn wind through dry grass. Not again, Hiram thought. Not again.

He had work left to do. The girl's father and mother would want to see her and she was in no shape to be seen. Not yet. He put bleach-soaked cotton pads on the bruises on her face and neck and hands. He was placing the last on her swollen eye when she spoke again:

I'd already picked out my dress.

He pulled his hand back. Cleared his throat.

Can you hear me? he asked.

Bobby told me one time when he walked me home that his

daddy was steppin' out on his momma. He cried when he told me. I wonder if Amy will hold his hand when he cries like I did?

Plink.

Hiram clutched his head in both hands. He squeezed his eyes shut. Then he realized he knew how to find out if all of this was only in his imagination.

He went to the mudroom. Lew's tackle box sat in the corner and he opened it, dug through until he found a tin that had once held throat lozenges. It was heavy, too heavy for cough drops. He opened it and pushed the sinkers around with one finger, and there it was, gleaming gold-mellow in the light of the sinking sun coming in the back windows. He picked up the ring and clutched it tightly in his hand. Then, confused and frightened, but satisfied he wasn't losing his mind, he went back to work.

As the summer wore on into fall, and the fall gave way to winter, Hiram saw more bodies on his table. Eb Greely's son Gabe tripped on a stump and his chainsaw clipped his femoral artery. Gabe bled out before he could even call for help. As Hiram stitched the gash in his thigh, Gabe told him how his daddy had wanted him to go to school and that he wished he had listened. He told Hiram that when he was twelve, he'd stolen a neighbor's ball glove and then was too afraid to use it so he'd buried it in the woods where it rotted. He told how he had later loved the neighbor boy and that when his mother had caught the two of them in bed together she had said nothing that night but forbid him to ever hang around the neighbor again. He told all of this and much more as Hiram stitched and washed, waxed and powdered, punctured and rinsed and dressed his flesh. The sink dripped steadily. *Plink.*

Why are you telling me these things? Hiram asked, little more than a whisper.

Because you will listen, Gabe replied.

The widow Eames—choked on a bit of Christmas ham—told Hiram of the teenaged girl she had been, night rides she had stolen away on her brother's horse to meet with her sister's husband—for a night ride of another kind.

Sara and Jesse Dunkle's new baby, not three months, fell from his crib and his not yet solid skull had crumpled like a robin's egg. Baby Dunkle cried and cried but sometimes Hiram thought he heard words in those cries. Once he thought he heard the word hungry. Then warm. When he heard the word daddy he tried stopping his ears with cotton but it didn't work. *Plink.*

Collin worked steadily and seldom came home for suppers. When he did, Josie would fuss over him and swipe a finger behind his ear, and cluck her tongue over its blackness. She told him he was filthy as a common guttersnipe. She would glare at Hiram and wait for him to say something, anything. But Hiram never did.

Emma Carthage lived up Glick Pass and died on Independence Day. She'd been a school teacher but never a loved sort. She'd been hateful in life and had died as she'd lived—alone. Once she was on Hiram's table, her words poured out of her as toxic as the embalming fluid that poured into her. She told of the dogs she'd poisoned, the horse she'd crippled, the children she'd punished. Listen to this—she said—when children misbehaved I just gave them a good damn case of what my daddy gave me. He strapped me, but good, and I turned out just fine. They will thank me for it someday. Listen to me now—my neighbors were always killing off my garden, letting their dogs shit where they may. Those animals had to be controlled. When that horse knocked down my back fence—

How is it that you can talk? Hiram asked.

How is it that you can listen? she asked. Listen to this—

Fall gave way to winter. Josie was darning in the sitting room when Sheriff Parker came to the door with his hat in his hands and told her that there had been a cave-in at the mine. Hiram let him in; Josie had fallen to the floor in a faint. As the sheriff stamped through the fresh laid snow that blanketed the ground leading to the Ephrams' gate, both his steps and his thoughts were leaden. Who cuts the barber's hair?

* * *

Seventeen. They worked for three days clearing the rubble and when they'd pulled out all they could, that's what Hiram was left with. He wondered where he would put them all, decided on the root cellar, and thanked god it was January and not July. They would keep.

Seventeen. They froze, black with dust, broken and crushed and some in pieces. He would have to sort them. Put them together the best that he could. Their families were waiting. Josie was waiting. *Plink.*

He put on his apron and opened the door that led to the cellar. The voices began immediately, rising in a chorus. One time when I was seventeen I there was a girl in the church had a horse named when the army kicked me out for always respected you even if I didn't agree with she was only twelve years old drunk and we went to Atlanta and saw the year my brother went to the war and he kicked me back listen to me I wish I had listened will you listen listen listen. He steeled himself against the onslaught of the voices and went down to find his son.

Hiram shone the lamp around. A familiar boot. An arm and there the hand he held often when the boy was small. There a face, too familiar, now badly broken and the hair so like his own, all matted down with blood. And the voice. There was that, too. With every piece Hiram held the voice grew stronger.

I always respected you, he said.

Plink.

Hiram put the pieces on the table, tried to wash them but his hands shook too badly. He was doing a bad job of it, just smearing the black around. None of this is real, he thought. I'm only hearing what I want to be hearing.

I respected you but I had to have my own life. Can you understand that?

You're not real, Hiram said.

It doesn't matter, Collin said. I wasn't real to you when I was alive, either. I've never been real to you. Me, Mom, none of us has ever been real to you. You'd rather spend your days with the dead than the living. None of us know you. How could we?

Josie found Hiram in the parlor. He held a glass in one hand, a small piece of wood in the other.

You can call someone in to help, she said.

Can't do that. Wouldn't be right.

If it's too much—

It's not, Hiram said. He drank what was left in his glass.

It *is*, Hi.

He knew what she wanted to say, what she wanted to hear. That he should not be the one to work on his boy, that someone else would put him back together again. She waited to hear these things but he couldn't give them to her. When she stood to leave him he stopped her with a question.

When he was small, he began, turning the wood in his fingers, how did you get him to be quiet? When he would squall and cry?

I sang to him, she said. I would sing to him and he'd just drift off. So peaceful. That's where he is now, Hi. At peace.

But Hiram knew better.

Hiram went to the hole and stood on the bank and watched the fast moving water rush past carrying leaves and branches and clumps of snow and ice. His fingers itched to tie a line, his arms ached to cast and pull. His fingers fiddled in his pocket, turning the piece of wood over and over. He pulled it out and tossed it into the rushing waters. *Plink.* The little animal that was not quite one thing and not quite another bobbed and floated down stream and out of Shook Rag.

Hiram stamped the snow off his boots and that's when he heard the singing.

Lay your head down now and rest, little one... He walked through the parlor to the mortuary door. *Let my voice be the last sound you hear...* He laid his forehead against the wood of the door and listened. *And I'll light a small candle to put you to bed...* And he opened the door and he went to her—*In the dark you'll have nothing to fear...* He went to her and found her, hands at work, needle flying and darting, over and under, over and under, her hands black and he heard the murmurs from the cellar door. Collin had come together under her needle and she brushed back the hair from her face, left a streak of soot high on one cheek. *Plink.*

I did what I could, she said.

It's enough, Hiram replied as he put on his apron. I'll do the rest.

Josie left him alone with Collin.

It's *not* enough, Collin said. You listen but it's not enough. I love you, Daddy, but that will never be enough. Why can't you see that that isn't enough? Daddy?

Hiram hung his head. He put one hand on his son's chest and then he spoke:

When I was thirteen my daddy brought me down here for the first time, he said. His daddy was a mortician and his daddy before him, so it was just right that I would be a mortician, too. So he trained me and I learned and I met your momma, and we had you, and I had everything I'd ever wanted. But then you wanted to be something else, and your momma hated me for not making you be something you're not, and then Lew died, and now nothing is was what I thought it was and now, and now you, and now you're gone and—

Plink.

The body was silent. Hiram listened. The chorus of voices from the cellar was gone as if it had never been.

Hiram cleaned his instruments and hung his apron on the door. He went through the parlor and he found Josie and he took her hand.

He said, Listen—

Jackson

Perhaps for the horses the journey is long, each hoof step stretching over frozen years. They have been carrying these two Southern generals for over a century now, riding at the edge of the city park, all the time heading for the unattainable Chancellorsville. The horses are still in their gait; they are Sunday driving. The men feel a calm, a relief, knowing that they will never reach the battles where one of them will die and where the other will be forced to surrender. These two invincible generals have eternity to struggle, to sense the awkwardness of being so close to each other, to feel the moments in which they confided in each other over the years sink into the wells of their bodies like strong brandy. If you look closely you will see a half-heartedness in their determination, a break in their concentration, like the laugh of a terminally-ill patient.

The generals have planned their location well, stationing themselves in the grove of oak trees at the edge of the park, so they may look, for most of the seasons, into a soft blanket of leaves, watching the tree limbs slowly stretch toward the sky. They are protected from the escalation of buildings that surround them. When headlights from passing cars, driving on the park road late at night, shine out over the trees, the generals remain undetected; they have hidden themselves well. And this allows them to draw even closer to each other.

When I walk out late at night, around the park, I almost pass by them as well, mistaking them for a drab curtain, an unshapened memorial, or a trunk fallen amongst the sleeping trees. But then I pause, click up the marble steps and stand beside the horses, my shoes covering the dark engraved letters on the marble base. I rap against the cast bronze, feel the metal, how the night has taken the heat out of it. I then circle the horsemen, raising my hand gently to the hind leg of a horse, touching the fur and saying cautiously to no one, *They are known to kick if startled.* Then I whisper down the body of the horse: *It's alright boy, it's just me.*

My hands grow numb on the ice-smooth metal as they run along the inside of the leg, down calf, over fetlock until I feel bronze shoe on bronze hoof. Despite the violent seasons, and their hollowness, these legs, I am certain, will be running for decades, will never need to be reshod. These horses will never tire.

These men and their animals are bigger than life, but up close, it is hard to tell: the generals' shoes half buried in the bronze leather, cupped stirrup filled with swollen foot, seem almost to be my size. But when I walk around to the front of the horses and raise my arms high to scratch the horses' ears, I barely reach their bits.

A car passes while I stand beside the statue, within the retreating woods. I see now that I have become invisible as well. I am a part of the curtain of trees.

I climb under their bellies, lowering, until I am in the cage of the horses' legs. They seem even larger now and I can almost stand under their bellies. I wedge myself up between the beasts, holding onto a sword handle and bracing against a general's knee. I want to ride with these generals, climb on the bronze bodies of their horses and feel the motion of their endless gait. For a moment I am a sack, a blanket rolled behind the saddle, then I work my way until I'm sitting upright behind one rider. I wrap my arms around the unribbed body of the general, lock my feet to the horse by catching my shoes on the ridge of the saddle, and prepare for the ride. The general's back is tall and I have to stretch my head up over his shoulders to look out across the night road.

I hug the cold, cold metal. My skin is numb and translates the feeling into heat. It is burning, this heat coming from this general's body, pouring out through his stiff metal clothes. I see the glistening fur of the horse in the cold night give off steam.

The headlights pass obliviously. I imagine it is snowing now, and already the sticks on the ground are nothing but vague moldings of themselves. But on this horse, I am safe from the snow, warm and dry—yet I can still smell from here the iron scent of the snow packing itself into the earth.

The tree branches behind us are bayonets, each tree trunk a soldier standing black against the trampled white. The general has made enough room for me now to slide onto his saddle and I do, pressing my body tighter against his.

Our horse's breath is loud, hot, living air, striking against the cold. I bring my head in close to the general's neck so as not to hear that sound, so as to hear only him instead. He is whispering, his voice curls around the side of his head and goes into my ear.

He is telling me about the men, how awkwardly their young branched arms hold their rifles, how easily they grow ill and start to march out of order. He says there are so many of them who are not with us now, who are instead further south, fertilizing the ground, forming mounds on flat fields. I sense he knows how each one died.

As he talks, he speaks as if he knows that he is now made of bronze and will be staying there forever while each of his men will remain vulnerable to the high winds, pestilence, lightning, swords, bullets, and saws.

He is talking to me alone, softly enough so that the other general cannot hear, as if over the years he has grown tired, or scared, of confiding in that other man. Or, as if he has something to confess that he could only say to a stranger, to someone he will never see again.

I reach my hand deeper into the general's vest to warm my hands, to secure my balance—for suddenly, I am jolted. We have broken free from the other horse and rider, the other general, and we are leaving them behind. We are riding alone in the forest of his men, the army of trees that before were behind us. I look up at them now and see their tired bodies standing bent. They stare at the general and straighten as he passes. They look as though they will follow him forever, as though they will fight for him always.

I hear them talk between themselves—they do not want him to go to battle. They want him to return to where he can make love in the rooms of his richly colored house and look peacefully out of his window onto victorious lands. They look at me, almost longingly, as though each has wished to be so close to this general as I am now. I cannot look back at them, for I know what will happen, how this general will never make love in the rooms of his richly colored house. I know it is this general whose face will come home dull and expressionless in a box.

But even more, I know that it is one of these tall, tall beautiful trees, one of his own men, who, confused in the dusk of not wanting to fight any longer, will accidentally shoot this general I am now with. It is one of them who will kill this man.

I know this, and perhaps the general knows it as well. That is why, for this moment, we have reined away from the other horse and rider and why we have ridden quietly amongst the soldiers as he whispers a confession about each one to me. And that is why he does not mind my body so close to his, my hand curled deep into his clothes against his hard, burning skin.

Michael Gray Baughan

Old Dominion

The road in was little more than a muddy path salted with just enough shale and fallen branches to keep Hale's battered Jeep from bogging down. Two flanking stone walls marked the property line but someone with great strength and determination had dislodged and regrouped an impressive number of the stones into a massive cairn that left no room to pass. He spent the better part of the afternoon dismantling the obstacle, and by the time he was done his hands were bleeding and he had sweat through his shirt. The way beyond led into a grove of old growth oak and sycamore that bent on both sides over the sodden track and canceled the daylight. Inside the Jeep, the GPS appeared to dim as a black mass of unmapped terrain inked onto the screen and swallowed the little car icon. Hale smiled, despite what lay in his back seat. For better or worse, he had found his terra incognita.

More accurate to say that it had found him. Still aflare with an anger he could not control or direct, he sat stiffly in the overheated office of the probate attorney and didn't hear the first time he was told a thousand-acre parcel of land at the foot of the Shenandoah now belonged to him. The second time he heard but did not understand. How is it possible that Polly had owned this much property and he didn't know? Had she known? Yes, said the attorney, she knew. So why didn't he? This the attorney could not answer. Just another secret, then, like the therapist in Alexandria, to whom she, and now he, owed a small fortune. Like the child dispatched without his knowledge and only discovered while sorting through her insurance claims. Like the reasons she had....

Well, now Hale had a secret too. Polly's will, what there was of one, was explicit. She wanted a direct cremation. Hale demanded to see proof of it when the attorney informed him. The wording was so odd and arcane. *No ceremony can mark my passing. If I fail, do not put me in the earth, or foul my body with preservatives. I must be burned. Leave nothing to find or make frolic.*

He knew better than to contest the law with a lawyer, but not everyone was so steadfast or wily. The grief of a husband is a powerful thing, made all the more so when backed by five crisp Franklins. The crematorium, as it turned out, was in arrears, the retort in dire need of replacement, and its owner was not a scrupulous man. Once the subject had been broached, the man freely admitted that his side deals usually involved discrete disposal, not illegal release, but who was he to quibble? It's not like he was giving her to some deviant to butcher or desecrate. Would the man put her in the back seat for him? "Sure, sure," the man said. "I can do that."

"She hasn't been embalmed," the man warned, breathing a little heavy from the exertion, "she won't last long." Hale promised to bury her soon.

Happy to have her back, Hale talked to her on the long drive. At one point, he even reached around and placed a hand on her, stroking her arm through the heavy vinyl of the body bag, the way he had before, to emphasize a point, but rigor had passed and there was a softness to her now that kept him from doing it again. He spoke slowly, reasonably, as if trying to convince a child. He could not bear to have her gone entirely. There must be a place to visit, somewhere he knew she would be. Even if in secret. Even if against her wishes. Surely she must understand. She had taken from him the future he had mapped out for them. He deserved some consideration. The needs of the living must outweigh the demands of the dead.

The tone was familiar and well-practiced. He had used it to talk her back from the night terrors that took her too often and left her brittle and rigid as driftwood, moaning words her dream-bound mouth refused to make. He used it to gently question her the mornings after, and whenever she locked herself in the bathroom or quit another job. He used it every Sunday when he asked her to join him for services at First Fairfax Unitarian, and when she told him she was not fit for a church, he used it again in his attempt to divest her of the notion. He was immensely proud of his reasonable calm and the emotional discipline it took to patiently knock on her wall of silence. He thought if only he didn't rush her she would come around eventually and let him in.

It wasn't always like that, of course. Far from it. When she wasn't brooding or scared, she lived life as if no heaven awaited her and she must wring maximum enjoyment from each new day before it died. Hale had never met anyone who savored food and drink the way she did, even the simplest things. A ripe peach, a cup of coffee, vanilla ice cream, even the cheeseburgers he cooked on the little charcoal grill on the little patio of his little townhouse— each was capable of lifting her chin, closing her eyes, and spreading a grin of almost obscene satisfaction across her face. And what a face it was. Uncharitable assessors might have deemed equine the overall effect, but to Hale her broad full mouth, her fine long nose, and her large green eyes all seemed designed to give her senses as much conduit as possible to give or take pleasure from this world, and that certainly did not stop at her face. Her breasts and hips were also superabundant, especially for such a small frame, and her apparent shyness evaporated shortly after she bared them.

As if in rhythm with his thoughts, just as the Jeep entered the tunnel grove, she surprised him by leaking a low moan, hardly audible through the bag and above the thrum of the engine. Hale had heard of such effects—the chemical vestiges of life leaving the body— but still he was startled and nearly swerved off the road.

"Now you want to talk?" he called back over his shoulder when he had recovered his composure. On those rare occasions when Polly said anything at all about what caused her to live life so desperately, she would only assure him he could not possibly understand.

"We all have our crosses to bear, honey. Sharing them lightens the load."

"If only you knew," was how she would end it. *If only he knew.*

a most fitting epitaph, for it spoke to more than just the unnamed cause of her troubles, this hidden kingdom in the woods, or the child she had killed without his consent. He also had not known how hard it was to maintain faith in the face of loss. It's so easy to be reasonable and calm when you don't need solace, when everything goes according to plan and life is nothing but a second-hand book of mazes already worked out for you. When Polly died, for the first time in his adult life, Hale found himself spinning and dizzy, clueless where to turn or look for a way out.

The Jeep hit a rut and bucked and she nearly slid off the back seat. Hale hated to think of her sealed in that bag, collapsing into herself. He wanted to unzip her a little and see her face, but he feared the odor might spoil the moment. He would have to bury her soon, but not before he found the perfect spot. Tomorrow, perhaps. It was still too soon to say goodbye.

Hard to believe they had only met two years ago. Walking in Georgetown, she happened upon his little store, Terra Incognita. She misunderstood and came in thinking he sold real, historical maps, made of paper and parchment, not the careful marquetry copies he assembled from pieces of exotic wood veneer. She couldn't hide the disappointment in her face, but she was polite enough to marvel at his craftsmanship and to ask how it was done.

"Little by little," he answered. Something in his answer kept her lingering, and they talked some more. She had an accent he could not place: Southern, sure, but also vaguely German and archaic. At the time he guessed she was a lapsed Mennonite and asked her what sort of map she was looking for. He closed up early and they continued talking over dinner in his favorite Mexican joint around the corner. She had her first taste of chili relleno and she showed him that appreciative smile of hers and he imagined how lovely it would look above him. They talked for hours, and he got his wish even sooner than expected, but she never really answered the question.

He was still lost in the memory and driving too fast when he finally emerged from the tunnel grove. The track dipped and dumped him into even wetter lowland choked with willows and reeds. A sudden bog stretched out on either side of the Jeep, through which snaked a narrow, knobby upthrust of rock like a scoliatic backbone. It was a lucky deformity, as otherwise the way forward was impassable and he would have pitched nose first into the mud. The tires hummed as they skimmed across the wet stone and he dared not break lest he swerve and hydroplane. An improbable stone track carrying him across a desolate swamp struck him as something out of the fantasies he read as a child and he wondered at the black knight's errand that had brought him here. The path gradually rose out of the bog and at last became certain and wide enough to lift his eyes from the immediate space in front of the hood, and he found another surprise when he did. Atop a small plateau, amidst a scattering of black walnut trees, he saw a little stone house hiding under a curtain of kudzu and creeper.

The lawyer said nothing of a house.

Hale only planned to bury her someplace nice, somewhere he could revisit in private, whenever he wanted, but a house changed everything. The moment he saw the place, that dizzy feeling of a stolen future started to fade and a whole new possibility rolled out before him like a mural, nearly complete in its particulars. He would close the shop in Georgetown and sell his overpriced condo. He would fix up this house and live out here. He would build a workshop and sell his wooden maps over the internet, making weekly trips to the nearest post office. He would plant a garden and put in a patch of lilies where he buried her, and each spring her favorite flowers would come up and remind him of her smile.

He was so wrapped up in this uncharacteristically maudlin fantasy that he almost didn't notice the furious buzzing that burst from the back seat like a cicada trying to shed it exoskeleton. The oscillations of the old Jeep engine would sometimes cause some item inside the cabin to vibrate and make a shocking racket, so at first he chalked it up to that, but when the buzzing got louder the closer he came to the house he was forced to admit it was coming from the body bag. By the time he reached a proper place to park the sound had so unnerved him that he cut the engine, threw open the door, and jumped from the driver's seat as if the vehicle might explode. Standing some distance away, he stared at the back window, eyes squinted and cocked hard

aslant, desperately trying to convince himself the fitful movements
he saw within were just swaying tree limbs, stirring the reflected glare
of the late afternoon light. If not that, then some other cruel effect of
decay unknown to him. In time the movements slowed and then ceased
altogether and when they did his mind pulled a little sleight of hand
by focusing on his new house instead.

Or the strange old house on the land newly his. In style and
make, it was more like something a medieval monk would inhabit
than your typical frontier cabin. For one, it was made of the same
mammoth fieldstones used in the property marker walls and the
cairn. For another, it was tiny and lacked all niceties—no sitting
porch or abutting shrubbery, no flower boxes or brick walks. The
heavy oak door bore a faded mark on its front, a dull red glyph
that meant nothing to him. In any case, it was locked and he had
no keys so he looked around back for some means of ingress and
found a creeper-covered window into the kitchen with a crosspiece
so rotted and soft the lock latch ripped clean out when he lifted it.
The smell within was old and earthy, as if he had cracked open a
cave or root cellar. The window was inordinately small and for a
moment he got stuck trying to shimmy inside, and he imagined
himself discovered that way by the next foolhardy soul to come
along. Which got him thinking: how long had it been since anyone
was here? Polly's mother was dead ten years when they met, and
her father had abandoned her when she was still a child. He always
assumed this was the basis of her issues. She had no siblings or
cousins, at least as far as he knew. All of which helped explain
why this Yarrow family plot had passed to him, but gave him no
specific answer to his original question besides a long, long time.

Once he'd freed himself and tumbled into the house, the state
of things inside certainly seemed to support that notion. A
potbellied wood stove shared the kitchen with a narrow pantry
cabinet, a freestanding wash basin, and a legion of dead insects.
That was it. There was no plumbing as far as he could tell. No
appliances either: no fridge, no toaster, no coffee maker. No
electrical outlets to support them. Silly to think of electricity
running all this way into the woods, but Hale was born and raised

in Reston, where nothing was older than 1964 and an acre was a fiefdom. He had wallpapered that historical void with pages from paperbacks about dragons and sorcerers, and grew up drawing maps to places that did not exist, dreaming in secret of conquering a kingdom of his own and building a place like this. Well, not like this perhaps, but still. The old adage about being careful what you wish for threatened to rise up and laugh at him, but he pushed it down with all the other things he wasn't thinking about.

It took five minutes to tour the rest of the house, and that included tying back the mildewed curtains in each room along the way. The kitchen led into a dining area, with a small oak slab table and several handmade chairs with woven reed seats. In the corner, by the door, was a short-handled rush broom only a bent-backed old hag would use. The eating area led to a great room, if you could even use the term, with a fireplace, a rocking chair, a small pine bed, and a plain pine dresser. On the far wall of this room hung the only item in the entire house that didn't look hand-hewn onsite. At first Hale thought it might be a dartboard cabinet, but that was ridiculous, and it looked hundreds of years old. It was a simple but handsome piece of figured walnut and incongruous enough to invite a closer look, but it would be dark soon and the temperature was dropping fast. He had a tent and a sleeping bag in the Jeep but there was no good reason not to sleep in the house. He just needed to get his things and gather some wood.

Back outside he was reminded of everything his things included. He couldn't leave her there, locked overnight in the back seat like a piece of fruit, fallen from a grocery bag. He gave himself no time to think or hesitate. He just opened the back door and hoisted the bag over his shoulder. No movement or sound attended the maneuver, only a small expiration of fetid air through the zipper that forced him to hold his breath as he lugged her inside. He laid her down as gingerly as possible and wondered whether now might be the time to steal a look at her. No, not yet, he decided. Better get prepared for the night.

There was no shortage of wood, but all of it was fallen branches that would burn hot and fast, so he collected seven armfuls and dumped them in a big pile by the fireplace. With each haul the sun dipped and reddened, tearing the horizon, until all that remained was a thin scar between the bruised sky and the bare trees. He stood holding the last load and watched until the color was gone and when it went he turned and went inside.

There was just enough light left to prepare the fire. Fearing it wouldn't catch without newspaper, he over-kindled and the dry tinder smoked for a while and then exploded, throwing flames high up into the flue. He stood too close and as the sudden warmth seeped into his face and body, he nearly fell asleep standing up, unaware until then how drained he was from the day's strangeness and rigor. He had not eaten anything since lunch, which didn't help, but he wasn't about to prepare something now. He washed down a granola bar with some water from a thermos, unpacked his sleeping bag, and collapsed onto the bed fully clothed. Fireborn sprites danced on the ceiling and stole the last of his will to stay conscious.

Something jerked him from a dream of vague rebuke into darkness utter and unfamiliar. He blinked and listened, waiting for the sound that woke him to repeat or its memory to manifest more clearly. He did not have to wait very long.

Something was in the room with him.

Something large that scuffed the floor in stealthy fits and starts. He sat up and extracted his head from the mummy sack and cold air poured down his neck as he strained to pick out anything in the blackness. The unstoked fire was long dead and lacked even the hint of embers to see by. In the end his ears were enough, as the whispery scuffling came again and a second, deeper chill sluiced through him as he arrived at a terrible conclusion. Attracted by the smell, some animal must have come to scavenge Polly and was trying to drag her off somewhere more conducive to eating in private. Only two animals native to Virginia were big enough to even attempt such a thing—a bear or a cougar—and despite the impossibility of either's entry into the house, let alone the lack of any animal smell or sound, the thought of a large predator trapped in a small space with him sent Hale's boy scout brain into badge-test mode, unpacking old trunks of memory for the proper response. Cower and play dead or bluff and shout? He was still vacillating between the two when he remembered his flashlight. Thankfully his backpack was on the bed with him and as the thing continued to scuffle he slowly reached for and extracted the light. What it revealed was far worse than a bear.

The body bag was unattended. And moving on its own. With a dreadful slowness it bunched and flattened like a black vinyl inchworm, until it reached a wall, where it worked itself upright and then paused a moment, as if to rest.

What the hell was happening? It only took a few seconds to run through the options and all of them were impossible. Save one: Polly wasn't dead.

Hale leapt from the bed, raced over, and unzipped the bag. When he pushed it back to reveal her face, the pallor and the withering stole his air, and when he inhaled to retrieve it the smell of her marched him across the room and sat him down on his ass.

Shuddering from the cold and the shock of it, he struggled to train the light on her face. Something was severed when she opened her eyes. A thin filament vaporized—the one inside the fuse that buffered his brain from information it could not process—and the failsafe forgetfulness that had protected him that afternoon gave way to a full and unfiltered awareness.

He watched as her long white fingers reached up and tugged open the bag wide enough to shrug it off her shoulders. He watched as she rose up naked and nearly translucent, burnt patches of her still glistening and the flesh sagging earthward with a rank over-ripeness that moiled his empty stomach. He watched as she took her first unsteady step, and then another, the gait clumsy and tottering, as if she were being tugged forward by an unseen force that was balancing her hips and leg bones atop each other without aid of muscle or tendon. And all the while she kept her gaze on him, milky eyes wide and chiding.

He continued watching, unable to move, as she lurched towards the door, where she stopped and passed three words through her wasted larynx before her limp hands struggled with the door and she staggered out.

Do not follow.

For a time, nothing at all went through his mind, and he sat quite still, motion and emotion robbed of him by the simple paradox that kept crashing his consciousness each time he tried to reboot: Polly was dead; Polly was out there walking in the night.

Little by little, bits of information surfaced to support each side of this illogical equation, but did nothing to balance it. All the strange and cryptic things she had said to him, the wording of her will, even the manner with which she had tried to end her life—they all presaged this. Hale recalled her difficulty with the alarm system at his condo, her apparent ignorance that such technology even existed. Surely she had not known about the sprinkler system that saved her from the immolation she desired but failed to prevent her asphyxiation.

As frightened as he was, he gave no thought to leaving. For one, he was inescapably culpable. By defying her last wishes, he had realized her worst fears. For another, those three parting words had only achieved an opposite effect. They proved that something of her remained, and whatever that something was, he owed it help and, if possible, salvation.

At that thought his inertia finally faded and he rose and waved the light around the room in search of some weapon or tool to give him enough courage to get out there after her. During the sweep, his light fell upon the odd decorative piece in the corner that had grabbed his attention earlier. Now that he was upright and moving again, every instinct told him not to delay, that each moment wasted was one in which he continued to fail her, but something about that hanging cabinet transfixed him and he walked over to examine it. It was too small for rifles but if he was lucky it might contain an antique pistol or dagger.

A simple iron catch held it closed. Once lifted, two stacked leaves opened up and away from a central panel on heavy hinges. Revealed inside was a triptych of painted woodcuts. They were primitive in the extreme, carved with hacks and gouges—clearly the work of a child—and yet obviously meant to function as some sort of primer. The only colors used were a dull red and a deep granular black, the pigments too crude and organic to be anything but dried blood and bone char. All of which was terrible enough, but it was the subject matter that truly disturbed him.

The left panel showed a trio of wagons moving through a wood. In the ground beneath the wagons was a tall, twisted thing surrounded by wormy squiggles and scattered pieces of stick people.

In the central panel the twisted figure was standing at the head of a wide clearing, ropy arms spread wide, and a lot of people were lying down before it, dead or prostrate, save two: a bearded burly man, nearly as large as the twisted thing, leaning over a cane and holding aloft the hand of a little one with long hair.

The last panel showed two scenes: on one side was a tight grouping of cabins, with chevrons of hearth smoke rising from their chimneys and smiling stick families standing in front; on the other, a small house all by itself in a thick wood. Nearby, in a small clearing ringed with gnarled shapes, the twisted thing and the little girl were entwined on the ground, their limbs jumbled and the girl's head turned away.

Hale followed her as closely as he dared, trying to keep quiet, but lugging a nearly full can of gas made it almost impossible to move gingerly, and the dead leaves crackled underfoot with each hitching step. Upon leaving the house, he manically scanned the lower ground in all directions and saw nothing but the circles of crosshatching limbs lit up by the flashlight. A half moon had risen while he slept and he realized that he could see without the torch. It was only when he cut the switch and stopped moving that he picked up the sounds of her lurching through the forest. Zeroing in took a few moments longer, but once he did he caught a glimpse of white skin between two trunks. She was still moving with that dreadful gait, like something dragged, and the slowness of her retreat eased off his throttle somewhat and allowed him to remember the gas can. He always kept it on hand, but typically empty. A quick map search before leaving Reston had warned him how few and far between filling stations would be out here, and he wondered, as he snatched it from the trunk and tore off after her, where the Jeep's gauge now sat. He had filled up halfway, but all those snaking country roads ate up a lot of mileage.

On the hill down below he saw another flash of white and heard the crunch as she pitched forward and fell. She must have lain there a spell, because he lost sight of her in the underbrush. At that point he probably could have closed most of the distance between them, but as he was maneuvering to regain a vantage point a rush of terror swept through his body and he involuntarily dropped to a crouch and remained absolutely still. His eyes widened and then bulged as he came to sense the other things moving all around him. He could not hear them, or see anything but the dimmest outlines of their shadowy forms, but he could certainly *feel* them. They were human in shape and size, but lacked all substance and seemed to flicker in and out of being. He could only detect them at all because of the way his body was reacting to their presence, and the slight distortion they inflicted on the space they inhabited, like the air above a hot tarmac or his little Weber grill. Something about the softness of their borders, their gentle bearing, and the slow steady way they moved through the trees suggested the feminine. What's more, there was a sameness to them, an ineffable affinity that evoked not just a gender but a lineage. He would be hard pressed to defend the impression, but it was aided when two of them reached where Polly had fallen and seemed to gather her up and help her rise. They waited until the others reached them and then they moved as one down the hill. Hale let them get a bigger lead on him and then he stood again and followed.

At the base of the hill, the land flattened out and the trees thinned. Polly and her specter escort shambled on a ways, until they reached a small clearing defended by a dense border guard of desiccated thorn bushes. They took no notice and plowed on through, leaving strips of Polly's skin behind.

Once inside the clearing they spread out into a circle and assumed the stance of dancers waiting for the music to start. For the specters this was but an abstract impression, a shadow play on the backdrop of the forest, but for Polly it was the cruelest indignity of all. Attempting a graceful posture, her discarded-puppet body and the abject defeat in her downcast stare was rendered too pitiable to bear and for a moment Hale had to look away.

When he looked back the dance had begun.

They circled the clearing at a dirge pace and lifted their wandering palms to the night. Without any conscious decision, Hale began to circle with them, but instead of mimicking their convoluted hand gestures he tipped his can to prime the thorned tangle that enclosed them. When their pace quickened, he quickened his own, and when the air took on the feeling of an approaching storm, without any hint of wind or moisture, and when in the center of their circle a darkness gathered and thickened and the sharp loamy scent of fertile earth and decay filled his nose, he reached into his breast pocket and struck a match and set fire to the circle and then he ran for his life.

He could not tell whether the dilating hiss that pursued him was made by the fire itself or the things it threatened. He only wished to get far from both, as quickly as possible. Running uphill with the can, even half full, was incredibly awkward and tiring, and as he leaned over to compensate he felt the flashlight shift and squirm from his front pocket. He stopped and turned, as much to catch his breath as to find it. Groping through the leaves with a desperation that bordered on hysteria, he might have laughed at himself if not for the chaos he had wrought down below. The ring of fire had both expanded and constricted and the specters were backlit and writhing as it closed in. Polly was on her knees, fully engulfed, and though he could not pick out her face from the flames, there was an attitude of something like supplication in her carriage. Not so for the twisted thing they had summoned, which stalked the contracting circle and seethed and mutely bellowed, like something watching its children slaughtered, and jutted its bulbous, misshapen head at him as if to mark him for what he had done. Then it sucked back into the earth that had birthed it and reemerged on the near side of the fire and stalked up the hill after him with great, terrible strides and an aspect so menacing it vaporized all thought of retreat and rooted Hale to his spot. When it was nearly upon him, and it spooled out its limbs, his mind went limp like a rabbit in the mouth of a dog.

A slight rain began to fall as the dawn came, and down below, the smoldering ash pile spit and sizzled. Hale remained on the hill where he had dropped the flashlight, bodily unharmed but still in shock and unable to convince himself it was over. Just before the twisted thing took him, Polly's body evidently burned enough to banish it, and it collapsed and disassembled into a squirming mass of saprophagous insects and annelids, which quickly burrowed out of sight. Hale was left to wonder what that meant, and whether the devil's bargain that Polly's ancestors had made with it was now broken or void, and if broken what new dominion it might seek to find the human carrion that invoked and sustained it.

When he finally rose, sodden, freezing and exhausted, his legs were stiff and bloodless and it seemed to take forever to climb the rest of the hill. When he checked the Jeep, he found it had sufficient fuel to use what was left in the can to burn the house, or at least its wooden infrastructure. He ripped the heinous triptych from the wall and piled his unburned kindling on top and doused the room with the gas and lit his third and final fire. He lingered long enough to dry away the chill from his body, and then he drove away with the orange glow of it flickering in his rear view mirror and the black smoke rising into the gray sky.

The drizzle turned into a downpour as he slowly made his way out, and when he arrived at the quaggy lowland he found the bridge of rock nearly submerged. No sane man would have attempted it, but he could not lay claim to that title anymore and he squeezed the wheel and skated across the swamp with a grim resolve that most would mistake as suicidal.

At the stone walls he got out and rebuilt the cairn in the rain, and several times he stumbled and collapsed into the mud under the weight of the field stones. When he was finished it was neither as tall nor as wide as its predecessor, but he draped the body bag over the top and weighed it down with a few more stones and trusted its meaning was clear.

David James Poissant

The Fox King

One morning, the girls went into the woods and by lunchtime were lost. The girls, whose names were Isabelle and Ellie, had long, blonde hair and eyes like movie swimming pools. The girls were friends and not twins, though people mistook them often for sisters. The girls were fine with this. Already, they'd done the hard work of gouging their fingers, pressing flesh to flesh, Isabelle crying at the cut, Ellie laughing, sucking her finger for hours when it was done for the tang like a tongue touched to a 9-volt battery.

The girls lived in white houses with blue shutters on a tree-lined street in a small county at the north end of a southern state. They lived in the mountains, took their water from wells, and in winter stacked logs on the porch for their fires. Sure, there was electricity, but electric was expensive and in winter went out often.

These girls, they knew their mothers by their aprons and their fathers by the black boots at the doorstep, the black clothes left in black piles on the porch, the tin helmets and the small lights that shone when the black was rubbed away.

All around the girls were woods, and, summers, they wandered the woods often. It should be noted that the woods here had a habit of eating people. Given this, you may be tempted to cite the girls' mothers with negligence. But, you who are not of the woods, you who buckle your babies into cars that will crash, who climb into elevators that will drop and planes that will fall from the sky, you who buy food you haven't prepared, food wrapped in plastic and paper and bagged, you of the suburbs, the cities, you more than anyone should understand that when you're of the woods, you trust the woods, even when you know what the woods can do. And so you let your children into them, just as you let your husbands tunnel into the belly of a mountain that might, any moment, close its mouth. To live is to walk a rope of risk, and so we let our children into the woods. Knowing what could happen, knowing full well, we let our children into the woods again and again.

Often, Isabelle and Ellie had traveled deep into the woods. They knew by the sun and the heat of the day when it was time to turn back, and always, it seemed, they emerged from the thicket just as one mother or another stepped through the door to call for them. The girls would sip tomato soup, eat sandwiches cut longways like wings, and with a nod were dismissed into the woods again, only to return for supper.

This particular morning, however, the girls had walked very deep into the woods, deeper than ever before. Twice, Isabelle had begged Ellie to turn back, but then a squirrel had leapt between trees, a bird had lifted from a branch, and home had been forgotten. They followed the animals until their bellies twisted beneath their shirts and hunger urged them home.

But where was home? They looked around. The woods were unrecognizable. Every tree, each rotted log and bend of root, was new. Moss furred the forest floor, and toadstools hiccupped from the moss, velvety and unbroken, as though no animal or man had passed through this part of the woods before.

Isabelle cried, and Ellie hit her. There were, after all, many things to eat in the woods. The woods would sustain them. So they found raspberries and ate them. They found a stream and drank from it. And, following the stream, they came upon a clearing.

The clearing was not wide, its reach that of two, three girls laid on their backs, heel to head. It was a circle of trampled grass littered by black twigs, a clearing unremarkable in every respect, save one. What was interesting about this clearing was what it held, and what it held was a red fox.

Never before, except in picture books, had the girls seen a red fox. They had seen the sly, orange variety. Those popped up often in their county. More than once, an orange fox had slithered from Isabelle's mother's hen house, its face a fireworks of wings. And, once, Ellie's father had shot an orange fox dancing in the street, its mouth busy with suds like an overworked horse.

But a red fox was a new and marvelous thing. Its coat was thin, the hair brittle looking, and its tail was black-ringed, the tip thick, white as unskimmed milk. The fox lay on its back. Its legs, three of them, hung stiff in the air, paws bent like the curled tongues of coat hangers. It was, to the girls, as though the fox had been pedaling an upside-down bicycle when someone had paused the movie and pulled the bicycle away.

The fourth leg was the crooked leg. It did not hang in the air but hugged the grass. A metallic half-moon gripped the leg like an enormous pair of silver dentures. Up the leg a ways, a band of white marked where the fox's fur and skin appeared to have been whittled away, whittled to the bone.

Here was a curious situation. Why a fox should sleep on its back, should let someone tattoo its leg in this way, why it should lie with its leg between teeth? But, of course, the girls' fathers hunted. Springs, trees bent with the weight of bucks tethered and spinning, necks open over buckets. And so the girls recognized death for what it was, that other kind of sleep.

In the clearing, the girls approached the red fox. They stroked its head, its black whiskers and the white stripe of its muzzle. Ellie followed the stripe down the neck of the fox to where it widened into the white of the animal's belly. There, a surprise. The skin of the fox *rippled*. It was, to Ellie, as when her father would lift the blue, hole-punched lid from a plastic tub before fishing, the feeling the pink things made on her palm tunneling through the soil inside. It was just that way. Through the stiff fur, through the cool, taut skin, she felt life, the tumble of little ones warm inside. She pressed Isabelle's hand to the spot, watched her eyes widen, and then all four hands were on the body, feeling and rubbing, then falling still.

The girls were not old, but they knew enough. They knew body parts by their names, both vulgar and proper, and they knew, when bodies came together, just where those parts went. And though they had yet to feel the first, hot stirrings in their abdomens, they had seen horses, seen chickens, had known, in the seeing, what was happening and what, done right, could come of the coupling. Thus, they knew the ripple for what it was, knew that, one way or another, the little foxes must come out.

In their play, the girls often imagined themselves princesses. The woods were where one went to become royalty, to care for the denizens of the kingdom, while home was the place to which one returned when one wished to be cared for. The girls would not have thought to express the situation in such terms. Nevertheless, these were the terms of the situation.

In the woods, then, the girls were no longer Isabelle and Ellie, but Princess Isabella and Princess Ella. In dreams, in games, in the woods, the girls were accompanied by a staff of friendly animals, rabbit and deer and squirrel and quail, all of whom spoke and allowed themselves to be ordered around by the princesses. Often, the animals were naughty and needed to be spanked. The girls were also accompanied by a prince, Prince Samuel, a boy with red lips and bright eyes, a boy shared by the girls in the way that the girls shared all things—toys, clothes, the last cookie pulled from the cookie jar and halved. Never had it occurred to the girls that there might be a prince apiece. One prince was sufficient. Like the animals, he took orders, and, as with the animals, a spanking was sometimes required.

Never before had the girls seen a red fox, and never before had the boy-prince appeared to them in the woods. Or, to say that never before had he appeared would be wrong. Certainly, the prince had appeared. Today, though, the prince *appeared*. His movements were not hazy, imagined. The woods moved to admit him, and then he stood before them. He was the prince of their imaginations, but real, *really* real.

Though the boy had the prince's eyes, his lips, he was not dressed as the girls had pictured him dressed. The boy-prince wore blue overalls with copper-colored buttons. His shirt was that shade of tan that indicated the material had once been white. His hair was cut close to his head and his eyebrows had been sheared. The girls knew this meant lice. Both had had lice, but both found it rather distasteful that a prince should allow himself to become the victim of such a common, un-princely pest. In the clearing, the prince stood very still. He breathed in and he breathed out and he watched the girls. His mouth worked as though to say something very important, but the first word was swallowed up by the crash of the King.

Limbs snapped. Bramble flattened, and then the King was among them in the clearing. The King was impossibly tall. He was long of beard and prodigious of gut and his eyes shone like buckshot. Dressed in white and red, he might have been mistaken for Santa Claus, except that his beard was red and his eyes were not the kind eyes of Saint Nick. They were the eyes of a man forced to lop off many a head in order to maintain the peace of his kingdom.

Never before, in play, had the girls imagined a king. Had they, the king they imagined would have been adorned in robes, a crown for his head, a scepter for his hand. This king carried no scepter. He wore red pants and boots of animal skin. The boots reached his knees and laces coiled the boots like snakes. The tops of the boots were fox-furred. His shirt was red and white and black. It was pink where the red and white met, and gray where the white and black met, and blood-colored where the black and red met. The word for the pattern was *plaid*, the word for the shirt *flannel*, but these were not the girls' words, and so the girls thought of the shirt as a checkerboard, pretty and precise and not a little hypnotizing. The man's face hung in folds, as though fishhooks bit into his chin and tugged, and fitted to the man's head was a covering like a coonskin cap, only the skin was the skin of a fox and the tail that hung between the man's shoulders was a fox's tail.

The King surveyed his surroundings, and then his eyes fell upon the girls. His eyes met the girls' eyes and burrowed into them like grubs, and here the girls felt a bob in their heads, a smoldering in their chests. The prince was their prince, but this king was not their king. He was a king, surely, but not theirs, for, had he been theirs, they would not have wanted to run. No, he was some other king, a king rare as the red creature asleep at their feet—a king of foxes.

For a long time, nobody moved, and then the Fox King asked the girls where were their parents. The girls said nothing.

The Fox King asked the girls when they had last eaten, and the girls shrugged. Their mouths, they knew from looking at one another, were berry-stained, their shirtfronts wet from the churn of the stream.

The Fox King asked whether the girls were hungry. They were, but Isabelle would not say it, so, at last, Ellie whispered, "Yes."

The Fox King then fitted his boot over the half-moon of bright teeth. The mouth unclamped, and the teeth, those perfect triangles, let go the leg. The boy hefted the fox by its armpits and slid the animal free from the teeth. Lifted, the fox's head did not loll. It was suspended, stiff as the end of an ironing board. Only the tail sashayed in the breeze. (And, here, you've caught me once again. *Sashay* would no more be the girls' word than *conciliatory* or *riboflavin*. Nevertheless, for our purposes, the tail sashayed.) The Fox King knelt to receive the fox from the boy-prince. He frowned, turning the animal in his hands, then he held the fox's stomach to his face. He closed his eyes and pressed his cheek, then his ear, hard, very hard to the belly of the animal.

He smiled and his teeth were green.

"Follow me," he said. "We will find your parents. But, first, we shall eat."

The girls, being girls, were trusting of adults—parents especially—and, though they did not trust this man, they considered the boy who stood, hands in pockets, looking up at the man, this prince looking up at his king, and each girl worked hard to imagine what bad could possibly befall her when nothing bad, it seemed, had befallen the boy. And, coming up with nothing, both followed man and boy across the clearing and into the woods.

They walked and walked. In one place, the woods grew thick, very thick, as though made up not of trees but of a single tree with many, many trunks. Times, limb and leaf blotted out the sun. More than once, the girls dropped to their stomachs and followed the Fox King through brambles and beneath low-hanging branches tangled by vines. By the time they reached the second clearing, the girls were very tired, arms and legs aching from the burrs and thorns, their skins calligraphies.

The house in the clearing was a small one. It was not brick and wood, like the girls' houses. No, this house was built of mud and stone. It looked the way the girls imagined the house of the third little pig must have looked, only less sturdy. Had the third little pig lived in this house of stone, the wolf no doubt would have huffed and puffed and eaten them all. The house—the stones were long and gray, river stones, and not stacked like hands, but piled, crowded together. Without mud to keep them up, surely the stones would have tumbled, as though the mud were magic and magic held the house up. A stone chimney rose crooked like the fourth leg of the fox from the house, and smoke twisted crooked from the chimney.

Into the house they went, the Fox King first followed by the boy followed by Ellie followed by Isabelle. Inside, the house was all one room and very small. There was a large pit for the fireplace. Settled into the pit was a black cauldron and beneath the cauldron white coals that ringed the cauldron red. One half of the room was a table and cupboards and many pots and pans and knifes in wooden blocks. The other half was a dresser and a bed, the headboard carved into the shape of two foxes wrestling, a bird between them, a pheasant. Stretched on the floor, at the foot of the bed, was the skin of a fox—all of it—the paws, the face, the thick tail, all but the eyes. Brown stones fitted the holes where the eyes belonged.

The bed itself was piled with orange skins, the pelts of a hundred foxes stitched together, though with no real care, so that a snout peeked out here, a paw clawed there, the quilt an almost-quivering puddle of foxes freed of meat and bone. The girls watched the bed and it did not move. But, when they looked away, from the corners of their eyes, they could have sworn they saw the quilt squirming.

There was no bed for the boy.

The Fox King moved quickly now, pulling a long knife from a butcher block. He rested the fox on the table.

"A red fox," he said. "A very special fox for our very special guests."

Then, with the tip of his knife, The Fox King unzipped the belly of the fox. The insides did not spill out. The belly opened like a purse, and the king reached in. What he pulled out were six sacs, smooth and wet. Dropped to the table, some of the sacs wriggled like fat worms. Others were still. The still ones looked to the girls like cocoons—gossamer, velvet—like what they'd found hung from the porch railing and torn open to find the black and yellow inside. They'd unfurled the antennae, unfolded the soft, damp wings, but the butterfly had never taken flight, and the next day, on the railing where they'd left it, they'd found only a shimmery, golden dust.

The Fox King moved to the cauldron, pulled a rag from a hook on the wall, and lifted the pot's lid. He stood beside the fire, and soon the room had filled with the scent of clover and thyme, of wildflowers and of honeysuckle and fresh earth. There was a smell like rot, like leaves raked into piles, and there was a buttery smell like cornbread crumbled into cold milk. The smell that was all of the smells was wonderful, and the girls' hunger doubled.

Now the boy, without instruction, carried the first of the six pouches to the cauldron and dropped it in. He repeated the ceremony twice, then he returned to the table. The three that remained were the three that wriggled. It had not escaped the comprehension of the girls that what moved inside each pouch, what pushed to get out, was the body of a young fox, nor had it escaped their imaginations what might happen should these bodies be dropped into the bubbling cauldron. What they were coming to understand, the girls, was an idea faraway-seeming as the most distant star, but it moved toward them, the star, racing their way and zeroing in at the speed of thought, which, after all, is a speed so many times faster than the speed of light.

Blood-slick on the table, the foxes pawed at their bags to be free, and it struck the girls that the Fox King was also the King of Death.

The girls thought, then—thought back to two summers past when each had lost her Grandpappy to a heart attack—and the girls wondered, if there was a King of Foxes who was also the King of Death, whether there wasn't a King of Grandpappys. They considered last month, when the ground had puckered like a kissing mouth, and their fathers' friends, ten of them, had been lost. Was there, then, a King of Coal Miners? And, if there was, then certainly there must be a King of Coal Miners' Canaries, in which case there would have been a King of Dogs Who Chased Cars and a King of Butterflies Too Soon Un-cocooned and a King of Little Girls Lost in the Woods.

The King of Death, then, went by many names and many faces, and who could say whether one king was not also another? If he could unzipper the belly of a fox, then who was to say that this king, this very king, could not unzipper their own?

The girls knew then that they must run. But running meant leaving the foxes, meant leaving the boy who was not a prince at all, but a servant of Death, perhaps Death-in-Training.

The boy's hands hovered over the table, trembled, and the King called to him, sweetly.

"Bring them to me," he said.

The boy's hands shook hard, and the King growled. "Bring me the ones that move!"

The boy leaned into table and a pouch slithered into his cupped hands. It turned and would not be still. But the boy was still.

The King roared. "Bring me my dinner!" His mouth twisted beneath his beard, but the boy would not move. He held the unstill thing close to him, cradled it in the crook of his arm. The girls moved forward, Ellie first, for in all things she was bold, and Isabelle second, for in all things she was timid. Each took a fox into her hands and marveled at the way it slithered, jellylike, in its warm, diaphanous bag.

"I will have my way!" the King bellowed, but by now his mouth was pulling in many directions at once. The lips tugged, and the mouth opened, and the face unfolded until the mouth had swallowed the face and the head had turned inside out. The fox-skin cap slipped to the floor. The body shuddered and collapsed like dropped clothes. And, from the pile, from the tangle of boots and pants, flannel and flesh, from the hole in the neck where the head had sunk like a deflated balloon, from the midst of all of this leapt a fox, crimson and sleek, the most beautiful fox the children had ever seen.

This new fox—its fur glowed like chrome and its breast shone like white sand. The fox curled before the fire and, following some instinct the children couldn't have put into words but trusted the way they trusted their mothers—the way you trust love when it enters a room—the children set what was in their arms before the fox who licked each bag open and licked clean what sprang free. The red fox licked and nuzzled and cleaned, and then she fell to her side, and the little ones took to her and drank until they were full, and, when they were full, the four foxes curled together and slept.

By now, the girls were very tired and very, very hungry, and so was the boy. He had been a servant of Death for almost as long as he could remember. But there had been another time, a time before this, distant but real, when he, like the girls, had had a mother and a father of his own. The girls spoke of their homes, and the boy nodded, for he'd had one of those too, a home and a bedroom and a bed all his own. He'd been in the woods a long time, but not so long he didn't remember his way out.

He would lead them home, the girls first, into the arms of fathers who would leave their faces black with kisses, into the arms of mothers who would know that the girls were too old to be rocked and who would rock them still. And the girls would be given big dinners and be drawn bright, warm baths, would be kissed more and rocked more and tucked into bed.

And then the boy would find his way home. The house would be darker than he remembered, the man and woman at the door older and looking sadder, sad because they had waited a long time, so long that they hoped now not for the return of a boy but for the return of a shirt, a shoe, evidence any that once a boy, their boy, had passed through this world. They would look on him sadly, would look and then watch him, until, unbelievingly, he would speak and in a word become their boy. He would be the answer to an already forgotten prayer.

Kevin Catalano

The Bad That Can Happen the Day Jesus Rose from the Dead

Bush tore me down the middle of Sweet Lane and I chased him, knees all blooded up, calling him low down. We sprinted through the peach orchard, my Easter dress raked once by his hands and now again by the blooming branches. I cornered him at Ruin Lake, brown like caramel and his dark shoulders.

"I'll bust you up," I screamed, knocking him over as he was getting a leg out of his trousers. "What Mom gonna say about my dress?"

"She'll call you a clumsy twit for falling all over yourself before church."

All gums and crooked teeth, he was down on the dew-grass, the sun glowing him beautiful. It made me hate him even more for leaving tomorrow. Last week he gutted Miss Hinshaw's poodle with a hunting knife. I didn't see him do it, but that night he came into my bedroom when I was sleeping. I made space for him in bed. Arms draping my ribs, he whispered me the story, all bitter breath and dark verbs that shot a hot cyclone through me. The story its own was hazy, but he made me feel that poor dog fighting from his hold and biting his fingers while the blade dug in. And I knew about how that dog licked Bush's fingers as it died for Bush tongued my fingers at the conclusion of his telling. I still swam in that stormy narrative when he pulled out the knife like out of the past itself. He handed it over. The knife, a kind with a bone handle, had white tufts of fur stuck to it, blood sticky like maple syrup.

He said to hide it, so I wrapped the blade in a pair of my cotton drawers and buried it in the back of my dollhouse thick with spiderweb. Just another secret to go with all our secrets. The hiding it didn't matter though, since Miss Hinshaw was witness to the killing and the police came by next afternoon. Judge gave him ninety days in juvie, starting tomorrow.

From on his back, Bush kicked out my legs and I crashed stupidly. He scrambled into the lake and splashed me.

"Fool," I spat. "You gone to hell."

He took out his noodly penis and pissed in the water. He cranked his shoulders back and made the yellow stream arc like a fountain. I pretended not to look but looked. Mom was hellbent on getting Bush's soul right with the Lord. She been talking about the Lamb of God all Easter weekend, and convinced the pastor to baptize his sorry butt before he went away. Now, in only a few hours, Pastor's going to dip Bush's head in pee while we all sing "Angel Band."

Bush jumped like he'd been bit and cussed the water. He scurried out and studied the lake.

"What is it?" I got beside him to look.

"A gi-normous scorpion, I swear it."

"Go on."

Just as I said it, a thick cloud of gold-flecked mud kicked up. When it cleared, the coiled tail of a lobster-looking thing was kicking around just under the surface. It was the size of a dog, not including its horrible red legs and claws. Its tail whipped and snapped, spraying both our shins. Then it crawled deeper until it disappeared into the lake's depths.

My whole body budded with hives.

"Come on, sis." Bush was trotting to the old aluminum rowboat upside down in the highgrass. "We're going to chase that thing. I want it. I could win something for having it."

He flipped the boat, pushed it into the water, and got in.

I stood in the grass with my arms folded. "There's no way I'm getting in with you."

"Might be others crawling round up by you," he said, pushing off.

"Bush!" I caught up to the boat and climbed in. "God knows I hate you."

His snapping muscles yanked the oars, his body different in the sunlight than it felt in the dark. I kept my eyes on his thready arms because I didn't dare look into the water. I repeated *Lamb of God* in my head. I thought nothing this bad could happen the day Jesus rose from the dead.

The middle of the lake, Bush yelped, "Good night," and pulled in the oars. He was big-eyed looking over the boat, and I couldn't help but look too. The lake around us bubbled and spit, and there was a swelling buzz like a million cicadas just beneath the surface. This swarm of whatever they were rushed the boat, nipping the sides and belly, the metal pocked like shotgun blast. Bush was frozen, not even breathing. I began to pee myself, and bunched the dress between my legs to sponge it.

I scrambled into Bush's lap and pressed my face into his sweaty chest, tasting its metallic saltiness. I pleaded with his body like I'd done on the nights when he'd hush me. His arms draped my shoulders. His heart slammed my temple like God had gotten into him and became frightened by what He saw and was punching to get out. Water coming into the boat licked our ankles. His heart it thumped fiercer than when he had promised me it was good love, and the water was the same cool as the bone-handle knife that still lay hidden in my dolly's room. My heart suddenly sprouted its tail which, seething poison, sought its victim.

I pushed myself from Bush, and lay back on the bottom of the boat to fire both feet into his chest. The loud white of his eyes caught the sun as he fell backwards, into the lake. I sobbed as the electric swarm bubbled around him, his arms waving like mad, his screams going from jagged to gurgle. The peach of his palms was the last I saw of him, descending quickly into the dark. As the lake went peaceful once again, I reached over the bow, screaming his name.

There Are More Things

There are more things in heaven and earth, Horatio,
Than are dreamt of in your philosophy.
—William Shakespeare, *Hamlet*
"There Are More Things" is also the title of the
Jorge Luis Borges story which he dedicated
"to the memory of H.P. Lovecraft."

I didn't have the time to take away from my portfolio to run an errand for someone else at the library of all places, but Lance was a roommate and a loyal friend, and there was the off-chance that I could wander across some creature-concept designs to steal from old books, so I went. I had to get some good ideas down on paper soon, sketches that the studio guys would finally call original, a true vision.

It was night. Closing time was soon. A few homeless guys woke from the library arm chairs and roamed like ghosts. I had grabbed the book Lance wanted, a book on prehistoric whale anatomy for a novel he was writing—I don't know why he couldn't have just researched some diagrams on the Internet—but then I found myself wandering through a labyrinth of aisles that had no orienting signage or numbering. As best as I could tell, it was the third and a half floor, maybe the fourth and a half floor. It wasn't a full floor: no elevator access, no windows. That's where I saw Jorge Luis Borges.

My brain tends to remember images well and faces even better, and I had seen two of his author pics in my college lit book, one in the upper left of the left page, another toward the end of the book in the middle left. Here in the library with me, like his old photos, he had a discoverer's face, half aglow with amazement, an old-world look that reminded me of the elderly version of Bela Lugosi, the Ed Wood years, or at least when Martin Landau played Bela in the Burton film.

It was Borges in the flesh, all right. And I could tell he was already blind by how he felt his way down the aisle of books, fingers crawling across the spines, feet inching forward darkly. I felt that in such a situation I should say something, and I watched him, trying to think of some impressive or profound statement, but I noticed the little can-shaped roll-stool in his way. I said, "Watch out!"

He startled, straightening tall and fanning both arms out on either aisle, searching around with his face as if to hear my location, or to sniff me out. He hadn't known I was there. I felt guilt for having used the idiom *watch out*, a thoughtless insensitivity toward his condition, but then I felt a far worse guilt for not having known enough about Borges before this moment. I couldn't seem to remember any details about his fiction or poetry that we read in college, and I hadn't touched any of his non-fiction, though I remembered a cool-looking monster on the cover of a book of his about imaginary beings—a thick-headed sphinx-pegasus with a peacock tail. Regardless, I just knew that Borges had to be full of original ideas since we did have to study him. I should have at least had a sense of his biography, or of when he had died, or something about his impact on the history of literature, but I was blank-page ignorant. I felt like an ass.

I neared him, warning while I did, "I'm walking closer to you," so I wouldn't give him another scare. I decided to come clean about my ignorance first-thing, just in case his blindness made him particularly apt at detecting bullshit. "Sorry," I said, "I know you're Jorge Luis Borges, and it's an honor to run into you, but I have to admit that I don't know much about you, literature-history-wise. And when we did read your work, I was kind of into other things at the time." Dark Horse Comics, Image, Marvel, lots of Jim Lee, some old-school Jack Kirby, anything by Mike Mignola—those four-color panels flashed through my brain faster than shuffling cards. "I guess I did pleasure reading more than college reading. But we did study you in a literature class."

He reset himself into a comfortable slouch and smiled. He said to me, "I have tried to disregard as much as possible the history of literature. When my students asked me for a bibliography, I told them, A bibliography is unimportant—after all. Shakespeare knew nothing of Shakespearean criticism. Why not study the texts directly? If you like the book, fine; if you don't, don't read it. The idea of compulsory reading is absurd; it's only worthwhile to speak of compulsory happiness." [1]

I liked that. And that's exactly what I was in need of, some compulsory happiness. This upcoming deadline to submit my portfolio, my creature concepts designs, my opportunity to get a real job with an fx studio—this was my last shot. There were only so many places in this industry to get rejected from. My unemployment checks were going to dry up soon. I hadn't opened my credit card statements in months. My girlfriend left me for a guy who sells smartphones to other guys who already have them. I had even considered reading up on how to operate the pistol I kept up in the closet. And while it was great to have my friend Lance helping out by living in my basement unit, I figured it wouldn't be long before his novel took off and he'd be gone. To top it off, I've been crumpling up page after page of my designs because I can hear the studio guys in my head already: *We've seen that monster before.* Or, *that's just this mixed with that. A bear with an owl,* or *a shark with a bird,* and so on. *What we need is something original.* As if that exists. I needed compulsory happiness, all right. And I needed some help with that.

So I asked Borges about his take on monster-making. "If you don't mind my asking, do you think it's even possible to draw an entirely new monster design? Like a really original vision? It seems to me, even back in ancient times people just accidentally came up with monsters just because they didn't know any better and ended up misunderstanding regular animals. I only ask because of the cover on that book of yours, the one with the human head on the horse body."

"The Centaur?" [1] he said, still seeming a little unsure about me. Or maybe he didn't know the book cover I was referring to, the sphinx-pegasus.

---

[1] Every line of Borges's dialogue in this story is quoted directly from his non-fiction, specifically from the following collections: *Seven Nights, The Book of Imaginary Beings, This Craft of Verse, Borges: Selected Non-Fictions.*

"Yeah, let's take the centaur for example," I said. "Like the first time ancient people saw a guy riding a horse, they just mistook it for a monster, and there you go. No real original vision, just a mix-and-match accident."

"But..." he said, "the Greeks did know the horse. It seems more likely that the Centaur is a deliberately drawn image."[1]

"So you think it's possible for an artist to deliberately come up with an entirely new monster, and it could stick around in people's heads? Maybe for thousands of years?"

"I think it is,"[1] he said.

And with the way he said it, the way he canted *I think it is*, with a kind of scoffing obviousness that didn't come off as much rude as it did patient—patient with my youth, patient with my ignorance, like an old magician—I think I was immediately convinced. If I brought him home with me and had him coaching me, I could churn out a portfolio that would blow minds and shake the world. He surely wouldn't be much trouble to keep around since he had been dead for so long. So I went for it.

"I tell you what," I said. "I'd really love it if you came and lived with me for a while. It's not much, but it's a warm place to sleep and some decent food to eat. I have lots of vintage movies from, you know..." I didn't want to say from his lifetime. "From your era. I feel like you could really help me out with some ideas I'm trying to get going."

He didn't seem immediately against it. But he said, "I would like to give you fair warning of what to expect—or, rather what not to expect from me." He rubbed the swollen knuckles of his hands. "The truth is that I have no revelations to offer."[1]

Of course I didn't believe his humility, but rather than argue I just said, "I don't mind. Come anyway. It'll be a nice change for me. Besides, I'm sure I haven't given you the respect you deserve, the writer you are and all. If I drew out some of the monsters that you tell me about, I could do proper justice to your writing."

"To do justice to a writer," he said, "one must be unjust to others."[1]

"Maybe so, but I guess I don't care anymore," I said. "Other writers haven't helped me out any, and it's time I focused on some artistic vision of my own. I have you here with me now, and you can help me come up with a monster that is…" An impressive word wasn't coming to me—a monster that is what?—but then I saw it written on the cover of the prehistoric whale book that I held. "A monster that is unfathomable!"

He wrinkled his brow.

I was excited, already feeling inspiration for the first time in months. I took him carefully by the hand and led him through the aisles, looking to find an emergency exit so we could escape from the library without anyone seeing us or asking questions to which the answers, at this point, would be too confusing for a stranger to comprehend and too insulting to say in front of a great man like Borges. And sneaking out meant that Lance wouldn't have to worry about returning the book I had picked up for him, though I wasn't sure how I would explain all this to him.

I wanted Borges to wait for me outside the house while I broke the news about his moving in with us, just in case Lance reacted poorly at first, which I thought might scare Borges away. I didn't know exactly what poor reaction to expect out of Lance, but he tended to be more skeptical and conservative than I, making my proposition to let Borges move in with us a shaky one.

Since it was sleeting, I had Borges wait in the cubby of the front porch. Also, from inside, I could see him through the window, and I wanted to keep him in the corner of my eye. I wasn't exactly sure if he was the kind of old man who might wander off, but since I had found him all alone and wandering, I assumed he was in fact that kind.

I yelled down the basement stairs to Lance, telling him that I got his library book but that I needed to talk to him. My plan was simple: tell him the truth, list the benefits of having Borges move in, and hope that he would agree. I was certain that, given a moment to consider the magnitude, the possibilities, he would agree.

Lance hopped up the stairs, skipping steps, asking me what was up.

"You have to promise not to tell anyone," I said.

Lance gestured toward the window at Borges outside, who was turning his head in the yellow light of the porch bulb, listening to the sleet. "Who's that?"

"I found him in the library. It's Jorge Luis Borges, the famous writer. He's going to move in with us. He's from Argentina, and he wrote all kinds of stuff, and he's an expert on monsters."

"I know who Borges is," Lance said. "And he's dead."

"Don't say that," I said, looking back to make sure that Borges hadn't heard that through the door.

"He died in the '80s. That's not him."

"It is him. Just look at him," I said. "If you promise to be cool about it, I'll let you talk to him, and you can ask him anything you want. Then you'll see. But you have to promise to help me keep him a secret."

"I have no idea if that guy looks like Borges or not, and I don't care. This is nutty, man. The pressure's getting to you." Lance took the library book out of my hand and flipped through pages. He let a centerfold fall open that showed an anatomical map of some atrocious version of a sperm whale, its skeleton, its muscles, its nasty teeth. He turned away from me toward the basement. "Just give that guy some food or liquor or whatever he's here for, and send him away. And get some rest, man. Jesus."

"No, Lance," I said. My stomach quivered, but I was determined to have Borges move in no matter what it took. "He's staying. He's going to live here. I don't want to be an asshole about it, but it's my house."

Lance faced me again, somehow amused. "You think he's going to help you with your portfolio, don't you? For the job?"

"Yeah, and who better?" I said. "They want monsters from me, don't they? They want real vision."

"I don't want to have to say it, but you're not going to get that job," he said. "You have to know that. You haven't had a single real vision in your whole life. Listen, you're a good sketcher and a good inker, but you're not a prophet, man. You're not John the Revelator. I'm trying to look out for you, and I've got to tell you that this is getting real crazy. I can't let you keep it up."

I tossed my hands and tried to yell, but I didn't know what to say. I couldn't believe he would say that. I could have real vision. I would prove it.

Apparently, he could tell I was upset. "Listen, listen," he said, softening his tone a little. "I'm sure you can get some kind of job in the industry, and you'll do fine, but you have to be realistic. I've seen you do this before. You get a glimpse of something great that's way out of your league, and then you totally obsess over it. It never goes well."

"When have I ever done that?"

"You're single again, aren't you? You're unemployed again. Look, if you're too uncomfortable telling that guy he has to leave, I'll do it." Lance started toward the front door.

I blocked his path. He was going to be mean to Borges. He was just going to hurt his feelings like he did to me, and while I could take it, I didn't know if Borges could, not given his odd condition. I couldn't have Lance tossing him out in the cold. I said, "You're not talking to him. And he's not leaving. You are."

"You can't seriously be kicking me out."

"You're either for me or against me on this, and you're against me, so you're out." My voice sounded stormy, and I liked it. I had never before stood my ground like this. Maybe I had just needed someone else to defend. I would be damned if I let anyone else run Borges off. He was with me now. Borges and I were in this together. We would draw forth a monster together. I told Lance, "Leave through the back door in the utility room. Don't even look at Borges anymore. I'm not going to say it twice."

"You know what, I don't need this." He tossed the book down on the couch and then pointed close to my face. "You know what you are? You're an Ahab, man. Yeah, you keep chasing after something you don't even understand, and you're going to destroy yourself."

"If I'm Ahab," I said, "then you're..." I wanted to turn his reference back around on him, and I was trying to recall the name of that prophet that Ahab fought with in the Bible. Was it Ezekiel or Elijah or something? The name wasn't clear to me, but I did remember an old etch-style illustration of the scene with a chariot in the background. "Then you're that prophet, the one who…"

"You know which Ahab I meant, you freak. You're not even making any sense. I'm out of here."

"Then you're overboard," I said. Although I was feeling the power of the moment, I knew I was terrible with the witty comebacks, and I knew that one was lame. Lance was always good with them, good at talking people down, but he even admitted once that it was a fake skill of his—a sleight of hand—so I knew not to take anything cruel he said to heart.

But I didn't expect him to leave just like that, without another word, without even collecting anything he owned from the basement, and yet he did, right out the back door. He had other friends, lots of them, so he probably just went to stay with one of them. I was suspicious for a moment whether he had planned to move out soon anyway, but, on second thought, I was sure he would come back in a day or so, and we would patch things up over a case of beer, and I would show him all the inspired art and monster designs that Borges would help me with. It would be fine. Until then, I had to make Borges feel at home in the basement, and I had to get him talking about monsters.

It wasn't long before I grew a little annoyed with Borges. In the basement I had prepared his cot, got a space heater ready, and brought down a lamp that he didn't even really require. In order for him to have something near the cot to set stuff on, or to reach out to, or to lean on, I even dragged a small dresser down the stairs. It was a bad decision to try to go down backward under the dresser, the steep wooden steps whining under the weight, the pipe railing loose like a stick in sand. I thought I would fall through, tap my skull on the concrete like a nutshell, and be dead in the basement with Borges for eternity.

But I didn't die, or even fall, and I had gone to a lot of trouble to build him a cozy little dorm. I also brought down my laptop to watch the original *King Kong* with him, one of the masterworks of American cinema. I knew he couldn't *watch it* watch it, but I tended to talk through films, so I described most of the shots. Borges remembered a lot of it anyway, as he told me, from when he had seen it during its original release in theaters in Argentina, back when he had sight.

Here was my basic plan: We'd watch the film, and then we would say wonderful things about it over a cheap bottle of cognac that I had, and then King Kong would get him talking about other great monsters, summoning all that mythical knowledge and all those original ideas that I could translate into art for my portfolio.

It didn't work. Borges hated King Kong.

"How can you hate King Kong?" I said.

He said, "A monkey forty feet tall—" [1]

"He's forty-five," I said. "Forty-five feet tall." I knew my King Kong. I owned the special edition DVD.

"Forty-five," he continued, "may have some obvious charms, but—" [1]

"But what?" I said. "Willis O'Brien, the guy who animated it, he created a real monster for the first time in the history of all humanity. Audiences back then hadn't ever seen anything like that. Kong was climbing on buildings that people in the theater really knew. The cinematographer was a genius, and O'Brien summoned a real, full-blooded ape up from primordial chaos!"

Borges paused and then started again with distinct punctuation, emphasis on the pick-up words, like a man delivering a lecture that ought not to have been interrupted. "King Kong is no full-blooded ape but rather a rusty, desiccated machine whose movements are downright clumsy. His only virtue, his height, did not impress the cinematographer, who persisted in photographing him from above rather than from below—the wrong angle, as it neutralizes and even diminishes the ape's overpraised stature." [1]

"Overpraised stature? He'd rip this whole house down, and then he'd scoop out this basement like a grapefruit and squish us into a bloody mess! He's massive. Look at him." I knew I was pointing at the DVD menu screen of an image of Kong fighting a wickedly strange-looking T-rex that Borges could not see, but that didn't make me any less right.

"He is actually hunchbacked and bowlegged, attributes that serve only to reduce him in the spectator's eye. To keep him from looking the least bit extraordinary, they make him do battle with far more unusual monsters and have him reside in caves of false cathedral splendor, where his infamous size again loses all proportion." [1]

"This is unreal," I said. "I'd love to see what kind of monsters could possibly impress you if King Kong—the greatest American monster—is just a little hunchback monkey to you. How big does a monster have to be?" My head was hot and heavy. It was the cognac and the lack of sleep, mostly the cognac, which had gotten me standing and slapping the cinderblock basement wall while I talked without thinking clearly. "Put King Kong in his place, why don't you? What do you got that's better? I'm ready to see it. I'm here in a basement with a guy who came back from the dead just so I can come up with a monster, so show me a real monster, then!"

"I timidly point out this monstrousness to my interlocutor." [1] Then he said nothing else. He took his cane and sat tapping the floor with it, with ticks like a waiting clock, probably indicating as politely as possible that he was ready to be left alone for the night.

I sat back down and wished I hadn't said what I said. I stayed silent for a while and kept swigging cognac. Then I offered an apology for my rude and aggressive manner—blaming fatigue and liquor—and I wished him a good-night with a promise that I would bring him breakfast early in the morning. I left him down in the basement, taking the bottle of cognac with me. I sat on my bed, drinking and sketching, coming up with one junk design after another. I could have cried. In the long mirror facing me on the back of my bedroom door, I looked pathetic and creepy, crouched up on the bed like the little demon in Fuseli's painting *The Nightmare*. I threw a dirty towel over the door to cover the mirror, and flopped back on the bed, giving up for the night, but just as I was drifting off, I got an idea for what to try next with Borges.

"Tell me about your nightmares, Borges."

It was mid-morning, and I had come back from with store, brewed some Columbian coffee, cooked some bacon, even cut up a grapefruit for him. I brought it down to the basement on a baking sheet, which was the closest thing I owned to a silver platter. He had apparently found a bathroom kit that Lance had left behind, and he was clipping his fingernails. He let the clippings fly on the floor.

"The nightmare," [1] he said as if he were making formal introductions. "Dreams are the genus; nightmares the species." [1]

"Exactly. Tell me about what scares you most in your dreams." I laid out his breakfast on the little dresser and then sat myself on the floor, away from his fingernail clippings, with my sketch pad in my lap, my Faber-Castell 9000 pencils at the ready.

He said, "I have two nightmares which often become confused with one another. I have the nightmare of the labyrinth, which—" [1]

"Wait a second," I said, stopping him so I could turn on the lamp for better lighting, also realizing that I wouldn't be able to do much monster-design work using something like a labyrinth as inspiration. "Okay," I said as I sat back down, "so the labyrinth is one, but what's your other nightmare?"

He found the coffee with his hand, sipped it, seemed disappointed, and went back to clipping his nails. "My other nightmare is that of the mirror. The two are not distinct, as it only takes two facing mirrors to construct a labyrinth." [1]

"Mirrors scare me too," I said, feeling quickly enthusiastic about the idea. "I had to cover up my bedroom mirror last night!"

"In the dream of the mirror, another vision appears… the mask. Masks have always scared me. I see myself reflected in the mirror, but the reflection is wearing a mask. I am afraid to pull the mask off, afraid to see my real face, which I imagine to be hideous." [1]

I was sketching like mad, liking what I saw for the first time in untold weeks. "This is good. This is good," I said.

Borges went on some more about some other writers, Coleridge and Petronius and whatnot, but I was deep into my lead, deaf with inspiration, possessed by ideas. I was filling up pages of stylized South-Pacific masks with cannibal teeth and even more pages of a mask design styled like a Victorian mirror. Maybe the concept was that the South-Pacific mask needs to be fed raw human flesh. Maybe it gives the wearer power when it gets fed, but maybe after the food passes the mask the wearer has to eat it all too. Maybe the Victorian mirror-mask steals the face of whomever it reflects. Masks always work for studios doing horror movies—Michael Myers, Jason, the *Scream* guy—and the cinematographers always squeeze in shots of seeing the killer in the mirror. Why hadn't I thought of using something in my sketches that actually creeped me out, like mirrors?

What I needed was a model to keep the inspiration flowing. I needed to stare into some mirrors and make exaggerated faces in them like masks. I told Borges this, and I let him know that he was free to wander around inside the house as he pleased but not to leave the house at all. He wouldn't be safe out there in my neighborhood, around the crazies and the thugs, around people who couldn't appreciate him like I did.

As I was on my way up the stairs, he warned me about seeing a fish in the mirror.

"A fish?" I said.

"The Fish," [1] he said, either repeating himself for emphasis or distinguishing a special fish—a capital F fish—from all other fish. Either way, he was not happy about it at all. He had turned serious. "An elusive, gleaming creature that no one had ever touched but that many people believed they had seen in the depths of mirrors." [1]

I told him that I didn't know anything about that Fish but that I would find out more later and that at the moment I needed to get to work and that he was free to adjust the thermostat to whatever made him comfortable.

He was slow with his words now, dark with his tone. "The first to awaken shall be the Fish," he said. He had stopped clipping his nails. He stood, facing the cinderblock wall, doing nothing with his hands, blind but seeing something. I didn't like it. "In the depths of the mirror, we shall perceive a faint, faint line, and the color of the line will not resemble any other." [1]

I had never before imagined what having visions or revelations actually looked like to an outside observer like me who was seeing the person having them. It was disturbing, like when a pet or some kind of animal is bristling and growling at an empty corner in an old house, you being the only one not seeing what there is to fear.

I told myself that whatever was going on with Borges at the moment was private—I was sure he had worries of his own—so I left him down in the basement, still talking to himself. I desperately needed to get to work while that ever-fleeting inspiration was still with me. I needed a full day of sketching, and I needed to put in an all-nighter on top of that.

I pulled all the mirrors in the house off their hinges and brackets, pulled them out of the drawers, even gathered some reflective glasses and bottles, and I surrounded my drafting table with them. I quickly realized that the morning sun coming in through the slits in the window blinds caught my eye through one mirror or another, so I had to take the time to pull out every sheet and coat and towel I owned and cover every window. I stood the couch up against the front door to block the light from its seal. It was so dark that I needed to turn on some lights, but none that would catch my mirrors directly, so I turned on all the flashlights that I had and angled them away from me. A few candles helped too. I had no idea what time it was when I finally got to sit down and grab a pencil, but once I did and started making monster faces in the mirrors, it was all the inspiration I needed, and I lost myself in the work, hours and hours of glorious blur.

The pilot light to the gas heater must have been snuffed out hours prior to my coming to, to my awaking out of a daze. My arms and legs shivered, and by the dull light I could see my breath. At some point during the drawing, and the intermittent sleep—against my own will—over my drafting table, and the staring deep into the mirrors, my nose had apparently bled on some of my best designs. It wouldn't matter much. The designs were good, and there were piles of them: masks and mirror-creatures and more masks.

Also I had apparently begun drawing parts of a fish, a big one. It was so big that it would never fit on a single page. I hadn't remembered specifically drawing those, but I did, and I couldn't quit looking back over them, using the tips of my numb fingers to piece them together at the corners in different combinations, trying to get a sense of what the whole fish would look like in a single vision.

I guessed it was about one in the morning. All but one of the flashlights had died, but the candles were still bright. The mirrors looked black beyond the hints of my face reflected in them.

That's when I saw the faint, faint line.

It showed up in the mirror that was on my left, the one I had taken off the bathroom medicine cabinet. The faint, faint line, it was something effable only by analogy. It was like it had a color, a compromise the perception of the brain might make between a spider and the rings of Saturn. The faint, faint line was like the slit of a closed eye, a nearly closed eye, like an animal dreaming. And I looked into the slit of that eye to get a glimpse of what was on the other side. I looked hard. My nose touched the mirror, and it was cold. I held my breath so I wouldn't frost it over. I thought my eyes might lose focus that close, but they didn't. It was just taking time for the image to sharpen.

And the image did sharpen.

I saw floating in a great deep. The line in the mirror didn't open, but I saw into it, and I saw floating in a great deep, hints of a vast fish.

I must have stopped breathing for I don't know how long because I found myself coming back to consciousness on the floor. The room was dizzy, and the faint line in the mirror was gone. I picked myself up and checked all of the mirrors, but it was gone.

I rushed down the stairs to ask Borges about it, yelling as I went. But he was gone too.

I ran back upstairs and checked the front door, checked the rooms, yelling for him, and then I checked the back door in the utility room. It was cracked open. That's where Borges had gone.

This was bad. He could run into anybody out there, crazy people. He could leave forever. He had to tell me about the Fish. I had seen a glimpse of it. I needed to see it again. I needed to see all of it. He had to tell me how.

Outside, I saw him just past the back lot, in the alley, where the street lamp just barely reached. He was talking to a couple of thugs—baggy clothes, weaving heads, flicking hands—and they were laughing with him.

I couldn't have that. They weren't capable of understanding the things Borges and I could see.

Back inside, with the last working flashlight, I found the pistol case in my bedroom closet, opened it, and removed the piece. I had no idea if the thing was loaded; I just knew that you pointed it and squeezed the trigger when you had to. I went out back toward the alley and yelled at the thugs to back away from Borges, to leave him alone and get lost.

It took them a moment to see that I was pointing the pistol at them. I think they were smoking weed right next to him. He didn't need that. He needed to be clear headed. The thugs said, "What the hell, dude?" and they called me crazy.

I repeated myself as I neared them. They didn't stick around.

There was a parked car nearby, in the grass to the side of the alley, and it looked like Lance's car. I had trouble remembering the image of his car for sure—all I could think of was the Fish—but I was pretty sure it was his, so he must have been staying somewhere nearby to spy on me. He was probably waiting for a chance to take Borges away from me. He probably called the cops. I should have never let him know that I had found Borges. But I knew I could scare Lance off if I left him a message, showing him that I was deadly serious. I used the butt of the pistol to smash out the driver's side window so he would know I was to be left alone, that Borges and I were to be left alone, and the thugs would know too, and the cops too.

The car had an alarm, which started blaring, and lights came on in neighbors' windows.

I grabbed Borges by the arm and led him back inside the house, accidentally smearing some blood from a cut on my hand onto his coat. "What were you saying to those guys? What were you talking about?" I was worried they had been mean to him or crude with him. I was worried he was telling them about the Fish.

"The art of verbal abuse,"[1] he said. "The middle finger and a show of tongue... 'Dog' is another very general term of insult."[1]

"You shouldn't talk to those guys. You shouldn't talk to anybody out here. They're dangerous." I pulled Borges to hurry him with me down the basement steps. It was a deep freeze down there, the cold coming in waves through the cinderblocks. He was moving slow, sliding his feet rather than picking them up, but we didn't have time for that. I had seen the vast Fish, had seen it in the mirror. Borges had to tell me more.

He had seemed amused since I found him talking with the thugs, not at all gloomy and nightmarish as when I had last left him in the basement. He was singing a poem when I sat him down on his cot:

"*Veinticinco palillos*
Tiene una silla.
Quieres que te la rompa
En las costillas?" [1]

I went back up the stairs to secure basement door, asking him what he was saying, what those words meant, what was the translation, whether they were ancient.

He said,

"Twenty-five sticks

Makes a chair.

Would you like me to break it

Over your ribs?" [1]

"That's got nothing to do with it, with the Fish," I said. From the inside of the door I shut it, locked it, and used the pistol to hammer the doorstop in the gap at the bottom to keep it wedged shut in the event that Borges figured out how to unlock it. In case I passed out again, down here in the basement, I couldn't have him wandering back outside.

Then I got close to his face and said, "Tell me more about the Fish. Tell me everything."

For a moment he kept that closed-eyed, pleasant look, but I knew that it was just a mask of his, because what I said had begun to sink in. His smile faded. He was getting back to the Borges that had scared me.

"That's right," I said. "I saw it. I saw it upstairs, a glimpse of it. I passed out but I saw a glimpse through the faint line in the mirror. It was vast. It was terrible and vast."

He lay down on the cot, now as serious as I was. He crossed his hands on his chest, and his voice sounded dead. "People speak not of the Fish." [1]

"But you did. You brought it up. You brought it here with you. You brought it to me." I knelt by his ear as if I were praying into it, my breath misting his skin. "Why didn't you stay dead, Borges? What did you see over there? Tell me about the Fish. Tell me what it is."

"The Leviathan," [1] he said. "The Bahamut… a Fish that floats in a bottomless sea." [1]

Someone was knocking upstairs now, knocking on the front door.

"What about it?" I said. I knew somehow that we were running out of time, that others would try to stop us, that creation would conspire against me now that I was seeing through it. "What is the Bahamut? What about it?" I didn't know the right questions to ask.

"A vacant god reeling in the barren centuries of the eternity 'before.'" [1]

"What does that mean? Before what? Before God?"

They knocked more.

"So immense and resplendent is the Bahamut that human eyes cannot bear to look upon it. All the seas of the earth, placed in one of the nostrils of its nose, would be no more than a grain of mustard in the midst of the desert." [1]

The knocking continued. I couldn't have anyone interrupting this. I flicked on my flashlight and turned off the basement lamp, knocking us into near darkness. I helped Borges up quickly and dragged him with me to hide under the basement stairs. I hit my head on the wood underneath the steps. There wasn't much space under there, but what we were on to was bigger than the universe.

I could tell there was yelling outside now, and they beat loudly on the front door with their bodies or their clubs or something, but they wouldn't find me and Borges down here, not if we kept our talking to a whisper.

I muffled the beam of my flashlight under my shirt, letting me see by the faintest glow, and I said softly, "If I keep looking for the Bahamut in the mirror, will I get to see it again? Will I get to see all of it?"

Borges kept his eyes closed as he huddled and shivered. I hadn't seen him shiver before. "Isa—Jesus—was allowed to see the

Bahamut, and when this gift was bestowed upon him he fell down in a swoon, and did not awake from the swoon that had come upon him for three days." [1]

"But I'm different, right? Human eyes can't bear it, but I'm a visionary, right? It was almost revealed to me. What would happen if I saw all of it?"

"Nothingness," he said. "As if blasted by a lightless fire." [1]

"Tell me, tell me the truth," I said. "If I look hard again, will I get to see it? Can I awaken it?" I was holding him close by the shoulders, like clinging to a pine box floating in an endless ocean.

"The first to awaken will be the Fish… Then, other forms will begin to awaken… they will break through the barriers." [1] He was turning his face away from me, and I didn't want him to. He was as scared as I was.

"Is it already awake?" I said. I was shaking. "Oh, God! Is it true? Has it now awoken?"

His eyes opened, and I saw my reflection in them. And in that reflection, I saw the Bahamut, and the Bahamut saw me.

Alexander Lumans

The Moonshiner

My shine doesn't get a man drunk. It changes him no less than a single regret burns him up, no more than years living alone chills his blood to springwater. And it's not cooked in a dead man still in the daylong shadow of Wolf Pinnacle, the way pap used to make his. A handful of skinwalkers know I sell it. They've bought enough boodles to keep my dog and me fed and fine for twelve years. Some stop, disappear. Plenty new ones take their place. The law don't know and the neighbors don't exist. Even on this bad leg, my business still carries me up and down the high hills with the help of a leaning stick. Late spring through early fall usually has the perfect conditions: clear night, the biggest moon, recent rain and a fine set of tracks. Put all those together and you get a pawprint filled with rainwater reflecting the full moon. *Moonshine.*

The sunrise after a boodle of shine has been kicked, the first thought to hit you is: *I need to stop before someone gets hurt.*

And the second? *I'm going to hurt someone if I don't get more.*

Now, October, going on six months since the last time I could collect any shine, my supply's dried up while thirsty skinwalkers are knocking down my door. That's a problem.

If I only had to dip a spoon into any old moonlit waters, like the springfed crick that runs through my backyard, then call it easy. Easy, I learned half a life ago, is always too easy. Shining got me plenty of geegaws to fill up the house. I've always been a sucker for trinkets and playpretties. So much that pap got to calling me Buzzard instead of Horace. I told him it was magpies that collected silvery things, not corpsebirds. "Simple pleasures," he'd say back to me, "simple mind." Maybe he was right. I don't know how to make a living any other way than by shining. Little else sounds good to a forty-year-old man stuck with only what he has.

That's why, here on this high granite ridge between two hollers with the evening sun turning the flat sky bloody, I know exactly how the wolf feels.

The iron trap has him by the big gray forepaw. Starving, wild-eyed with hurt, he tried chewing through himself to get free. His legbone shows. The skin around it's turned black and green. I'd bought these dozen foothold traps a week ago from Grim's Pawn down in the valley and staked them down into the ridgerock with heavy chains and some fresh roadkill for bait. The wolf's been caught for at least half that time. Brown stains of sick dried by his head. Nearest vet couldn't save this one.

He growls deeper each time I come close. As if he could scare me into giving him what's left of my strength, or convince me to set him free.

I nudge the trap with my ashwood leaning stick.

"You must think I wanted it this way," I tell the wolf.

He parades his bloodblack tongue over his teeth.

I did what Grim warned me not to do when I bought the traps: set the spring too tight. I wanted to make sure the traps worked. I couldn't afford any mistakes. Not with the last skinwalker's threats still rinsing me out. Now, thanks to my doing, all this wolf can do is lie here, as much use to me as a leaning stick is to a man with two broken legs.

Where someone else might leave the animal as is and let nature do her dirty work, when I turn to walk away, my bad leg turns me right back around.

Solutions? All I've got is my huntingknife. Antler-handled. Silver blade as long as my palm. I don't want a reason to use it. My old bloodhound Brutus used to be insurance enough, only he's back at home with that cast on his poor leg. I haven't carried a gun in twenty years. Back then, I stole a Saturday night special out of some from-off's glovebox. Nothing had taught me yet about too easy. The first time I shoved that hole puncher in my pocket turned into the last good step I ever took. My glockleg reminds me daily that some things don't come with safeties. When I run or when it's cold, I feel all twelve PEZ-sized screws twisting into my femur.

I draw the knife from my belt. I halve a few persimmons I'd picked on the hike up. All their kernels: white and blade-shaped. They predict icy winds all through winter. They don't tell me what I should do before that happens. The Ozarks have seen their share of weathers. They learned how to settle down and bear it. I like to think I'm like them. I took root in the very house where I grew up. I don't want to have to leave Arkansas. Knowing what's crossed the threshold of my home—good and terrible—makes it all the harder.

As if the dead season began that very moment, I feel a cold stare. Something other than the wolf is drawing a goose eye on me.

I scout the near and far timberbreaks. I listen for bear huffs, or a hammer creaked back. Could be crankheads, hunters, the lucky sheriff. A certain skinwalker following me to see where I collect my shine. Still, there's more than rumors about what runs in the Greater Ozarks—just like men here aren't like men elsewhere, there's more in the mountains than your average wolf.

With those eyes still on me, I toss up the knife, hoping I'll look unworried.

On the way down, it slips through my hand. The blade pings off the rock. The echo turns into a low toll that makes the mountains sound unhappy with me. The wolf flicks his white-tipped tail. He knows a weapon when he hears one.

Make it quick, he's saying. Make it count.

When you're waiting for the right conditions to gather moonshine, anything but *perfect* won't do. Over the past half-year, most times it was weatherless and I knew the place for some old pawprints, but we were in the middle of a drought; or it rained solid the whole week, but come the right night the sky still teemed with thunderheads; or worst of all, no clouds in sight, full moon in blazes overhead, and the ground was plain sopping from the afternoon's t-storm, yet I couldn't sniff up a single track. Having my own wolf chained up in the backyard would have made my shining life much simpler.

Do I cut the throat or break the neck? Either way, killing a mostly-dead wolf on a mountain pass as the October sun goes down with someone else watching—this wasn't my plan.

I recover the knife. I crouch behind him. My empty hand hovers over his side, as in *Easy, boy*. I hadn't the heart to put down Brutus even though the vet said he was already near the end of his days and he'd never walk right again. I will admit, standing there in the vet's house at three in the morning with him holding a syringe of something blue and Brutus splayed out crooked and quiet on the kitchen table, I was just as afraid, if not more, for my own well-being. Someone had once made the same decision about me.

A week and a day before, I'd had a midnight visitor.

The first time he darkened my porch steps, months prior, I didn't know he'd prove to be different than the other skinwalkers. He moved into these black hills from some flat state without trees. We get too many of his kind: adventurous, but greedy and green. Daily they roll into Arkansas in their RVs or rice burners with headless hula girls on the dashboard. Every one of them from off somewhere else. So many that that's what we call them: *from-offs*.

That first time, this from-off smelled fresher than most. His black hair he shellacked with serious grease. I could picture him sucking on fancy-shaped ice in a tower taller than the Pinnacle. I learned later that he used to be something called an occupational therapist; I had no idea what that was and still don't. Before I got the chance to tell him he had no business here, he held out his hand. It looked soft from a lifetime of lotion.

I declined.

I declined and asked his name. Giving a name means you're prepared to have it wiped from the slate.

"Johnny Zoo," he said, lying.

"Magpie Skiles," I said, lying.

I declined his shake because I'd heard of too many men letting their guard down just long enough to have their guts clawed out. Pap taught me so. When I was six, after the fever took mom, on Sundays he ran whiskey around Eureka Springs in his shocked up

Cutlass Sierra. With the rear windows curtained like a hearse and the seats stripped down to the chassis, he fit in four whole barrels of his homemade hooch. We'd both sit on them pretending they were comfortable. He brought me along because I made him look innocent. He then parked in old motel lots and sold that ruckus juice to rich from-offs. They'd line up in front of his car with whatever they could carry it home in: teakettles, oilcans, some just their big hats. But whenever somebody offered to shake pap's hand, that's when he moved on. One Sunday drive I told him he was losing money leaving like that. He looked straight up at the Oldsmobile's ceiling where the vinyl was starting to bubble. He mashed his earthworm lips together. Then his whole bony body sighed. "This business, Buzz," he said, "you'll learn friendly turns to wicked all too quick." I didn't know how or why that mattered to moonshining. Only later, once I was on my own, did I finally gather some sense from the pool of his words: stay in one place long enough, corpsebirds start to circle. After that, you deserve what you get.

Pap never left Arkansas.

I wanted to tell this new from-off on my steps to go away. He wasn't going to find this state any less godforsaken. Even without the offered hand, his gravy-colored suit and fat money clip on his belt told me all I needed to know: yonder stands trouble, begging for a toehold.

But a man's giving in to weakness was on what I'd banked my living for twelve years.

Zoo became a regular. In a matter of months he drained me dry. I usually cut my supply with crickwater to make it stretch. But the last boodle I'd sold him was pure, and he paid hefty for it with that nice huntingknife. Not ten hours later, midnight, there he stood on my walkway.

Crank will turn you into a live wire, but on my shine, you become wholly yourself.

Your lips are the same. Your face is the same. Your guts are the same. Your bones only grow a little. Your eyes turn one shade yellower. Your eyebrows stay your eyebrows but they meet in the middle. You open your mouth and bristles swell under your tongue. You sprout fur all over, as dark as pinetrunks after a brushfire. Your hairy skin moves in the wind. You grow two long nails at the end of each limb and each limb doubles in circumference. You are as strong as you think are. You walk in a swinging stride when you're not loping on three legs, holding your fourth behind you so that it looks like a tail.

Your voice don't change either. "Shine," Zoo said. His was a butter-slick tone that liked to draw things out. I'd bet my good leg he'd never once yelled at the moon.

With me on the porch and Brutus inside and Zoo standing in middle of the walkway, I said I'd already sold him the last of my stock. He'd have to wait until the end of the month, at least.

He took a step forward. "Shine."

I'd never had a skinwalker come in the middle of a binge and demand more. Enough was always more than enough. And I'd never seen one with that silver stripe of fur cutting Zoo straight down his middle. I already had my huntingknife out and my stick ready to swing.

I told him to go home.

He took several more steps.

Before I could raise my knife, Brutus clawed open the door. He tore between my legs and upended me onto my back. He about threw me onto my own blade.

At my feet, he howled twice.

Zoo said nothing.

Brutus leapt.

It took one backswing of Zoo's to pitch Brutus into the blackberries. The bloodhound yelped when he hit ground. Zoo followed him into the bushes. By the time I got to my feet, he strode back into the middle of the walkway. He held woofing Brutus by the scruff; the hound didn't look too hurt.

With his free hand, Zoo lifted up one of the hound's paws. It lay tenderly in his clawed hand, like a thing he meant to keep safe and sound. He showed me the leg. How beautiful it moved. How much it resembled his. He said to me in that buttery voice: "Shine."

The sound that followed—of him sundering Brutus's legbones with one quick, effortless roll of the wrist—I hear every time I look at the crick in my backyard. How it flows one direction parallel to the house, then turns sharply left, downhill.

At noon I'm still dead tired from hauling my ass off the ridge emptyhanded. Killing that wolf still doesn't sit right with me. I keep nodding off in my easy-chair and waking up holding my own wrist like that antlered handle. I grab my neck to make sure I've not slit it too. I know, more than ever before, that the end to my shining days is all but nigh. Even so, I still collected some ditchwater under the quarter moon. Don't know what it'll do. No different than selling brown sugar with baking soda and lye, calling it crank.

What finally rouses me isn't Brutus or my hand around my own neck, but that black Sunfire's twin cam going quiet at the road. The car door's closing pop as haunting as a shotgun in the distance. I take to the porch with my knife in my waistband.

Before he's even crunched halfway down the shale walkway, Brutus smells him and comes out onto the porch in his lampshade and cast. He tries to leap down the path. I catch him before he can. He tries again, and I hold down him by his neck. "Easy," I say. He sinks to his belly. His plaster cast slides out in front of him like a white flag he doesn't have the strength to raise. I feel weirdly thankful; Zoo could have done us both much worse.

Today, he looks like any other skinwalker.

His flannel and corduroys hang in strips like someone twice his size tried them on. Gone is his nice suit. His once-black hair now a sandblasted gray with twigs in it. To his pale forehead he tries to glue his hand. He shivers like the heart of winter's not still months off. Some sick or blood or powder burns dot his shirtfront in a tight grouping. And he wears one of those bladder backpacks with the blue spouts.

The only thing that looks hopeful about him hangs at his waist.

His black belt bears this new, pristine buckle: a silver saucer inscribed like a rifle's receiver. The picture looks to be a girl's face or a waterfall—hard to tell. The metal positively gleams. A piece of the sun fallen right into his crotch.

"Zoo, I already told you."

He sucks on the spout and squints sideways at me.

"Even if I wasn't out, I wouldn't sell you any."

He says, "I got it."

The first time I laid eyes on this from-off, I gave him the same look I'm giving him now. "You break my dog's leg one day and come begging the next. Yeah," I say, "you got it."

Zoo reaches into his backpack.

I quickdraw my knife.

He sighs through his nose at me. Instead of a gun or a blade, he takes out a cheesecloth pouch. Into my hand he pours about twenty grain-sized gems. It goes against horse sense to ask where a skinwalker's goods come from. Don't matter if they're family heirlooms or hot. I keep the ones I fancy. The rest I pawn at Grim's. Zoo probably jiggered these jewels out of a picture frame that once hung over his great granddad's mantle in that big city tower. In my palm they flash more than pretty.

"Well," I say, "well." I shuffle from foot to foot, making a ten-step process out of scratching a bloodspeck off the knife's edge, pretending like I don't already know what I'm going to do.

We trade: jar for gems. I can't stop staring at his buckle. My gums water. Would have only been a matter of time before he gave up that geegaw for some shine.

Zoo takes two long pulls on his spout. He holds up high the half-full mason jar of shine.

"I'm *done*-done," I tell him. "Don't think you can break Brutus's leg any time you want more. I won't be here." Only after I've said this does it hit me that I have no idea where I am going to go or what I'm going to do, if not here and this.

If he weren't so rough-looking today, I might have mistaken his grin for encouragement. "You don't mean that, Skittles." His long accent is too good at smoothing out every word.

"I do," I say. "Can't squeeze blood from stone."

"I'm still waiting for the part where you explain what that has to do with me."

"I can't make it anytime I like. You know that."

"You're a resourceful character."

I squeeze the gem pouch until it hurts. "It means I don't want you here."

He swishes the jar around. Its glass throws the big sun. Around the two of us the shale turns into the glittery bottom of my backyard crick. "I'm not asking for blood," he says.

"You say I'm resourceful, but it's resources that's the problem."

In both Zoo's eyes, burst vessels. I wonder just what the hell an occupational therapist does for a living, and if he's still one here. He says, "A problem's only a problem for the unwilling. You'll scare up something, I'm sure. Otherwise—" when he stops swirling the glass, the light and ground freeze around us "—how're you ever going to get your hands on this buckle you can't peel your eyes off of?"

"Pull it off your dead body, I guess."

He laughs, spit flying. I see the wolf from the night before: how he bared his bloody teeth at me and I couldn't do a thing to save him. "I'll hold you to that," Zoo says. "See you soon."

Back on the porch, I give Brutus a deep rub. He all but melts through the planks. I don't want to think how quiet this house will be without him. Maybe I'll get fortunate. Maybe this bad boodle will kill Zoo. He's too right about the buckle; I want it as bad as he wants my shine.

I only drank it once, back near I'd first started selling. Cut it with a little of pap's leftover whiskey and some apple slices. A good shiner needs to know his own boodle's strength. I wanted to go into shining the same as pap had because it seemed easy and profitable, but I discovered my own recipe. And I didn't want to end up like him. He'd started to break his own rules.

Shine only works at night. But it works the whole night. While on it, some skinwalkers say they get the urge to eat dead things. Others just run through the mountains as fast as they can. Even coming down from it, you still have the strength to break bones easy as sticks. The ones that got to be my regulars say that after a few binges, the craving for more never really leaves; it begins to hurt so bad they want to shatter the moon with a stone or hide forever from the light. Withdrawal can go on for days. I have only half a mind to believe them. But they all agree: after that first swig, you get thirsty. And you stay thirsty. No matter how much water you chug.

I woke up after that first and only binge the way a dog does: outside in the dirt with a mouthful of feathers and a bodyache no worse than having been runover by a chickentruck. If he'd still been alive then, pap would have kicked me in the side and said he was proud of me, simple mind and all.

Unlike rain and birdshit, good fortune only falls into open palms.

With knife and stick, I head back to the same granite ridge several days later. The harvest moon glows south over Wolf Pinnacle. It's half-full. For the first time I can remember, I thank myself for being lazy. I'd left all the traps up here; hauling them down last time would have only further sunk in my failures. Make no mistake, I did throw the wolf's body off the ridge. But the trap that caught it: still there, clamped and worthless.

Admittedly, I have Zoo to thank for the trap idea itself. If he hadn't broken Brutus's leg, it would have never occurred to me that an animal—a wolf—with the same wound might be tamable. The thought of Zoo's belt buckle warms my fingertips. Here's hoping I don't have to cut one more animal's throat to get it.

Three other traps are sprung. Nothing in them. Roadkill's gone.

Come December, if not tonight, that bad wind the persimmons predicted will begin to blow. Zoo won't kill me. But I can feel my own body breaking up at the thought of what he could still do to Brutus. Best case scenario: Zoo gives up on me, moves to some new habit or state, and then I'll be stuck inside my house with Brutus the Lame, the two of us having a starving contest that lasts until March thaw. The few breezes up here already feel barely over freezing. They turn the screws in my leg to tiny hot nails.

With nothing to show for my work, I look up at the moon. Half-black-half-butter-colored, it's saying, "Fuck you, Horace."

So that's what I yell back: "Fuck you, Moon!" I want it out of the sky. I want it in ten thousand pieces. "Fuck you!" I hurl my huntingknife straight up at it.

Those eyes again. The ones I felt before. They bore into the back of my neck like the bonedrill that must have holed out my femur. Hands over my head, I scramble out of the way. I don't hear where my knife lands. The moon's still there, fuller and brighter than a minute ago. I make my way across the ridge away from whatever's staring me down.

Near the treeline: the right-sized shape crawling downhill, like it's hurt. I want to shoot myself in the foot for not having the guts to own a gun. With only my ashwood stick I tear after this lone wolf.

I run harder than I have in years. Maybe the cold has numbed my leg. Maybe I'm twice as quick as I thought. The distance between us closes fast.

Right before I can catch a clear view of it, the shape banks into the timberbreak.

In the moonlit persimmon grove, where the leaves have turned but not yet fallen, everything hums violet. But for a few blown branches, nothing moves. On a knee I crouch to catch my breath. I stare down the forest floor. I listen. No sounds but the dumb mutterings in my heart. The wolf is gone and I have grown old in a single night.

More branches move in the breeze. A scared bird overhead makes a scared bird-noise. Then I'm looking not at these branches pushed by wind, but at something pushing them, hiding in the crotch of one persimmon tree twelve feet up.

I whack my stick on the ground to get the wolf's attention. I have no idea what I'm doing. The animal ducks out of sight. Crackling leaves above me. Then a sudden blur I barely leap clear of followed by a solid *tump* at the foot of the tree where I'd been standing.

There on the violet ground, dropped practically into my lap: a girl.

Teenager. Dirty and pretty. Knocked out on a root.

I look at my stick. I look back at her. I consider the possibility that my knife never fell back to earth.

* * *

On my back steps, I'm stroking Brutus where the lampshade digs into his throat. He won't quit whining. In that shade, he sounds so old and helpless. I'm no closer to knowing what to do about Zoo; yet I won't admit, even to my dog, that I'm much further than I was yesterday.

He keeps wanting to go over to the girl. I have to keep telling him *No.*

His leash I cinched around her wrists. One of the legtrap chains holds the leash to the trunk of the ash tree that leans out over the crick. If she's going through what I think she's going through, she'll still have a lot of strength left in her for the next half-day. I'm not happy about caging her like this. But I didn't know what kind of mood she'd wake up in. Nor do I know what she'll do if I untie her just yet. I already made the mistake of dropping my leaning stick within her reach when she came to. Now the ashwood lies in three perfect pieces at her bare feet.

She keeps lashing around like the links will break before her arms will. Already she's rinsed herself a couple times in the crick's bend, clothes on. I don't care to watch. I told her what happened. That the leash is temporary. After dunking herself in the crick, she'd look refreshed if her face wasn't wrinkling up with good old-fashioned hate. Her soaked Pepto-pink top's torn at the shoulders and her knee-length green skirt probably won't ever come clean of mud. Where her shoes have gotten to, who knows. But all her toenails are painted with a broad white stripe across their tips. She busies herself picking them clean; she must have been taught proper at some point.

The towel's still where I hung it for her in the ash's lowest branch.

"Last thing I need," I say to Brutus, "is one more thing to take care of. Am I right?" He drags his cast across the steps like he's drawing the line that I've just crossed. He doesn't believe a word of what I've said, and neither do I. He limps inside. Someday soon, he's going to die. When that happens, I'm thinking more and more that this girl will be just the thing to keep me going. If anything, as hard as it was on my bad leg, hauling her down off the mountain felt like the first right thing I'd done in as long as I can remember. She needed saving as much as I do.

I keep asking her name.

She won't face me fully, let alone answer me.

"Becky?"

"Kelly?"

"Brittney?"

When she finally speaks, it's to tell me: "The only girls' names you know have two syllables and end with a Y, huh?" Her voice sounds twice as sweet as I expected.

"You could have died up there. Least you can do is tell me your name." When she doesn't, my stubbornness can only rise up to meet hers. "Fine," I say. "Fine. No name: no food."

"What's yours?" she asks.

With what's remaining of the family pride pap left me after he died, I puff up my chest and tell her, "Horace Virginia Skiles." The moment those three words are out of my mouth, I want them back in. Not only have I shot myself in the leg and hurled my one good knife into the night sky, I've given this girl the only info she needs to give me trouble if she really wanted to. I never fail to fail myself.

Hate still clouds her face. "You look like an Ashley," I say, trying not to sound worried. Short copper-colored hair, rag-baby cheeks, very skinny. She wobbles on her legs like they're new to her. A forty-year-old and a fourteen-year-old don't make much of a match; still, the night I brought Brutus to the vet's house, he told me he'd just been to visit a barncat mom who'd adopted a lost cockatiel chick. "Ashley," I say, "yeah." She immediately feels like mine to protect.

Ashley kneels at the crick's bend. She dunks in her pixiecut head. If she's trying to drown herself, I don't know how to tell her she's doing it the hard way.

Then I recognize what it is she's doing. My suspicions harden into certainties. She's not trying to wash herself or take water into her lungs; she's drinking desperately. Like all the skinwalkers that have shuffled up to my porch, she's in shine withdrawal. I just didn't know how bad it was.

I pull her out by the chain. "That won't do you any good."

She looks straight at me, for the first time, without that face full of hate. She opens her eyes wide. They're no different from a cat's on the windiest day, and they're as gold as boiling butter.

"So give me what will."

There's reasons a dog is a dog and a wolf is a wolf. Why one comes to your call and the other runs. I can only hope that one will turn into the other with the right kind of concern shown for it. If not, my options are shrinking by the hour.

Shoot her? Yet one more reason I should have had a firearm in the house.

Leave her in town? She'll either drop my name to the sheriff with claims of molestation or get picked up by someone who will deliver on those claims.

Give her some shine? Even had I any left, I'd not feed what's eating her up inside.

In the house, Brutus works to claw open the back door. "She's dangerous," I tell him as much as remind myself. His ears perk up. He gets to three feet. I expect to look out the window and find her hanging from the towel. Instead, the hound half-darts-half-rolls toward the front.

Not just on my porch steps, but in the door's peephole: same ripped flannel, same blasted hair, same backpack.

Johnny Zoo.

A long slurp on his side of the door. "Skittles," he says coolly. Between the girl and Brutus and everything, I didn't think I had the kind of perfect fortune where all my problems show up at once. Yet here is the biggest one, asking for me by name. "Skittles. I told you I'd be back. Where's the welcome wagon? Where's my complimentary cocktail?"

I keep quiet, to the side of the door.

"Honestly," he says. "I can feel your heart beating through the floor."

I glance back at Brutus. His tail is batting the pineboards over and over. I raise my hand toward him. He doesn't stop.

If pap saw me like this, he'd open the door. Make me face the thing head on. He always wanted me to be honest with myself. But pap also died like this: another moonshiner, his oldest friend, knocked on this very door and when dad opened it to let him in, the Mossberg hidden in the shiner's duffel peppered him with buckshot at a range of four feet. I came home, found him crooked and quiet on the floor, knew exactly what had happened. Best thing I could do was keep on as best I could. I bought Brutus to help me.

Zoo's steps and slurps retreat from the porch. I fold up against the door, staring down at the floorboards with thanks. My stuck feeling flees me like a corpsebird does a woken-up hiker. I want to stay in this position all day.

A magpie chatters in the backyard. It sounds like an all clear.

"Shit," I say. "Shitshitshit." By the time I've burst through the back door, Zoo and Ashley have already made their introductions. They face each other like they're trying to pick out their own reflections in runny water. I shove Brutus back inside. I don't need him going berserk with a cone for a head and a club for a leg.

"Skittles," Zoo says. "You never told me you were running a halfway house."

Without my stick, I stumble badly across the yard. "No. What? Get away. Don't. Please."

Ashley starts to say something but Zoo cuts her off.

"You are ten times as crazy as I thought." His eyes haven't lost their bloodshot sheen but his face is haunted by a kind of happiness. "That's why I keep coming back."

Half my options involve me trying to knock Zoo unconscious, the other half me begging him to forget all this. The only words that end up dribbling out are "We can make a deal."

He's wearing the buckle; best I forget about it. If Ashley weren't already a heap of possible problems, having Zoo know about her piles it on double.

He's shaking his head, pacing, slurping, leading her with the chain, patting her shoulder, running a hand down her arm. She backs away. She wobbles on her feet even more than before. But compared to this morning, she looks to have calmed down some.

I barge between them. "I'll get you more shine. Wait for the full moon, of course, but I can get you a lot more. All you want." How I'll deliver on this promise, I have no clue.

"I'll do you a turn better," he says. "I will make you the best deal ever." There's that grin of his again: encouragement or scorn, I can never tell. It's the kind of grin that doesn't show a single tooth. Like a legtrap that's hidden in the leaves, the look's friendly on the outside, but wicked just under the surface. "This girl here?" He flicks his wrist so that his thumb points at her; it's the exact same motion he used to snap Brutus's leg. "I won't make a call to the sheriff that says you've got her chained up in your backyard. I won't let everyone know that you like them way too young. I won't tell a soul. Easy as that."

"How much shine?" I ask, already wincing at the number he's about to demand.

He twists his lips up. He takes a couple pulls on the spout. He watches the crick flow under the ash until I can't stand it anymore. Then he says, "Zero." He waves his hand. "No more shine." He starts to unclasp his belt buckle. "All you have to do is let me take her."

"Take her? Here? This is my backyard, not the Crescent Hotel. This is no place for fucking."

"Christ." He tilts his head back and looks straight up. Pap did the same thing, as if he were always asking for something he didn't already have.

Ashley says, "I'm standing right here."

He says, "Quiet, Missy."

The girl snaps to attention.

"Missy?" I ask.

Even with her wrists bound together, she can still give me the finger.

Zoo is talking again. "I said, '*Take care* of her.' Undo the chains, bring her home, feed her and everything. Look at her, Skittles. Look at those toes. This girl's a runaway. You think anybody but a runaway would still care about her feet? She won't tell anyone about you. She's got no one in the world," he says. "Now she's got me."

If I let him have her, who knows if he'll keep a single one of his promises. But man's constant giving into weakness was how I'd gotten in this deep to begin with; I'm not about to let it go one step further.

"Okay."

I'm afraid that the girl is none too pleased with my answer. But after Zoo unknots the leash, she stops her wobbling. I expect her to come at me for tying her up in the first place. But she rubs her wrists and wrings out her damp hair. She's young, but she manages to look practiced, resilient. Those pretty white toes will one day walk her down the straight and narrow again.

If it's true that she's a runaway, I'm starting to wish that I'd be the one to help her along, not some from-off skinwalker. But regret seems at times a natural law.

Zoo closes the few feet between us. He locks eyes with me. I am afraid he's about to add some extra condition or pull a hidden gun. His eyelashes are tiny black claws. In the cool shade of the lawn, with the crick dribbling in the background and the wind doing its thing, Zoo strikes me as nothing worse than someone stuck in a bad rut. No different than me. He'll go through bad withdrawal, but maybe he'll make it. Maybe she's just what *he* needs.

Zoo extends his hand.

I don't know why, but I take it.

"I don't have to tell you this," he says, gripping my fingers until they hurt, "but you won't ever see me again."

Pap didn't have enough of a chance to learn this, but you cannot shake someone's hand and look him in the eye without knowing that the world, if you stick it out long enough, will hand you exactly what you want. Long after the two of them leave, Zoo's fantastic grasp stays with me. He'd pressed the buckle so hard into my palm my skin still bore its inscription: a wolfpack running across a bald mountaintop.

Days later, I walk into Grim's Pawn, polished buckle leading the way.

Grim doesn't look impressed. But he takes a liking to my pouch of gems. He tries to talk up an alarm system he's recently acquired.

The man's a wrecking ball: hairless, iron-black, and heavy as all get out. Nothing about him says, "Allow me to parley with you over the value of your eighteenth century candelabra." Besides Brutus, he's as close to an ally as I've got. And he's always ready to rip me off.

Across the shop a youngish couple plucks two scythes from a barrel of field tools. It's their Winnebago out front dressed in Oregon plates. They twirl the scythes while singing, "*Swing low, sweet cherry top, calling home to carry my phone.*" Grim and I glance over, both hoping they'll do each other in.

He spreads out part of the alarm system between us. Whoever'd collected the green and red wires stripped them badly. Their ends are short copper hairs. Grim says, "New, the package runs twenty-two hundred." I tell him I don't want it. "Sure, this one's a bit used, but it's legit. Trust me." He cups his fat chin in a display of what he must *think* thinking looks like. He hefts his gut onto the counter to lean over and whisper: "Couple weeks ago, they found the front door of the McDermott place wide open and the alarm system off. *This* system. High quality. As for the good Dr. and Mrs. McDermott? Slaughtered on the kitchen floor like lambs."

The McDermott place I know only by name: a recent McMansion on the Pinnacle.

"So what you're telling me all this alarm system needs," I say, "is another alarm system."

"Horseshit." He shoves the wires in a box and that box on a shelf behind him. "It's a steal at eight hundred."

"I said I don't want it."

"Then how about the next best thing?" From under the counter he pulls out a blue steel Smith & Wesson .357. No price tag.

Before I can throw a solid *No* in his face, from the Oregon couple comes a shriek that lights up the place. I half-want to see an arm split open as a lesson I'm all too familiar with: never pick up the weapon you're not prepared to use. A series of clangs follows the shriek. The two of us find the young man pointing at this tiny cut in his palm, the woman pointing at the scythe on the floor, and a terrific scratch down an antique armoire's front door.

After they've paid the damage and gone on to terrorize the next town, Grim and I come back to the revolver on the counter. It's pointing at me.

"From-offs," I say, shaking my head.

He says, "They'll off themselves before any of us do."

"And they say we're dumb."

"Ditch-dumb."

"Dumb as a bag of hammers."

"They got it total bass-ackward," Grim says. "But there is one thing I like about them."

"There's one?"

"Their money." He jerks a thumb back at the box on the shelf. "You sure about the alarm?" he asks. "Cops said their daughter Missy turned it off. Get rich girls angry enough, double homicide's easy as 1-2-3. Zoo told me all about it. He's the one who sold me the system."

I'm doing fifty on a bad mountain road with no guardrail between me and the loblollies below. Grim sold me Zoo's address, but not before charging me twice the book price for that revolver and a box of hollowpoints. It killed me that I also had to throw in all twenty gems.

I don't believe what Grim said about Missy killing her parents. And I don't believe I have a plan for what to do with her once I've got her back, but anything will be better than her living with the from-off who got her drinking shine in the first place. My insides lurch with a boiling kind of emptiness. Pap was right again. I thought I'd gotten away with something, but Zoo still gutted me with that single handshake.

Maybe she'll want nothing to do with me; I'll buy her a train ticket and that'll be that. Or maybe she'll let me be the one to take care of her.

On Zoo's road, I slow down to load the revolver. Its weight feels ten kinds of wrong.

His Sunfire's outside his log cabin. His front door stands wide. I keep the gun out and pointed at the sky because I don't want to come off as either unarmed or wanting a firefight. Up the porch steps and in his doorway, I'm too late.

The first tipoff's the smell: soured tang of roadkill, but worse.

His white oak split chairs flipped on their sides. Dead leaves all over the place. A slice of moldy bread on the windowsill. And on his table: the mason jar, perfectly intact and empty.

I cock the revolver. I call out: "Zoo."

I wouldn't expect him to keep her body in the house, especially on shine. Again, louder: "Zoo." I've brought the gun to level with the ajar bedroom door. I nudge it open with the revolver's nose. That sour stench blows over me double-strong.

"Zoo?"

In the dim windowlight, sticking out from behind his two stacked mattresses: feet.

I squeeze the trigger. I shout my head off. I hear the shot bang between my ears. I stumble back into the main room and drop to my knees. All the screws in my leg are rattling loose.

No response. No return volley. No wonder.

"Fucking safety." I push off the revolver's hammer block. I'd only imagined the shot.

"I didn't want this!" I yell into the bedroom. But I'm too late in a different way.

Zoo's dead. Half-naked, his throat's torn out from chin to collarbone. A couple days this way. I can see the whole terrible event. They dip into the ditchwater shine together. He starts to paw at her. Missy takes to the mix in a bad way. Before he knows it, her two clawed hands are around his throat and, hello Back of Beyond, he's bleeding out on the floor and she's running out the door, as free as she was the night I carried her off the ridge.

By the time I'm halfway up my own walkway, it's evening, cloudy, and I've come to new terms.

I'm done shining. I'm done feeling regretful or guilty. I'm done with Arkansas.

I smashed the jar in Zoo's cabin. I dropped that silver buckle into the hole in his neck and chucked the revolver off his porch.

Don't matter anymore what has or has not happened in this place I call home. I'll pack this old Sierra with what little I need, call Brutus, and we'll shag ass to some place without mountains or towers or pack animals.

Inside the house, Brutus is bowed up at being cooped all day. I let him out back; I'll not have him bonkers while I'm trying to drive at midnight away from everything I've ever known.

My mouth goes desert on me. In the ash branch over the crick, a big corpsebird preens one wing that shines violet in the cloudy dusk. Maybe it's the branch creaking under the bird's weight, but I swear I hear Brutus's legbone snapping again and again. The bird keeps one eye down on the waters. At the crick's bend, as if nothing'd changed in five days, Missy's knelt down with her head in the current. Only this time blood, not mud, stains her green skirt. I watch as Brutus drags himself over to her, sniffs her, then retreats quickly back to my side. She doesn't move at all. I don't know whether to let flow my tears or be glad I can finally make a clean exit.

Either way, I'm limping over to take care of her body when she lifts her head from the water.

I hold dead still. The corpsebird takes off to circle higher and higher. What looks at me from the bank is only half-Missy though. Dark coppery hair's sprouted in patches around her neck. Her eyeballs are that bloodshot gold. One arm dangles limp at her side. She tries to stand, can't. The bad shine has fucked her up in ways I can't imagine.

She manages to whisper something.

I tell her it's too late. I can't do anything for her. I turn, limping, leaving her for good.

Once more, my bad leg whirls me right back around. I can't see the corpsebird anymore, but I feel it up in the sky somewhere, watching us. Something Zoo said about problems hasn't left me: how they're only problems to the unwilling.

She says a little louder, "No." Up on one knee, she holds out her empty hand like she wants to give me something I don't have: strength, love, a second chance? "I don't want—" She collapses, wheezing. Her bare feet she's thrown out to the side.

Her white-tipped toenails are chipped to hell. Those imperfect white crescents, the fallen shards of a shattered moon: she starts to wiggle them like that's the last thing she has control of. Make it count, Missy's saying, make it quick.

"Easy, girl," I say as I stagger toward her. But she's making it too easy.

Contributor Biographies
& Story Notes

 **Michael Gray Baughan** is the author of *Charles Bukowski* and several other books of biography and literary criticism. More recently, he has returned to fictively baiting the imp of the perverse. Other anthologies featuring his stories include *Richmond Macabre*, volumes 1 and 2, *No Rest for the Wicked*, and *Body of Evidence*, a limited edition art-lit collaboration with Chuck Scalin. He hails from Philly, lives in Richmond, and can be found online at michaelgraybaughan.com and wondercabinet.net.

Story Note: I married into a Virginia family with deep roots and by default became the caretaker-in-training of a large plot of land where no one above ground lives full time. Only later did I learn that a substantial branch of my ancestral line hailed from parts nearby. Long stretches spent alone at the old homestead have occasioned uncanny interactions with a *genius loci* that has yet to fully define itself. "Old Dominion" is the first, but won't likely be the last, of my attempts to bottle that genie and make it do my bidding.

 **Helena Bell** is a poet and writer living in eastern North Carolina. She is a 2012 Nebula Award nominee and her fiction has appeared or is forthcoming in *Clarkesworld*, *Indiana Review*, and *Shimmer*.

Story Note: This story was written as an antagonistic response to a podcast in which a physicist complained about the use of scientific concepts as metaphors.

Lynne Buchanan is a writer, teacher, painter, and special-effects makeup artist. She won "Best Fiction" for her short story "Indelible" in *The Coraddi*. She earned her MFA at the University of North Carolina at Greensboro. She lives in North Carolina with her two dogs, a furry musician, and too many books. She is currently working on a novel.

Story Note: This story found its beginnings in two unrelated events. First, I found a mortician's handbook. It covered everything from facial reconstructions crafted from wax, to how to speak with surviving members of the family. The second event occurred when I purchased some fishing flies as a gift for a friend. I knew nothing about fly fishing and was fascinated at the detail, at the precision involved in making these tiny pieces of edible art. Both events stirred my curiosity and I thought long about morticians and what they see and what they might think as they work.

For me, this was a natural lead in to the surreal aspect of this story: What might the dead think? What would they say if given a voice?

Kevin Catalano, the author of *The Word Made Flesh* (firthFORTH Books), was born in Chittenango, New York, the same birthplace as *Oz* author L. Frank Baum. His fiction has appeared, or is forthcoming, in *PANK, Booth, Pear Noir!, Atticus Review, Gargoyle Magazine, Used Furniture Review, Fiddleblack, REAL: Regarding Arts and Letters,* and others. He has an MFA in fiction from Rutgers-Newark University, where he also teaches literature and composition. He lives in New Jersey with his wife and two children.

Story Note: A summer years ago, I'm on the back porch of my parents' house in North Carolina, watching my father pick up felled branches from the yard near the shoreline of Lake Norman. Maybe it's the heat, or some metaphorical fear, but I have a sudden, nightmarish image of Dad turning his back to the lake, and a giant scorpion scuttling from the murky water and latching itself to his back. This horrible lake scorpion became an unshakable part of my thinking until I finally wrote about it. "The Bad That Can Happen the Day Jesus Rose from the Dead" is one of the few pieces that I wrote in one sitting, without any pre-thought of who the characters would be, or the plot, or its ending. I typed the first sentence, and discovered a voice and cadence was gifted to me. It was that mystery voice that told me the rest of the story.

 **Katherine Lien Chariott**'s work has been published in literary magazines including *Post Road*, *Sonora Review* and *The Literary Review*. The story in this anthology, "Introduction to the Unofficial Reports," was first published in a slightly different form in *Fiction International*. She holds an MFA from Cornell University and a PhD from UNLV, where she was a Schaeffer Fellow in fiction. She is a Special Educator in New York.

Story Note: "Introduction to the Unofficial Reports" was inspired by two news reports concerning cases of severe child abuse, one about the starvation of foster children and the other about similar abuse of a biological child. In both cases, the charges were denied by the accused, and many people from the community stepped forward to argue that the parents could not commit such terrible crimes, though there was a great deal of physical evidence of the abuse. These stories stayed with me, not because I imagined that I would use them as the starting point for fiction, but because I struggled to understand what could motivate such treatment of children. Another thing that stood out to me was that, in both cases, there was at least one other child in the family who was treated well. My attempt to understand these two instances of child abuse, perpetrated by parents who were also, apparently, capable of forming loving relationships with their other children, failed as long as I thought of them as taking place in the real world. However, when I began to imagine them as happening in a fictional world, one that existed outside the mode of realism, I was able to come to some sort of understanding, or at least become comfortable with my lack of understanding. As I took the story through many revisions, I was inspired by the writings of Kafka, Cortazar and Borges, all three of whom have helped me understand the power of fiction, which does not attempt to faithfully mimic the real world, to help readers understand their own reality more deeply.

Josh Eure is a thrash-metal vocalist and fiction writer from Hertford, North Carolina. His stories have won the Dell Award and the Brenda L. Smart Prize, and reached the finalist list in *Glimmer Train*'s Short Story Award for New Writers. He has also won *Sundress Publications*' Best of the Net Award for 2010, and has appeared in *Oxford American*, *Southern Cultures*, and *Raleigh Review*, among others. He earned an MFA in creative writing at North Carolina State University. He currently lives in Cary, North Carolina with his wife and daughter. He is shopping his first novel.

Story Note: "Shivering" is a story inspired in many ways by the neighborhoods I grew up in. I wanted to explore the foolishness of lust as I've experienced it, while occupying an immediately recognizable setting. Characters are as familiar to me as family, but I wanted to trouble them with matters elemental to mankind overall. In this story I endeavored to bring a celestial down to Earth, to backwoods North Carolina even. What happened there was completely out of my control.

Kendall Giles, PhD, is a writer and tinkerer of many things. Bred and buttered in Virginia, he worked his way through college and continued as an engineer in a variety of fields, including medical imaging, defense intelligence, and knowledge discovery. As a university professor, he has designed and taught business, engineering, and mathematics courses. As a writer, he has an MFA from the Stonecoast MFA Program in Creative Writing at the University of Southern Maine. He also has publishing experience at the literary agency Foundry Literary and Media in New York. His stories, articles, and research papers have been included in *The Dead Mule School of Southern Literature, InYo: The Journal of Alternative Perspectives on the Martial Arts and Sciences, Breaking Muscle*, and more than a dozen academic publications. He writes regularly at his website, kendallgiles.com, and has a fondness for coffee, travel, critters, and things that creep in the night.

Story Note: While the Civil War is, for some, just a few bullet points to be regurgitated for standardized tests in high school, the memories and ghosts of those participants linger there, still, in the hills and fields where those distant battles and events took place, where people fought, died, struggled, and cried, all in the name of our country. We who are living in the U.S. now, the reunited, continue on, stronger and clearer of purpose, for all the trials of our ancestors.

Having recently moved to Appomattox, Virginia, I could not help but think about that era, and the modern one, as I walked the old battlefields, looked at faded Civil War photographs, and felt strange winds blowing through forests dark and close. Something shimmered in the periphery of my vision, and I wondered, "How thin actually is the veil between the present and the past, especially at certain focal points of such historic, hopeful, and heart-rending significance?"

I believe that the land holds many secrets of the past that we today do not know how to hear, even if we could be bothered to tear ourselves away from our gadgets and schedules long enough to even try. And the dead—sometimes they have a desire to give us counsel and warning, sometimes they have their own agendas. But they grow frustrated, even angry, when we forget them.

Many of the events, places, and people in this story are real. Perhaps all. I just listened to the wind and peeked behind the veil.

Adam Joseph Goebel III was born and raised in Henderson, Kentucky. His four novels have been published in sixteen languages. Though hardly known in his own country, he has (for whatever reason) found an audience in the German domain.

Story Note: My old high school friend Robert Gilliam actually threw a "surrealist party." If I'm remembering correctly, he did so because some friends of his were living in an incomplete house that they considering a surreal setting. I did not go to the party as it was in Lexington, but he told me about it, and I thought it would make an interesting little story.

Becky Hagenston's first collection, *A Gram of Mars*, won the Mary McCarthy Prize; her second collection, *Strange Weather*, won the Spokane Prize for Short Fiction and was published by Press 53. Her fiction has appeared in *Prize Stories: The O. Henry Awards*, *Indiana Review*, *Crazyhorse*, *Moon City Review*, *Gettysburg Review*, *Alaska Quarterly Review*, and many other journals, as well as several Press 53 anthologies (including *Surreal South '09*). She teaches at Mississippi State University.

Story Note: When neighbor kids were doing a scavenger hunt several years ago, I thought: What if someone comes to my door and asks for something weirdly specific, something I have but that no one could possibly know about? As with most stories I write, I had no idea where "Scavengers" would go when I started it. Every time Delores showed up, she surprised me, too—and it wasn't until late in the process that I understood who she was, and what she was really after.

Blake Kimzey's work has appeared in *FiveChapters*, *Puerto del Sol*, *Mid-American Review*, *The Los Angeles Review*, *Short Fiction*, and *PANK*, among others. His collection of short tales, *Families Among Us*, won the spring 2013 Black River Chapbook Competition and will be published by Black Lawrence Press in fall 2014. He is currently a student in the MFA fiction program at UC-Irvine, where he teaches creative writing. He is working on his first novel.

Story Note: When I was writing "The Boxer and the Bear" the bear just showed up, dressed and ready to fight. The closest explanation I have for it is this: I had hiked the Ouachita Trail, the third most secluded trail in the US, with my wife and brother. We started the trail in Oklahoma and came out of the woods in small town Arkansas six days later. The trail was wild. In the woods there was evidence of black bears everywhere, (overturned rocks, tracks, dens, etc.) but we didn't see one bear. When we emerged from the wilderness into a clearing, soiled from our journey, we happened upon a biker gang. They were drinking cans of Keystone and staring at us with some kind of awe. The three of us looked a lot rougher than the assembled bikers. We found showers and fresh clothes, lost our edge, and later that night walked into a dive bar. Cleaned up, we looked out of place. We got sideways looks, reserved for out-of-towners. Then I thought about bears hiding in plain sight, and what would happen if one showed up. I think this is where the story came from.

Tawny Leech grew up in Southern Illinois. She got her GED when she was seventeen. For a few years, she lived in L.A. Now she lives in Makanda where she is raising two children and a cat, Meow, and a rabbit, Aragorn. She graduated with a BA in English from SIUC and was recently accepted into their MFA program for fiction.

Story Note: "The Quillman Girl" was a real person. And she died the same way she died in the story. To the point, I think this is about Little Girl trying to figure out how to be a woman, but her examples are pretty extreme, and it's her kid who keeps her anchored. I don't think he saves her, but I think he reminds Little Girl that she'll always choose to struggle rather than do what's easy. And then there's a creepy carnival and some ghosts.

 Although **Nathan Alling Long** now lives in Philadelphia, he grew up in a log cabin in rural Maryland, lived for four years on a commune in central Tennessee, and spent nearly a decade in Richmond, VA. His stories and essays have been published in over fifty journals, including *Tin House, Glimmer Train, Story Quarterly, The Sun, Crab Orchard Review, Salt Hill, Camera Obscura,* and *Indiana Review.* His work has also appeared on NPR, in a dozen anthologies, and in a chapbook of short stories published in 2005 by Popular Ink Press. Nathan's stories have been nominated for a Pushcart Prize and Best Non-Required Reading award, as well as been finalists for the *Glimmer Train* Very Short Story Award nine times. He teaches writing and literature at the Richard Stockton College of NJ.

Story Note: This story is based on a real event. I was living in Baltimore just after graduating from college. While walking by the Baltimore Art Museum, I saw a large metal statue of Lee and Jackson just in the woods. I investigated and somehow fell under its spell. I seemed to become invisible to the cars that drove by just a few feet away. And the horses were so exquisitely rendered, I couldn't help but pet them, as though they were alive. I'd grown up with horses. And though the metal was cold, I felt some sort of heat radiating from the statute, from the animals and men. I climbed up, and from there, who can say what was real and what was imagined?

 **Alexander Lumans** (Associate Editor) graduated from the MFA Fiction Program at Southern Illinois University Carbondale. He will be the Spring 2014 Philip Roth Creative Writing Resident at Bucknell University. He has been awarded fellowships to the MacDowell Colony, Blue Mountain Center, ART342, and Norton Island Residency. He received scholarships to Bread Loaf, RopeWalk, and the Sewanee Writers' Conference. He received the 2013 *Gulf Coast* Fiction Prize, 3rd place in the 2012 *Story Quarterly* Fiction Contest, and the 2011 Barry Hannah Fiction Prize from *The Yalobusha Review*. His fiction has appeared or is forthcoming in *Story Quarterly*, *Gulf Coast*, *Blackbird*, *Cincinnati Review*, and *The Normal School*, among others. He is co-editor of the anthology *Apocalypse Now: Poems and Prose from the End of Days* (December 2012, Upper Rubber Boot Books).

Story Note: The seed for this story came from a chapter in *The Foxfire Book*. The book discusses all these unique solutions to problems that Appalachian folk use—things would seem surreal to anyone outside the region, like using spider webs as gauze or rubbing a black cat's tail over your eye if you have a sty. My personal favorite: if you are bitten by a spider, drink heavily from 3 p.m. to 7 p.m. ("You will not get drunk, you will be healed."). The "Moonshining" chapter describes in perfect detail all the ways these mountain people used to (and still do) make moonshine. Plus, I'm a sucker for work stories that focus on a particular process. I knew the story was going to be stranger than just a typical moonshiner, which got me thinking about the word "moonshine" and how I could play around with the expectations it created. Then it just became a matter of having a great deal of fun with skinwalkers, addiction, and this moonshiner's voice.

Alice G. Otto is currently pursuing an MFA in Creative Writing at the University of Arkansas, where she has received the Walton Family Fellowship in Fiction, the Carolyn F. Walton Cole Fellowship in Poetry, and the James T. Whitehead Award. She attained her BFA from the University of Evansville. Her work has previously appeared in journals including *Harpur Palate* and *Yalobusha Review*.

Story Note: About six years ago, I told a friend that I was going to write a story about a woman who gives birth to a litter of puppies. It was the kind of weird, offhand declaration that's easy to both make and forget in the course of an hour—but, it stuck with me. Hard. Over the next four years, I made reference to "my puppy story" from time to time, but it wasn't until I entered my first MFA workshop in 2011 that I finally began to give it serious thought. I had never worked beyond the naked premise of "woman births puppies," which sounds, and sounded, astonishingly silly—and the one thing I knew was that I didn't want this to be a silly story. Jotting down the first sentence of the first draft turned out to be half the battle. That line, "Charles and Maggie lived deep in the hills of Kentucky," still opens the story. Not a legendary collection of words, sure, but seeing them on paper mapped it all out for me. It became clear that these two characters were a young, married couple leading a simple life in an isolated terrain; the woman was devout; the man was pragmatic; an unearthly blizzard would allow the incomprehensible to unfold just how I wanted it to, in spiraling claustrophobia; the characters' deepest beliefs would be pushed to the brink, and one of them, at least, would snap. Drafting, researching, and revising "my puppy story" wasn't a joy from start to finish, because any author who claims such a thing is possible is either lying or delusional, but the process came close.

 **Adam Padgett**'s short fiction has appeared in *Appalachian Heritage, Roanoke Review, Cold Mountain Review, Santa Clara Review, SmokeLong Quarterly*, and other fine journals. He has recently completed a short story sequence (which includes "Out from Under") set in Southern Appalachia for which he is seeking a publisher. He currently resides in Charlotte, NC, where he is at work on a novel.

Story Note: I spent my high school years in a fairly evangelical Christian church after spending the first thirteen years of my life outside that atmosphere. So I felt as though suddenly hurled into a foreign country where I had to quickly pick up a new language and learn customs just to survive. Many years after high school, "Out from Under" came to me after viewing the 1967 documentary *Holy Ghost People* (which you can find in its entirety on YouTube). While I certainly had borne witness to enthusiastic worshiping, I had never witnessed snake handling, which the documentary depicted. What struck me most about the documentary is that it did not depict the people there as caricatures of snake handling mountain folk that maybe we imagine them to be (or as popular culture may have depicted them). Instead, they were people seeking the same kinds of universal things everyone seeks: love, forgiveness, acceptance, belonging. That kind of caricaturization is something I hope I've avoided here. The story seemed obvious to me in that it was the obvious conflict, the obvious resolution (or lack of). I can't imagine what else I could have written. As for the ending, I'm not sure I will ever be able to write another one like it. Which, I guess is a terrible thing to say since I have, at this point, only published a handful of stories. The ending that is simultaneously wonderful and devastating. But I think this is the way life tends to be, or can be at times.

I first wrote the story about four or five years ago, and it has undergone a tremendous amount of revision since then, probably the most any of my stories have undergone, and so I'm thrilled to see it printed here in *Surreal South '13*.

David James Poissant's stories appear or are forthcoming in *The Atlantic, Playboy, One Story, The Southern Review, Ploughshares, Glimmer Train*, and elsewhere, as well as in the anthologies *New Stories from the South* 2008 and *Best New American Voices* 2008 and 2010. His collection, *The Heaven of Animals*, will be published by Simon & Schuster in 2014. He lives in Oviedo, FL with his wife and daughters, and teaches in the MFA program at the University of Central Florida

Story Note: I've never been lost in the woods, but I was once lost in Rome. I was twenty, there on vacation with my parents and brother, and, one night, I walked alone to the Trevi Fountain. I watched the fountain a while, ate some gelato, spoke to some kids, then headed back. It was a straight shot to the hotel, but the streets, I swear, took strange turns in the night, and I became hopelessly lost. I wandered Rome for an hour. What's worse, I couldn't remember the name of the hotel where I was staying or the cross streets to even catch a cab back. And then, somehow, I was standing before the hotel doors. The next morning, I attempted to retrace my steps, but I couldn't find where I'd lost my way or where I'd been. It's an hour of my life, lost, and, to this day, I can't explain it or imagine how I got back.

This was the impetus for "The Fox King," how the familiar becomes unfamiliar, sometimes quicker than we can blink. I can't say where the rest of it came from—nightmares and daydreams, the startling things that hover behind closed eyes.

Ron Rash is the author of the 2009 PEN/ Faulkner Finalist and New York Times bestselling novel, *Serena*, in addition to four other prizewinning novels, *One Foot in Eden, Saints at the River, The Cove*, and *The World Made Straight*; four collections of poems; and five collections of stories, among them *Burning Bright*, which won the 2010 Frank O'Connor International Short Story Award, and *Chemistry*

and Other Stories, which was a finalist for the 2007 PEN/Faulkner Award. Twice the recipient of the O.Henry Prize, he teaches at Western Carolina University.

Clint Stevens (Associate Editor) is a writer living on a small farm in southern Illinois with his wife and two children. He received his PhD in English from the University of Illinois and is currently an assistant professor of English at Kaskaskia College. His scholarly work has appeared in *The European Romantic Review*, *Eighteenth Century Theory and Interpretation*, and on the *Modern American Poetry* website. Recently he has ventured into more imaginative terrain by writing for *The Dark Mountain Project* (dark-mountain.net).

Fred Venturini grew up in Patoka, Illinois, where he survived being lit on fire by a bully, a neck-breaking car accident, and being chewed up by a pit bull. His first novel, *The Samaritan,* was published by Blank Slate Press in 2010, then disappeared from print, but will reappear as *The Heart Does Not Grow Back* in 2014. His short fiction has appeared in the anthologies *The Death Panel, Sick Things, Noir at the Bar 2, Booked.* and the upcoming *Burnt Tongues*. He lives in Southern Illinois with his wife, Krissy, and their daughter, Noelle.

Story Note: When I was a teenager, a cute girl at the mall approached and I was too much of a schlub to say no when I figured out she was lassoing me into taking a survey. I don't remember any of the questions, just that they were boring, I lied on a bunch of them just to get done with it, and the place I took the survey was downright scary. It felt like a secret hallway that led to a secret room in the mall. I'm not sure if they do those cold-call, in-person surveys anymore—something tells me the Internet probably destroyed the need for them.

In "Survey," I tried to capture the Twilight Zone vibe I felt in the atmosphere of the mall that day. The only thing missing from making that setting an actual story was some hideous survey questions. I have to admit I had fun coming up with the most awful questions and putting Frank through pure hell. Things got worse for him in every draft, and his answers may make him seem like a terrible person, but everyone is terrible if you ask them the right questions.

The story firmed up for me when I realized that Frank had it too easy if there were only repercussions for telling a lie—I needed to save the most awful repercussions for when he finally told the truth.

 **Jeff Weddle** grew up in Prestonsburg, a small town in the hill country of Eastern Kentucky. He has worked as a public library director, disc jockey, newspaper reporter, Tae Kwon Do teacher, and fry cook, among other things. His first book, *Bohemian New Orleans: The Story of the Outsider and Loujon Press* (University Press of Mississippi, 2007), won the Eudora Welty Prize and helped inspire Wayne Ewing's documentary, *The Outsiders of New Orleans: Loujon Press* (Wayne Ewing Films, 2007). His work has appeared in many venues, including *Port Cities Review, Chiron Review, Beat Scene, Midday Moon, Hawaii Review, Journal of Kentucky Studies, Publishing History,* and the anthologies *Mondo Barbie* (St. Martin's Press, 1993) and *Stovepiper Book One* (Stovepiper Books, 1994). Weddle is the author of a poetry collection, *Betray the Invisible* (OEOCO, 2010), a limited-edition, fine press book handcrafted by master book artist Mary Ann Sampson, and a chapbook of Barbie poems, *Not Another Blonde Joke* (Implosion Press, 1991). With Beth Ashmore and Jill E. Grogg, he is co-author of *The Librarian's Guide to Negotiation: Winning Strategies for the Digital Age* (Information Today, 2012). Weddle is an associate professor in

the School of Library and Information Studies at the University of Alabama.

Story Note: I wrote "An Ugly Monkey" quite a while ago—twenty years, maybe?—when I was a grad student in the Department of English at Ole Miss. At that time, I had four major influences: Charles Bukowski, Ernest Hemingway, Barry Hannah, and beer. I'm not sure how much Hemingway is in evidence here, but I can certainly see Bukowski, Hannah, and beer. Barry, may God rest his soul, was the Ole Miss Writer in Residence back then and I took his fiction seminar a couple of times. Maybe I wrote this one for Hannah's class, though I doubt it. More likely, I wrote it sometime after I was through with his classes and just reading all of his work I could get my sweaty hands on, re-reading Bukowski and Papa, avoiding Faulkner like the damned plague, hanging out with my friends at a wonderful bar called the City Grocery night after night after night, arguing about writers and poets and all those silly, essential things aspiring writers and accomplished drinkers argue. Where did the monkey come from? I don't know. I've always tried to follow Hemingway's advice of writing one true sentence, then following it with another. That monkey, Bobo, was true for me and his story oozed from the cracks in my brain with no conscious plan or agenda. I certainly wasn't attempting to construct a high toned metaphor or explain the human condition. For what it's worth, I had been in helpless love with a sweet and beautiful girl named Margaret, who had exercised the good judgment to break up with me not long before I wrote the story. Other than a shared name, she has nothing in common with the Margaret in this story.

Josh Woods is also editor of *The Book of Villains* and *The Versus Anthology*. His work has appeared in *The Nevada Review, Apocalypse Now: Poems and Prose from the End of Days, Black and Grey Magazine,* and *Prime Number Magazine,* among other places. He is a Pushcart Prize nominee and winner of the 2008 Press 53 Open Awards in Genre Fiction.

He graduated from the MFA program at Southern Illinois University Carbondale and is currently an Assistant Professor of English at Kaskaskia College in Illinois.

Story Note: It was astronomically more difficult to have my back-from-the-dead version of Jorges Luis Borges speak only direct quotes from his nonfiction, as happens in this story, than to simply make up all of his lines, but I've been wanting to take up this writing challenge/homage for years, so when *Surreal South '13* came along, I accepted that it was time to do it. Nearly everything Borges discusses in my story—indeed, nearly everything he discusses in all his own non-fiction, and, indeed, in his own fiction—is about other writers and works, and I've always loved that about him, so that is the tradition I'm participating in with this story. And in case my surrealist literary parody—offered in extreme and honest reverence—is not apparent enough in the body of the work, I take as my title the same quotation from *Hamlet* that Borges used in a story of his that was his homage to H.P. Lovecraft, whose tradition I'm also working in with the vision of the Bahamut. And about the Bahamut, or the Fish, or the Leviathan, or the Cthulhu, or the Great Dragon, or Its other names, I must not speak.

Cover artist **TERRI YESKE** has been creating art in many mediums since she was a child. She graduated from the Nova Scotia College of Art & Design and lives and works in Alberta, Canada. You can see more of her work on her Flickr page at www.flickr.com/photos/mrs_dj_deh/.

www.ingramcontent.com/pod-product-compliance
Lightning Source LLC
Chambersburg PA
CBHW020549020726
47494CB00006B/1986